BROWSING COLLECTION
14-DAY CHECKOUT
No Holds • No Renewals

IWO, 26
CHARLIE

———————————

IWO, 26 CHARLIE

P. T. Deutermann

ST. MARTIN'S PRESS
NEW YORK

First published in the United States by St. Martin's Press, an imprint of St. Martin's Publishing Group

IWO, 26 CHARLIE. Copyright © 2023 by P. T. Deutermann. All rights reserved. Printed in the United States of America. For information, address St. Martin's Publishing Group, 120 Broadway, New York, NY 10271.

www.stmartins.com

Library of Congress Cataloging-in-Publication Data

Names: Deutermann, P. T. (Peter T.), 1941- author.
Title: Iwo, 26 Charlie / P. T. Deutermann.
Description: First edition. | New York : St. Martin's Press, 2023. |
     Series: P. T. Deutermann WWII novels
Identifiers: LCCN 2023016832 | ISBN 9781250284990 (hardcover) |
     ISBN 9781250285003 (ebook)
Subjects: LCSH: Iwo Jima, Battle of, Japan, 1945—Fiction. | United States.
     Marine Corps—Fiction. | World War, 1939–1945—Campaigns—Pacific
     Area—Fiction. | World War, 1914–1918—Naval operations,
     American—Fiction. | LCGFT: War fiction. | Historical fiction.
Classification: LCC PS3554.E887 I96 | DDC 813/.54—dc23/eng/20230424
LC record available at https://lccn.loc.gov/2023016832

Our books may be purchased in bulk for promotional, educational, or business use. Please contact your local bookseller or the Macmillan Corporate and Premium Sales Department at 1-800-221-7945, extension 5442, or by email at MacmillanSpecialMarkets@macmillan.com.

First Edition: 2023

10 9 8 7 6 5 4 3 2 1

This novel is dedicated with greatest respect to the 27,000+ Marines who became casualties of war on Iwo Jima in early 1945.

ACKNOWLEDGMENTS

I am indebted to the US Navy's History and Heritage Division; E. B. Sledge's memoir on the Peleliu and Okinawa invasions, titled With the Old Breed, *published in 1981; Chuck Tatum's book on the battle for Iwo Jima, titled* Red Blood, Black Sand, *published in 2012; Hal Buell's book about the Iwo Jima campaign, titled* Uncommon Valor, Common Virtue, *published in 2006; and the* West Point Atlas of War: The Pacific, *edited by Brigadier General V. J. Esposito, published in 1959. Several YouTube videos about this battle also gave me a good idea of what the terrain actually looked like and the extent of the hardships suffered by the Marines, some of whom describe what it was like in these videos because they were there. As usual, I thought I knew a little bit about what happened at Iwo, but, again, as usual, I discovered that I knew next to nothing. I am grateful to have had the above books and the YouTube videos to explore.*

PROLOGUE

The late afternoon had turned gray and gloomy as we sat out on the front porch of our home in Hancock County, Georgia. Low-flying rain clouds were scurrying over the plantation and it was actually getting colder. February in the Georgia countryside trying to assert itself, I guessed. My wife had just come back outside with hot rum toddies and a couple of car robe blankets. The mugs contained Tennessee whiskey instead of rum, but it worked just as well.

The view from the colonnaded porch hadn't changed since I'd gone off to the Pacific a million years ago. A long gravel drive traversed the half mile to the two-lane, with field fences and double lines of oak trees on either side. A lonesome-sounding wind tried to drive us back inside, but I'd wanted to tell this story to my bride of one year out here in the lowering darkness. It wasn't the kind of story that belonged in the brightly lighted rooms of the interior.

There should have been flares, I thought, as I scanned the uneasy skies.

It was the early spring of 1948. I'd been back for just over two years and had studiously avoided any talk about the war, even with the other vets that I occasionally ran into. They all asked the same question: Where were you? What outfit? Most quit after that, understanding that all of us felt pretty much the same about where we'd been and what we'd seen and done. We shared that look of gratitude that we'd been able to come home at all, and that was usually enough. Plenty of time to think about the past, should any of us ever want to. When I said I was at Iwo, that name usually created a sudden, respectful silence and an end of the questions. Everyone—Navy, Marine, Army—knew about Iwo Jima.

My wife, Née Libby Miles Thornton, was the second daughter of the family whose plantation bordered ours across the Little Ogeechee River. Her older sister, Rebecca, was a famous Georgia beauty, if one with a somewhat scary personality. She'd married into one of the wealthy families up in Atlanta. Libby was pretty, maybe five three on a tall day, and exceptionally sweet and caring. Gentle, retiring, with none of her older sister's pretensions and with a Northern education to boot, she'd swept me right off my feet with her warmth and those deep blue eyes.

Her mother, no slouch herself in the world of powerful Southern women, and a wickedly funny individual, had quietly advised me that I might as well propose because I was so obviously "all four on the web," as she put it, and didn't stand a chance of escape. I was more than happy to accommodate her. Their land holdings were larger than our family's, but we owned over two thousand acres, so I supposed that made me minimally socially acceptable. It was kind of funny in a way, since both our families had descended from enterprising carpetbaggers, not the blue-blooded "Southron" lines that everyone who was anyone in the county claimed. After the Civil War and Sherman's march, the blue-bloods were mostly in the ground, as were the previous owners of our estate, and not that far from the house, either.

In fact, I now owned the two thousand acres, since my father had passed away one month after my return from the Pacific. My sister had disclaimed any interest in inheriting half the plantation, having long ago moved into the top layers of Atlanta society. Miz Mary had few fond memories of our rather woolly, increasingly run-down, plantation home, and the burdens of the rustic business of trying to make money out of all that played-out red dirt that made up most of our holdings. So now I was a Southern land baron, of sorts, with as yet no clear plan for the future prosperity of my acquired semi-ancestral home.

"Are you very sure," I asked Libby, "that you want to hear this?"

"Lee Boy," she said, using the nickname I'd had in the county before the war, "I think it's mostly important that you tell it, if only to get that great big black ghost off your back. You're back, you're alive, and we have a future to embrace. I need you to look ahead, and I don't want to see you weeping when you think I don't see. So, yes, I'm sure. Please."

"Cuddle up, Bunny," I said, calling her the name that had come to me after our wedding night. "This will take a little while."

I shuddered at the prospect of bringing so many much-missed ghosts back to life, even for her.

Back to Iwo Jima, I thought. Great God Almighty, and, please God, just this once.

PART I

WAR AT A
DISTANCE

ONE

The battleship *Nevada*'s gunnery officer, Commander Brent Willson, frowned as he stared down at the circular radar scope. "This picture isn't exactly useful," he said, shaking his head. "Look at all that clutter down at the entrance. Can we maybe tune it?"

"Actually, sir, that's a pretty accurate picture," I said. "I looked at a chart of these straits this morning; the western entrance is a cluster of a couple dozen small islands and exposed reefs. Once they get up into the straits proper, their formation will come into better focus."

"I sure hope so, Mister Bishop," he said. "The bridge says it's darker'n a well-digger's ass out there. The primary optical range finder can't help us tonight until we hit something and make it burn."

"Yes, sir, I know," I said. "This'll be a radar shoot all the way. The OpOrder says the admiral wants to open on them at twenty-seven thousand yards. By then they'll be in the narrowest part of the straits. And, we'll have crossed their T."

Willson smiled. "Admiral Jellicoe would approve. Assuming they keep coming after the PT boats and the destroyers take their shots, this will be a slaughter."

"Just like Pearl Harbor," I said. "Not like those bastards don't deserve it."

"Amen to that, Mister Bishop," Willson said, quietly.

I looked around at the fifteen men manning their various stations in the space called Main Battery Plot. I was the ship's fire-control officer, which was a principal job in the Gunnery Department aboard USS *Nevada*. Most of the Plot crew were tending to the hundreds of dials, brass cranks, and switches on the three-thousand-pound analog computer squatting in the middle of the space, the Mark One-Able gunfire computer. It was relatively cold down in Plot. We were three decks down from the main deck. Armored decks and massive, hydraulically operated hatches built into them sealed us inside the protective steel envelope that encased our battleship's vital spaces. I recalled the instructor at gunnery school calling it the "armored box." Think of a battleship as a giant shoebox-shaped steel enclosure, he'd said. Surrounded by a ship's streamlined hull. The "box" contains all the vitals—the machinery for the guns, the Main Battery magazines, Plot, the four engineering spaces, vital interior communications centers, and the ship's gyro and stable element. The rest of the ship—the weather decks, topside superstructure, berthing compartments, mess decks—could get hammered in a gunfight with another battlewagon, but as long as that armored box is intact, you can shoot back.

A battleship fight, I mused. There'd only been one other in this Pacific war, when USS *Washington* wrecked IJN *Kirishima* off Savo Island in the Solomons. Some of the ships in tonight's battle line, including my ship, USS *Nevada* BB-36, were survivors of the attack on Pearl Harbor, and had been raised from the mud around Ford Island and sent back to the States to be rebuilt. They were antiques, of a sort. Top speed of twenty-one knots, so they couldn't run with the big dogs—the new, thirty-three-knot, sixty-thousand-ton *Iowa* class battleships, who could keep up with the growing fleet of big-deck fast aircraft carriers. Some in our task group, like us, carried "only" fourteen-inch guns; the four *Iowa*s sported nine sixteen-inch guns.

Nevada was suitable mostly for shore bombardment these days, but not much else. The older battleships were more like the armored dragons who'd fought at Jutland in 1916, not to be trifled with, but ill-suited to today's grand scale fleet engagements, where carriers fought each other at distances of hundreds of miles. On the other hand, now that the so-called Big Blue Fleet had transitioned to a campaign of island assaults, like this attack on the Japanese-occupied Philippine Islands, I knew that those poor bastards charged with going ashore to hit well-defended beaches were most appreciative when one of the elderly dragons materialized out of the offshore mists and started belching fire and throwing seventeen-hundred-pound high-capacity shells into Japanese defensive positions. And, truth be told, even the Glamor Girls, the *Iowa*s, were seeing their mission transformed into serving as massive floating anti-aircraft gun platforms. Japanese battleships, having had a taste of massed US Navy carrier air, tended to remain far from the fray here in late 1944.

I checked the bulkhead's ten-foot-high illuminated status boards. The information was displayed in vertical columns of amber-colored, backlighted plexiglass. The first set of columns listed our ship's movement and ambient conditions: course, speed, true winds, barometric pressure, real-time pitch, roll, yaw, air temperature, relative humidity, powder magazine temperature, projectile magazine temperature. The second column listed target information: ship type—which in tonight's engagement was actually going to be Japanese battleships—their plotted course, predicted speed of advance, range, and bearing. The third column listed what other ships would be in company with them, along with their gunnery reach. The fourth listed information on what we were going to shoot at them: the type of ordnance, the predicted time of flight, the predicted interval between salvos, how many of our ten fourteen-inch guns would be firing.

We knew tonight was going to be special: we were going to shoot the "good stuff," armor-piercing 2,300-pound shells that would be capable of piercing fourteen inches of the best Vicker's armored steel. With the evolution of our mission from battle line to shore bombardment, *Nevada* only carried 250 rounds of the AP ammunition; everything else now was high-cap except for some white phosphorus rounds, known as Willie Peter (for the letters WP), used for spotting. The high-cap shells were general purpose, point-detonating crowd pleasers that would throw tanks and artillery pieces a hundred feet into the air and collapse bunkers, tunnels, and other fortifications buried as much as fifty feet deep. Tonight was special because most of the ships in our formation had been battered down into the mud by the attack of 7 December. This was going to be revenge of the best sort, and definitely enjoyed cold.

All of the light panels showing data were being fed from the massive computer and its daughter, the Mark Eight-Able rangekeeper, sitting right next to it in the middle of the Main Battery Plotting room. Some of the panels were dark because we had not yet established our own radar contact on the anticipated Japanese formation. Our ambush battle line had been established at the top, or northeastern, end of the Surigao Straits, which itself was the gateway from the southwest into Leyte Gulf.

There were five other battleships in the American formation: *West Virginia, Maryland, Mississippi, Tennessee,* and *California.* The other, western, end gave access from the straits out into the Sulu Sea, where an Imperial Japanese Navy task force, consisting of two battleships, IJN *Yamashiro* and IJN *Fuso,* and their escorts were expected to enter the straits around midnight and head northeast, in an effort to surprise the Americans who were making an amphibious landing on the eastern shores of Leyte Island.

Waiting for them at the northeastern end were our six battleships (invisible to the Japanese, who purportedly did not have radar), twelve heavy cruisers, and twenty-eight torpedo-firing destroyers. As the Japanese came up the straits, they'd initially be harassed by a swarm of PT boats, then attacked by two squadrons of destroyers. And then, once they were within our range, the big boys would get into it with radar-controlled salvos of fourteen- and sixteen-inch shells plunging down on them from a range of thirteen and a half miles. Plus, we would have "crossed their T": the entire battle line of American battleships would be able to bring all their guns to bear on the entire Japanese column, which, because they were advancing up a relatively narrow channel straight at us, could only return fire from the lead ship of that column. With any luck, it would be a much-deserved slaughter, indeed.

"*California* reports radar contact," the fire-control chief announced. "Bearing two four five true, range forty-six thousand yards." That's a good radar, I thought—twenty-three miles.

The talk between ships (TBS) radio speaker, mounted in the overhead, came to life. "Nemesis, this is Ranger: enemy in radar contact. Change one to the OpOrder: I intend to open fire, at my command, at *thirty* thousand yards. Remember Pearl Harbor. Acknowledge."

Ranger was the call sign of Rear Admiral Jesse Oldendorf, commander of the battleship fire support task group, telling his force of six battleships what his latest intentions were. I listened as each of the dragons replied in turn, acknowledging the admiral's message. Remember Pearl Harbor, I thought. Nice touch. Thirty thousand yards. Fifteen miles. *Yamashiro* and *Fuso* were elderly remnants of the interwar battleship construction campaign in Japan, just like we were. Fifteen miles was beyond the extreme end of their own gunnery range.

"Range is now forty-three thousand yards," the chief announced.

"Do we have radar contact yet?" Commander Willson asked.

"Negative, sir," the chief replied. "*California* has the new surface-search radar; ours won't see 'em until about thirty-five thousand yards. *California* will report range and bearing once every three minutes until the rest of the group acquires."

I walked over to the main tracking table to examine the plot, where *California*'s reported radar contacts were being plotted on a navigational chart of the straits. It looked like they were just approaching the area where they'd be jumped by a swarm of PT boats. The captain had said at the morning's planning session that the torpedo boats weren't expected to accomplish much in the way of torpedo hits because the Japanese had their first-class cruisers and destroyers screening them. But they'll raise hell and take names, the skipper had noted. Hopefully throw their formation into confusion, shoot up some of their bridges and pilothouses, scare the hell out of all the topside AA gunners, stuff like that. And while the Japanese are dealing with all that excitement, two squadrons of our destroyers will be coming at them from each side of the strait at thirty-three knots, each of them capable of firing ten torpedoes into the Japanese formation.

"Will there be anything left for us?" the executive officer had asked innocently.

The captain had smiled. "Once the destroyers hit 'em, it'll turn into a melee," he'd said. "Hopefully that will happen when they're fifteen miles from us. You remember that the Japanese coded signal to attack Pearl Harbor was: East Wind Brings Rain? We're going to deliver a different kind of rain tonight. Six battleships firing full salvos. Just the prospect warms the cockles of my icy black heart."

"Range is now 39,500 yards. Track indicates steady bearing of two four degrees true, closing."

I picked up a sound-powered phone and called the director officer stationed at the top of the ship's forward director tower, some 120 feet above the water line.

"See anything?" I asked. The director officer was Lieutenant (junior grade) Marty Cullen, my roommate. His battle station was inside the Main-Battery director, a squat steel box at the very top of the tower. The director contained the ship's stereo optical rangefinder, a circular beam some thirty feet in length and a foot in diameter, which housed the optical telescope and mirrors that allowed its operator to give a precise range to the target.

"Lightning, white and red," Marty replied. "Long way off. There's so much humidity that I've got guys hanging out on the optical beam, wiping the lenses."

"This is gonna be a radar shoot," I reminded him.

"Hell, yes," he said. "But I'm gonna have a ringside seat unless we run out of lens tissues."

I grinned and went for some coffee. Lieutenant (junior grade) Jackie Beamish took over supervision of the main plotting table. He was the assistant fire-control officer. He hadn't been aboard for Surigao Straits, but he had been with us for the previous island assaults on Saipan and Peleliu, so he was no novice. The ship was barely moving, steaming at five knots on a course perpendicular to the enemy's axis of approach. We just had to wait. Eighteen miles down the straits, there was a fierce battle taking place, as American destroyers fought it out with Japanese heavy cruisers and destroyers to get close enough to launch their torpedoes at the two Japanese battleships.

Soundless lightning, white and red.

For a moment, I felt some comfort in being where I was: deep inside the armored box of a battleship, instead of in the middle of that thirty-knot running gunfight, with ships blasting away at each other at point blank range while maneuvering to avoid being hit or even run over. I'd secretly always envied the destroyermen, with their fast, nimble ships, negligible armor, and daring maneuvers. I felt slightly chagrined that I was here and not there, twisting and turning in the midst of a flashing confrontation between tin cans and much, much bigger ships. I could just see it: our 2,100-ton destroyers dashing through the Japanese formation, pumping five-inch rounds against those towering, armored pagodas while white-hot eight-inch shells sought out their own unarmored sides. If you lived through it, you'd by God have some stories to tell, I thought.

Admittedly, that could be a big if.

"Nemesis, this is Ranger. The enemy formation has slowed. Ships in radar contact and with stable solutions may expect to commence firing in about five minutes to give our destroyers time to clear. At my command, regardless of range. Acknowledge."

The six battleships again acknowledged the order. It was clear what the admiral wanted: if you have a fire-control solution, start shooting when I give the order. If you don't, wait until you do.

"Fill the Main-Battery hoists," Commander Willson ordered.

The fourteen-inch gun turret officers acknowledged. *Nevada* had four Main-Battery gun turrets. Two mounted down on the main deck—one forward, one aft—contained three fourteen-inch guns apiece. Two more—also mounted one forward and one aft, just behind and above the three-barreled turrets—contained two guns each.

Down in the magazines the hoist elevators would begin to whine as powder bags were lifted four decks up to position the silk bags on one side of the ten open breeches. On the other side, the projectiles, each weighing more than a ton, began their ascent, stopping just above the transfer-tray fire doors where the elevator machinery rotated them to the horizontal position. When the "load" command finally came, the projectile would be pushed through the flash-fire prevention shutters onto the transfer trays, which would then lower the shell onto the rammer tray, after which the hydraulic rammer would come forward and force the projectile into the breech and all the way forward, until the shell's copper rotating bands engaged the rifling in the sixty-eight-foot-long barrel, leaving only the very back end of the shell, called the boattail, visible.

The rammer would then withdraw and as many as six silk powder bags, depending on the anticipated range, would be rolled down onto the rammer tray The powder bags, each filled with nitrocellulose powder grains the size of cigarettes, would then be pushed a lot more gently forward into the breech chamber, snug up against the boattail. The rammer would again withdraw and the breechblock would start rising into position. The chief gunner would lean down over the gleaming stainless steel maw of the breech and place what looked like a hot-pan holder against the back of the last powder bag just as the breechblock came forward to lock into the face of the breech. The gunners prided themselves on knowing how long to wait before placing that fabric patch, containing simple black powder, up against that last bag, just before the block closed and rotated into locked position.

Once the shell and its propellant were safely locked into the gun barrel, the gunner would press the ready button. Up in the control booth, at the back of the turret and one level above the gun pits, the turret officer would watch for all three barrels to report ready. When he had three green lights on his console, he'd press *his* ready button, which would light up the fire-control display boxes for unloaded/ loaded/ready on the electric status board down in Plot. That was the signal for the Mark One-Able computer to begin producing continuous train and elevation orders. The guns themselves wouldn't swing out until the ship's captain gave the order.

Commander Willson nodded at his phone talker, who reported to the bridge that the Main Battery was loaded and ready. At that moment, the chief announced that our ship's radar had gained a solid contact on the lead ship of the Japanese formation. This meant that the crew who'd been inputting ranges and bearings manually, based on radar reports from other ships, could step back and let the radar electronics communicate directly to the Mark One-Able. Our senior talker then reported to the captain up on the bridge that the ship's gunfire-control system was now in full automatic and locked on.

Once that report reached the bridge, the Captain gave the command we'd all been waiting for: Surface action, port. Commander Willson nodded and then the word went out to all four turrets to sync to the Mark One-Able, at which time a deep rumbling sound permeated the entire ship as the four three-hundred-ton turrets rotated out to the ordered bearing and the barrels elevated to the ordered range.

"Commence firing!" the talker shouted. The chief pulled the firing key back to the first position, which sent a three-part tone into every announcing system speaker in the ship. Beep-beep-*beep*. When the third tone was heard, he pulled the trigger back to the second position, and all ten fired, sending ten *tons* of armor-piercing steel at the Japanese column, now some fifteen miles distant.

The giant barrels recoiled, and by doing so pressurized the hydraulic reservoirs and cylinders that then pushed the barrels back into the load position, even as they lowered from the firing elevation position back to the flat load angle. A thirty-second blast of 2,500-psi air was sent into the breech and down each of the barrels as they came back down in order to push out any products of combustion that might still be lingering in the barrel. The whole point of making the powder bags out of silk was that silk left nothing in the way of ash or hot residue, but just to make sure, the blast of air was always applied.

Once the barrels stopped descending, their breechblocks were commanded to unlock, rotate to the open position, and drop down out of the way. The chief gunner would visually inspect the breech to make sure there were no hot sparks visible, and then the next shell would be lowered into ram position and the entire cycle repeated. As soon as the ready lights blazed in Plot, the barrels would lift again to the ordered elevation, the three tones would go out ship-wide, and then the big booms would come.

I knew that the time standard for fire, reload, fire again was optimally forty-five seconds. I hadn't been timing the salvos, but Commander Willson had. The cycle was taking almost seventy seconds. Normally he would have been yelling about speeding things up, but this time he kept quiet. That time standard was for a ship-on-ship engagement where another battleship was firing back. Tonight's situation was different. Only the lead Japanese battleship could shoot back, and do so only with her forward two turrets. Our formation could bring many more barrels to bear. The other Japanese battleship, locked into their column formation behind the first battleship, could not safely shoot back. Slaughter, indeed, as it should be.

For a moment, I felt that the whole scene was slightly surreal. Here I was, in the cool, antiseptic, air-conditioned fire-control plotting room, watching the wheels, gears, rods, cranks, and pinions of the Mark One-Able responding to a dozen or more inputs from the ship's many sensors, and then transmitting electric servo orders to the four giant gun turrets, which in turn translated them into even smaller servo signals which put huge gears, motors, and hydraulic rams in motion. And at the other end? Literally tons of red-hot armored-steel projectiles were falling from the night sky, punching through ships' decks, and detonating deep inside, setting off secondary explosions, lighting big fires, and killing everyone locked below decks.

"Nemesis, this is Ranger: Cease firing," the TBS speaker announced.

I looked at my watch—we'd only been shooting for nine minutes. Was that all it took?

Nothing had changed in Plot, or in the whole ship for that matter, except that we caught a whiff of gun smoke in the vents. We were still steaming in a column formation at five knots just inside Leyte Gulf, moving across the eastern entrance to the Surigao Straits. It was 0235. The sound-powered phone talkers up in the Combat Information Center (CIC) were saying that what was left of the Japanese formation appeared to be retreating back out into the Sulu Sea, pursued now by a pack of American heavy cruisers. I called Marty way up in the director.

"What can you see?" I asked.

"Nothing," Marty answered. "All dark. There was a lot going on downrange until our big guns got into it. Then our own muzzle blasts wiped out my night vision. Now there's nothing to see. I'm guessing we nailed the bastards."

"Yeah, we just got the cease-fire order. Sounds like our cruisers are down there now, hunting cripples. I wonder where the rest of their fleet is?"

TWO

We found out where they were the next morning. I was having breakfast in the junior officer wardroom at 0630 when the general announcing system lit up with the bridge boatswain mate piping an all-hands call. Then the announcing system shifted to voice mode.

"This is the captain speaking; we've just received word that a formation of enemy battleships has entered the Leyte Gulf amphibious operations area and is engaging the jeep carriers. We're headed north at top speed, but we're at least two, three hours away. Apparently, Admiral Halsey has taken his four *Iowas* north on a hunt for Jap carriers, so only the amphibs' screening destroyers are now facing *Yamato* and three other battlewagons, plus several heavy cruisers. They appeared out of the San Bernardino Straits at around 0500. I'm afraid we may be much too late, but we're gonna give it a try. GQ in about ninety minutes. If there's any AP ammunition left, we'll start with that. That is all."

The officers in the wardroom looked at each other in wide-eyed horror. *Yamato*? The world's largest battleship was coming south to annihilate MacArthur's landing forces with her *eighteen*-inch guns? Great *God*! How did that happen? There were literally dozens of relatively helpless transports, hospital ships, oilers, and cargo and ammo ships anchored off the landing beaches. As massacres went, this would make Surigao look like a minor scrap.

No longer hungry, I hurried back to the bunkroom I shared with Marty to get my GQ gear, a sick fear growing in my stomach. *Yamato*'s eighteen-inch armor-piercing shells would punch easily into *Nevada*'s guts, while our own fourteen-inch shells, especially if we'd indeed run low of AP, would bounce off that monster's sides.

Ten minutes later I arrived down in Plot and found the space buzzing with activity. Commander Willson was instructing the magazine crews to check and double-check how much AP ammo was left. The turret crews were already in their gun houses, cleaning the barrels, fixing any small hydraulic leaks, and checking the high-pressure air-ejection systems. I found out that *West Virginia* and *Maryland*, with sixteen-inch guns and better speed, had been dispatched to go ahead of the older, slower dragons. They also had spotting planes embarked, which they could launch and send ahead to see what was going on off the island of Samar. I prayed they wouldn't be reporting a lot of sinking American ships.

Throughout the ship just about all hands were on their way to or already at their general-quarters stations, responding to the captain's announcement. The control stations in the main turrets and in the line of anti-aircraft five-inch gun mounts bristling along each side were making phone checks and pre-positioning ammo. Then, well before the captain's predicted ninety minutes, the GQ alarm sounded. Commander Willson called the bridge to find out what was going on. To everyone's surprise in Main Battery Plot, he found out that the general quarters alarm had been sounded to deal with an incoming *air* raid, not Japanese battleships. Our group's cruisers, which had the newest versions of air-search radars, had detected unidentified aircraft closing in on the lumbering shore bombardment group from the direction of Luzon Island, where the Japanese were known to have several outlying air bases.

The battleships had been directed to maneuver independently to defend themselves while their escorting cruisers and destroyers formed up into anti-aircraft formations to concentrate defensive fire against whatever was coming. I could only glean snippets of information from internal communications circuits because the Main Battery, our ten fourteen-inch guns, could not be used in an air-defense mode.

I felt the ship heeling slightly as she went into a turn and then heard several double detonations as the twin-barreled five-inchers began firing. There were four five-inch mounts on each side, along with two dedicated secondary battery directors, each with its own radar, to control the AA fire. I now felt somewhat like a supernumerary down here in Main Battery Plot, while the gunnery action was being handled by the CIC and the individual AA guns' plotting room located one deck above us.

Commander Willson ordered Plot's comms technician to ask Radio Central to patch the force's formation tactical radio frequency to one of our overhead speakers. Plot could not talk on that circuit, but we could eavesdrop and thereby have some idea of what was happening topside. There was a lot of radio chatter, mostly warnings of incoming bogeys and claims of splashes, the term used when a ship shot down an attacking aircraft. But then came one statement, addressed to the collective call sign of the entire task group, that got everyone's attention. I didn't catch the call sign of the ship making the announcement—probably one of the heavy cruisers—but the warning was perfectly clear: these guys are *suiciders*, repeat, *suiciders*; alert your peashooters.

Willson hurriedly called Secondary Gun Plot and told them to warn the ship's 40mm and 20mm gun mounts to be ready to deal with straight-in targets if one of the suiciders came at *Nevada*. The ship carried eight four-barreled 40mm and *forty* single-barreled 20mm mounts along her main decks and some of the upper levels above the five-inch mounts. Given that the ship's main armament consisted of 356mm guns, the forties and the twenties were affectionately referred to as peashooters. I had once dismissed them while talking to a gunner's mate chief, who'd immediately corrected me. They're designed to deal with a suicider, he'd said, and those bastards have to fly straight at the ship they want to crash into. One peashooter can't down a bomber, but twenty or thirty of them can tear the plane apart in that last thousand yards before impact. They're the *only* guns we have that can do that, by the way, Lieutenant, as in, don't open your yap unless you know what you're talking about. Sir.

Yes, Chief.

The fire of the five-inchers became more sustained and then came a significant thump somewhere aft along the starboard side, strong enough to dislodge coffee mugs and make the lights in Plot flicker and most of our crew wince. CIC reported a near-miss to starboard; the big thump was the suicider's underslung bomb going off underwater. There was a lull in the five-inch fire while the mount crews called for more ammo. I could only imagine what it was like down in the five-inch magazines, where sweating crews were manually stuffing the elevator hoists with projectiles and powder cases as fast as they could.

"Where the hell is *our* carrier air?" Willson complained. "We should be well within range, and there's supposed to be a dozen CVLs and CVEs up off Samar Island."

No one had an answer. Stuck down in our darkened armored steel cave, nobody in Plot knew much at all about what was really going on topside. Even the eavesdropping phone talkers couldn't provide any good dope. I once again had the feeling that our battle station was somewhat surreal. Topside guns were blasting away at enemy bombers, whose pilots probably were already dead and their planes blazing brightly, but who were crashing into the water fifty feet away while down here, in the dim light and cool air-conditioning, I was sitting around on a metal stool with a mug of coffee in one hand and an unlit cigarette in the other. I felt like a guy listening to a baseball game on the radio from his living room.

The five-inchers began pounding again. One of the phone talkers listening to the CIC circuit reported that there was a second raid inbound. The ship once again began a slow, ponderous turn, to port this time. All the Plot crew could do was wait and listen and try not to think about torpedo-bombers. Even if a suicider managed to crash out on the main deck, his delayed-action bomb couldn't reach us down in Plot. Then I remembered the report about those Japanese battleships headed for the Leyte landing area. Were they still out there?

THREE

The captain came up on the 1MC announcing system after another suspenseful hour to bring the ship's crew, 2,020 officers
and enlisted, up to speed on what was happening. Many of that number had been sealed in steel vaults inside the ship for more than three
hours now, and the captain had always been good about keeping us
informed.

"This is the captain speaking. We've now arrived in the vicinity
of the Leyte invasion beaches. We are proceeding to join up with
Admiral Sprague's carrier support group between where we are now
and the island of Samar. They've had a bad morning. Japanese battleships, along with a crowd of heavy cruisers and destroyers, descended
upon the escort-carrier formations at around sunrise. Admiral Sprague
ordered his screening destroyers to lay down a smoke screen between
the enemy and the carriers, and then to attack the Japanese formation.

"The destroyers went in with guns and torpedoes, and apparently none of them came back. We've lost two, possibly three escort carriers, but here's the good news: for some unknown reason, the Japanese turned around and went back into the San Bernardino Straits. We have no idea why—they absolutely had our entire invasion fleet at their mercy. Ten minutes ago, a suicider came down out of nowhere and hit the jeep carrier *Princeton*, which exploded and went down. Admiral Sprague wants a battleship to join each of the three carrier formations to assist with anti-aircraft fire. We'll have to stay at GQ until we *know* there's no more air threat from suiciders. I'm authorizing ventilation temporarily, and gun crews may stand easy on station. But if they come back, button up everything immediately. That is all."

Commander Willson smiled. "Typical of our skipper," he said. "He's got half the crew, a thousand or more guys, locked in compartments with no fresh air until we stand down from GQ, so he orders the vents to be turned on."

The ship's interior ventilation systems were always turned off when General Quarters was sounded to prevent battle damage fires from spreading. Captain Henderson, our skipper, was taking chances, but I was grateful for it. The air down in Plot was cooled but still only on a recirculation loop; some fresh air below all those steel decks would be very nice indeed. Our commanding officer was Captain Dorian William Edwards III. He'd been a battleship officer for twenty-eight years, with service in both the Atlantic and Pacific fleets, so there wasn't much he didn't know about battlewagons. He was trim, just over six feet tall, gray-haired, and sported a neatly trimmed Vandyke-style beard. He'd been aboard another battleship when she was torpedoed at Pearl Harbor, where he'd been awarded a Silver Star for bravery during the ensuing damage control and rescue efforts. He was popular with and much respected by the crew.

It took two more hours before the ship secured from general quarters and set the standard, wartime condition II underway watch. I went topside just like everyone who'd been buttoned up down below.

Nevada was steaming in company with the four destroyers that normally accompanied us in a screening formation. There were several other ships nearby, including two light cruisers of the *San Juan* class, specialists in anti-aircraft gunnery, and of course, the escort carriers. One of them had a destroyer tied up alongside assisting with battle damage aboard the carrier. The word quickly spread throughout the ship about what had happened that morning. There was a tall plume of heavy, black smoke drifting across the sea about five miles away where the *Princeton* (CVL-23) had gone down after a suicider hit her and ignited a magazine. Another ship, the escort carrier *Gambier Bay*, had been shelled by the Japanese battleships until she, too, rolled over and sank, and the escort carrier *St. Lo* had also been sunk. The cruiser *Birmingham*, which had been alongside *Princeton* helping to fight fires, had been severely damaged when the light carrier eventually blew up. Two destroyers were now attending to *Birmingham*, who'd suffered more than six hundred casualties when the carrier exploded literally in their faces.

The light breeze blowing across *Nevada*'s decks smelled of burning oil and other things. Navy fighter planes droned overhead. I recently learned that the new name for the suiciders was *kamikaze* and that the Japanese had recently formed entire squadrons of pilots willing to fly their planes, usually armed with a single large bomb, right into American ships. It felt a bit strange, standing out here on deck in the sunshine, while all around us, all the way to the horizon, there were damaged ships being tended to and smaller craft from the amphibious forces searching for survivors of the morning's battle. We knew that there had to be men still out there in the water, injured, burned, and in shock, fighting off sharks, thirst, sunburn while spitting up fuel oil. In contrast, here I stood, in clean khakis, like a passenger on an ocean liner, taking it all in.

Last night *Nevada* had been in an old-fashioned prewar battle line of capital ships, pushing slowly through the darkness while our huge guns bellowed into the night, sending enormous projectiles miles downrange to shatter other warships, turning them into flaming wrecks that never stood a chance. It was all well and good to mouth the words "Remember Pearl Harbor," but I wondered about my role in all this: watching the dials and the wheels on a soulless machine, cranking out gun orders to waiting synchros, which in turn directed one-ton electric motors to drive three-hundred-ton turrets to move, however slightly, before unleashing the next salvo. It had been "sort of" exciting to participate in a real battleship versus battleship action, but the knowledge that the Japanese battleships wouldn't be able to fire back because of the geometry of the battle had taken the element of fear out of the situation. I'd been much more worried about my fire-control machinery screwing something up than about return fire from the Japanese. News that one of their super-battleships, along with three others, had burst into Leyte Gulf, headed for the amphibious objective area, had electrified everyone, but even that had fizzled out during *Nevada*'s valiant effort to get up to the landing beaches, knowing in advance we'd be too late to save the escort carrier formations, only to hear that the Japanese had turned around.

Part of me yearned for some real combat action. A smarter part reminded me that there were many good things to be said about several inches of armor plate between you and the bad guys. At that moment, I met up with one of my junior officer buddies, whose GQ station was down in one of the engine rooms. We eagerly exchanged the latest hot rumors and then headed for the JO wardroom. There was nothing *Nevada* could contribute to the search and rescue efforts going on around us, so lunch seemed the best option. That said, as I watched what was happening around us while trying to ignore the smell of burning oil and burned bodies, I was hard-pressed not to feel just a bit embarrassed that I was headed for the junior officer wardroom for lunch, while hundreds of men were bouncing around in small boats not that far away as they searched the sea for the living and the dead.

FOUR

S o that's Iwo Jima," I said. "Not a whole lot to it, is there?"

At sunrise, I'd climbed all the way up to the Main-Battery director, a combination optical and radar station that looked like a five-inch gun without barrels. It was positioned high up, above the bridge structure, some 120 feet above the water. I was sitting on the side of the main hatch leading into the director. The stereo-optical range-finder's arms extended out to either side but their optics were capped today. Marty, now a full lieutenant like me, nodded. The wind blew with a steady whistling sound this high up, but the whitecaps down below us didn't seem to impress *Nevada*'s thirty-two thousand tons.

"They've been bombing and shelling this island for more than four months," Marty said. "We're gonna join the party at zero-nine-hundred this morning; word is that the Marines are gonna go in tomorrow. I swear to God, can't be a whole lot of enemy troops left alive over there."

"Over there" lay a flat and desolate-looking small, black island.

We were five miles offshore, steaming at a bare five knots, but I'd thought I could smell sulfur down on the main deck. At one end was an ugly, supposedly still active volcano; at the other end were some hills that looked like they had been smashed by a giant's hammer and reduced to a jumble of house-sized boulders. In the middle of the island there were supposed to be two, maybe even three Japanese airfields, which supposedly was why we and fifty or more of our ships were here. The entire island looked and smelled dead. I couldn't see green anywhere. We'd passed the invasion force of three Marine divisions fifty miles south of here on our way to our fire-support station. The plan was for a general bombardment for a day and a night, and then call-for-fire missions once the troops went ashore. I didn't think we'd be here long if we'd been bombing and shelling this desolate hunk of cinders, black sand, and sulfur pits for four months.

Four other battleships and a gaggle of heavy cruisers and destroyers were deploying into their fire-support stations. Word was, there were some escort carriers even farther offshore to provide local air support. There were a half-dozen small minesweepers inshore right now, dutifully plying their dangerous task. Two destroyers were prowling the inshore waters with them in case the defenders decided to start shooting at the 'sweeps, but the island remained ominously silent. I wondered if they were all dead: four *months* of softening up bombardment? Even from out here, ten thousand yards offshore, we could see that the volcano and its island had been well and truly worked over. There wasn't a single piece of green vegetation in view.

"Where they gonna land?" I asked Marty.

"Between that pile of rocks there and the volcano," he said. He'd attended the main operations briefing in the wardroom a day ago. I'd had the bridge watch, so I'd missed it. "A hundred thousand Marines are going ashore," he said. "Hardly seems like there's room enough."

I had to agree. We were going to set a modified general quarters in about thirty minutes, mostly to get any rubberneckers off the weather decks before the big guns started up. Commander Willson had told me that we would be doing area fire on the eastern slopes of the volcano, where there were supposedly a bunch of Japanese six-inch guns embedded. It was clear why they'd think that—the volcano overlooked the entire landing beach area. But gun emplacements dug into an active volcano? It was obviously not erupting, but there was a definite smoky haze hanging over the top. Up here on the director, there was also a whiff of sulfur and other noxious gases, so maybe it was active, after all.

The beaches seemed to be composed of black sand and appeared to be ascending from the sea in terraces. We were loaded to the gills with high-capacity ammunition. I wondered if that stuff, big as it was, would be effective going off in what looked like a sandpile. One of the guys called from inside the director: Lieutenant Bishop, boss wants you down in Plot. I waved goodbye to Marty and started the long climb down to the main deck and then through the armored hatches to Plot. Down was easier than going up, but not by much. I passed the hatch crews standing by their assigned hydraulic machinery, ready to lower the two-thousand-pound hatches into their holes in the armored box once GQ sounded.

Commander Willson was waiting for me in Plot. "Lee, I want you to get set up as the Marines' GLO responder on the spotter's net," he said. "You remember how to talk?"

"Yes, sir, I do," I said. "But I thought we were going to start up with preplanned area fire?"

"Yup," he said. "Go study the plotting table. We're gonna give 'em sixty minutes of walk-it-around fire within our sector on *Suribachi* and then switch to call-for-fire. The spotting chart's on the main table. The main concentration for the battlewagons will be on those parts of *Suribachi* that can shoot directly at the landing beaches. High-cap, all day."

I was confused. Marty had said the Marines were going in tomorrow. Willson saw my confusion. "Supposed to be tomorrow, I know, but the big bosses apparently got tired of waiting. Today's the day."

"Aye, aye, sir," I said, and headed for the other side of the Mark One-Able. The plotting room crew was just about fully manned up and there was a quiet buzz coming from the various stations as they got ready for our first fire mission.

A preplanned area-fire mission didn't require any ship to shore communications. The guns would do all the talking. Our job at the plotting table was to establish a precise navigational track for *Nevada* on the table chart, using visual bearings sent down by the quartermasters on the bridge using topographic features ashore and even radar ranges, if needed. The Main-Battery optical director would get us confirmation bearings, which would come down via sound-powered phones to the plotters. Between the inputs from the bridge and the director, they'd get a navigational "fix" every three minutes.

Once we were confident that we knew where *we* were, the next step was to develop ranges and bearings to the various parts of our assigned target sector and feed those into the big computer. Basically, we'd divide our assigned sector into small squares, a hundred yards on a side, and then proceed to plant a single fourteen-inch high-capacity shell into the middle of each square until we'd covered the entire sector. Three other battleships would be doing the same thing, along with several cruisers and destroyers, so for a while, Mount *Suribachi* should look like it was erupting again.

The Marines would go in as soon as we stopped firing, landing while the shell-shocked defenders were still trying to dig their way out of the blasted landscape. Spotter planes would be loitering high over the island as the troops moved in; any guns that opened up on the waves of boats headed toward the beach would be called in as targets and one of us would take the mission and suppress the defensive fires coming from the island. That's when I would have a job, manning the naval gunfire support (NGFS) radio net and talking to a spotter in the airplane. He'd give us a rough estimate of the target's position from us and we'd shoot a spotting round. We never expected to hit the first time around, so the spotter would call in corrections. We'd reset the computer and fire another round, hoping to land closer than our first attempt. This would go on until our shells were landing on the target; then we would fire a three-, five-, or even a ten-gun salvo, which should neutralize the problem.

My role was to talk to the spotter in the plane, or, once there were Marines on the ground, a shore fire-control team in a regimental command post, known as a CP, using a highly choreographed and scripted vernacular developed over the past three years of fighting. It wasn't really a code but more of a way to standardize the commands and information flow so that any spotter could talk to any ship or artillery battalion, regardless of Service. It was traditional in Navy–Marine Corps NGFS procedure that the spotter's radio call sign would always begin with a randomly selected word, such as Baxter, or Treetop, followed by the number two-six, and ending in the military phonetic word for the letter "C," Charlie.

As the Gunnery Liaison Officer (GLO) responder aboard *Nevada*, I would be listening for any radio calls on the spotter net directed to our own call sign, which today for *Nevada* was "Avalanche," from any spotter. This might come across as: "Avalanche, this is Boystown, two-six Charlie. Fire mission, over?"

I would answer, we'd exchange a two-letter challenge code of the day or even hour, and then the spotter would call in the mission: what the target was, where it was, how close it was to friendly forces, what kind of rounds he wanted, how many rounds, how many guns, and when. I'd repeat all that back to him verbatim, and then say the word: out.

Our plotting crew would then enter the data into the Mark One-Able, compute a firing solution, and give me a thumbs-up. I'd come back up on the air and say: "Boystown, two-six Charlie, this is Avalanche. Ready, over?" He'd come back and say: "Ready, break, fire." We'd shoot one round from one of the guns in one of the turrets. When we fired, I would say the words "Shot, over?" on the radio. He would reply "Shot, out," meaning he acknowledged there was one on the way. Then, five seconds before the round should actually land, I'd say the words "Stand by, out." That phrase alerted him to look for an explosion on the ground on or at least near the target. When he saw it, he'd come back and say "Spots: right two hundred, up eighty feet, add three hundred."

Spots were corrections, from his point of view, to bring the fall of shot closer to the target. They were always given in the precise order of: deflection, elevation, and range. Deflection meant bring the computed impact point right (or left) X yards. Elevation meant move the target's position being generated by your computer X feet higher (or lower), and range meant move the target's computed distance from you, the shooter, by X yards. But: those spots were from his point of view. Those corrections had to be converted into the corresponding numbers from our point of view, since we were the ones doing the shooting. The target he was seeing might be west of him, but, since we were out at sea, east of us. Hence the need for geometric conversion. The spots would be entered into the computer, and then I'd say: "ready," and he'd again say: "ready, break, fire." We'd do this until our rounds were landing on or near the target.

That was the moment we'd been waiting for. He'd say the word: "target," meaning we were right on. Then he'd tell us again what he wanted: nine rounds, Main Battery, three guns, high-cap (or armor-piercing, white phosphorous, or even fragmenting air-burst ammo), fuze quick, meaning point detonating, at my command. I'd read all that back to him, and when the guns were loaded, I'd go back and once again say: ready. The spotter would then look hard at the target, which might be a half-dozen enemy tanks in a staging area, to make sure they hadn't moved, and then give the familiar: "ready, break, fire" command. We'd send three salvos in succession, using three of our fourteen-inch guns, and then I'd report: "rounds complete." We might then get more spots, or a request: "repeat," meaning do it again. Or we might get: "target destroyed, mission complete." And then, ten seconds later: "Avalanche, this is Boystown two-six Charlie: fire mission, over?"

All this time we'd be cruising at five knots offshore on a straight-line course to maintain position stability. The spotter might be in a light plane, orbiting at ten thousand feet above the battlefield, or just behind the front, peering through a set of stereo-optic binoculars from behind a convenient pile of rocks. More likely he was on the ground right up there on the front line while dodging incoming bullets. This was called indirect fire, which meant we'd never actually see the target, but rather compute a virtual target location based entirely on what the spotter told us. We could be firing on invisible (to us) targets as much as fifteen miles away. We didn't need to see them: we'd shoot into their general neighborhood, and the spotter would walk us on.

When the Japanese suddenly began seeing large explosions erupting nearby and then starting to get closer and closer, they'd know exactly what was happening and, quite often, they got the hell out of there. But not before dispatching a team of snipers to go find the spotter who was bringing the end of the world down upon their heads.

There were three of us in the Gunnery Department who'd been trained to do this stuff. I was the most experienced Gunnery Liaison Officer responder onboard. The other two were trainees, coming along. I always made sure one of them was with me for actual fire missions so he could soak up some firsthand experience and become qualified to "talk."

We had to have memorized these highly choreographed commands and responses. If a spotter called in a mission and the GLO read it back to him and missed one word, the spotter would angrily declare: wrong! and then we'd have to do the whole thing over again until the dummy on the ship got it right, word for pre-scripted word. Only commissioned officers could be a Gunnery Liaison Officer responder, and if he was good at it, he was known as someone who could "talk" NGFS—naval gunfire support.

There were all sorts of arcane artillery terms and words with precise meanings. The spotters ashore were usually Marine or Army artillery officers who knew all those terms by heart, but we kept a large cardboard poster down in Plot so if something strange came in, we had a ready reference. Fire missions were almost always the result of an infantry unit that suddenly found itself in dire straits and desperately needed help to survive, so none of this was done casually. Occasionally, it was the ground spotter himself who was in trouble. The Japanese had special teams organized to hunt down artillery and naval gunfire spotters. There were stories told at the Marine Corps naval gunfire support school of spotters calling down naval gunfire on their own positions as the vengeful hunters closed in on them.

We fired our area-fire mission for ninety minutes, finishing up fifteen minutes before H-hour, when the Marines, who'd been milling about their transports offshore in a variety of amphibious boats, finally turned in toward the beach and began the actual invasion. There was a line of cruisers that had been assigned to begin firing all along a line some five hundred yards ahead and parallel to the actual landing beaches once the first boats hit the shoreline. The idea was to walk a continuous line of eight-inch gun fire in front of the troops as they jumped off their amphibious boats and headed inland. The battleships would move farther offshore and wait for the calls-for-fire to begin once the troops ran into targets worthy of fourteen- and sixteen-inch shells.

Our captain, recognizing that it was going to take a while for the literally thousands of Marines to get ashore and start inland, relaxed general quarters and ordered chow to be made available to the gun stations. We were sufficiently far enough offshore as to not be able to see in detail what was going on up and down the various beaches, other than that the entire island was now obscured by clouds of dirty brown gun smoke. The sea offshore was covered in small boats as wave after wave lunged at the beaches.

I'd gone topside to get some fresh air and to see the spectacle that was taking place to the west of us. Once again, I felt more like an observer than a combatant. Whatever hell that was erupting as those Marines spilled out of their boats and charged up those black sand beaches was literally not our direct concern. Supposedly there were bigger guns up there on that volcano that could reach out to where we were, but we were confident that, if they did, we could move even farther seaward until we outranged them, and soon crush their emplacements with shells twice the size of theirs.

As far as that went, I still found it hard to imagine that there were any Japanese left alive along those beaches after *days*, much less months, of preliminary bombardment. The volcano at the southern end of the island might be a different problem, assuming the Japanese had had time to bore into it like armored termites and fill it with artillery. Inland, however, on that long, narrow swath of flat volcanic wasteland between the volcano and the rockpile on the north end of the island, there didn't seem to be much going on. I wondered why. Supposedly that was where the military airfields were, which is why we needed to take this crappy little island in the first place.

I was about to head down to the wardroom to grab a bite when suddenly that low-hanging dust and smoke cloud along the beach mushroomed up into a maelstrom of explosions. Hundreds of bright white waterspouts began rising in the surf among the incoming landing craft, and streams of tracer fire were converging right along the beach. The GQ alarm went off and everyone hustled back to their battle stations as *Nevada* began a ponderous turn to port and the main turrets began to rumble as they trained out. My last glimpse of the beach as I dashed into the protection of the "box" was that the landing zone had become an expanding mass of erupting shells, incandescent boils of fire, and flying debris that consisted of wrecked landing craft and the shredded remains of Marines. All along the black slopes of the volcano gun flashes winked red and yellow and the growing roar of artillery rose to a crescendo we could still hear until the weather-deck hatches were shut. Men were running to their battle stations, sliding down the companionways like spawning salmon to the decks below as fast as they could before the heavy armored hatches began to lean over into their four-inch-thick coamings.

They waited, I thought. The bastards had waited until hundreds, maybe thousands of Marines were concentrated on those black beaches in an increasingly chaotic traffic jam of boats, tanks, support equipment, and men, and *then* they had let fly. I felt an impact and then a second as something hit the ship. I just about flew down the next companionway, my feet barely touching the rungs of the ladder as a bunch of us cascaded down to our GQ stations.

Plot. I've got to get back to Plot. Those impacts meant only one thing. Even way out here, the Japs were shooting at *us*—and getting hits.

FIVE

The noise level down in Plot was out of hand when I got there. One of the loudest voices was that of Commander Willson, who was berating the director officer to give him a bearing to whoever was shooting at us. I went immediately to the plotting table; I knew what was coming next even as I felt the ship leaning into another turn. The deckplates were beginning to rattle as our four huge propellers started to thrash the water in earnest. Whenever enemy shore batteries had opened fire on us, we'd now go into the so-called counter-battery mode. If we could see the enemy gun emplacement, the director officer would get an optical range and bearing to it. The big fourteen-inch guns would train out onto the bearing, elevate to hit that range, and reply. The enemy gunners would lose their enthusiasm for pricking the dragon as everything within a two-hundred-yard circle of them went skyward along with their cannon.

Even if we only knew the general direction of where the enemy's rounds were coming from, we could fire back. We'd shoot back down the incoming bearing and then start walking the salvos inland until things went quiet. But today, we had a problem: the director officer way up on the rangefinder tower was reporting he couldn't see *anything* along the shoreline or even on the slopes of *Suribachi*. The entire island had disappeared behind an immense cloud of smoke and fire as the Japanese came out of their holes and unloaded on the landing beaches with everything they had.

"Whaddya mean, you can't see?" Willson shouted into his telephone. "Gimme a fucking bearing, goddammit!"

I was listening in as Marty tried to explain that the entire island was obscured in gun smoke. "One minute ago, I could see the individual boats landing; now I can't see *anything* ashore," he reported. "I suggest we open the range, Commander. That shit could be coming from anywhere."

Willson slammed the phone down and glared. A talker handed him a second phone. The captain, the man mouthed.

Willson listened and then began to shake his head. "We have no idea where that came from, Captain. Iwo Jima, that's the best I can do." He listened, frowning at whatever invective was coming down that phone line. "Yes, sir, we can do that, but what we really need to do right now is open the range and then get set up for area shore-bomb. The Marines're gonna be screaming for help here real soon."

He listened some more and then nodded. "Yes, sir, exactly. Get us out to twenty thousand yards. If I get a lull, I'll lay some rounds on *Suribachi*."

He hung up the phone and looked around. He knew we'd all been eavesdropping hard. "Captain wanted a hundred high-cap on *Suriba-chi*," he said with a cold grin. "On general principles, I think. We're going out to twenty thousand yards, then getting set up for fire missions. I don't think they have fourteen-inch guns on that island. We do."

The admiral commanding the bombardment group apparently agreed with putting some distance between us and whatever cheeky bastards had shot at us. All the battlewagons were decamping, but not too far out. The five-inch were effective out to eighteen thousand yards, or nine miles. They could shoot farther than that, but with decreasing accuracy. We could hit Iwo from a range of almost fifteen miles with the big guns, if we had to; six-inch shore guns could maybe get reliable hits at ten miles. If we'd been dealing with another battleship, our radar could have put the Mark One-Able on target in seconds. But with an island? All the radar could see was a five-mile-long line of green light on the scopes. It was clear that the big boys had all crept in much too close to the island, probably for sightseeing as much as direct fire missions. Then the phone talker connected to main engineering sounded off.

"Damage Control Central reports a Class B fire on the port catapult; the spotter plane is over the side. Mount fifty-eight also took a direct hit; multiple casualties."

That sobered everyone up: multiple casualties? I think we'd all been feeling somewhat outraged that some peashooter in a cave had taken a shot at *Nevada*. But they had, and now we had people down and one of our two spotting seaplanes over the side. Everyone in Plot went from how-dare-they to oh-shit-this-isn't-an exercise-anymore. I could see it on their faces. They could probably see it on mine, too.

"Fire mission," one of the talkers yelled. "*Emergency* fire mission," he added. "Channel seven."

In our haste to open the range to the enemy's shore batteries, we'd momentarily forgotten our primary mission. Now we had to quickly establish that slow, steady offshore track which would allow any GLO ashore to send us initial coordinates, ranges, bearings, and, eventually, spots to flatten whatever it was that was killing Marines in great numbers.

They'd waited, I reminded myself. Let as many Marines pile onto the beaches as the Americans had to offer and then, and *only* then, turn on the meat grinder they'd been building for two years. The problem was that we were still en route to a more distant firing position. We'd have to wait until we got there and then begin the tedious process of establishing our track and precise navigational position before we could help anybody back there. I took my place at the plotting table and told the spotter to delay thirty for repositioning. He immediately called another ship, as we were no help. I felt embarrassed, but unless we knew precisely where we were, we couldn't hit anything reliably except maybe the island itself.

It took forty-five minutes because the salient navigational points on the island that we'd use to determine our position were no longer visible. The volcano was the only visible nav point above that huge blanket of gun smoke. The rest of the points were being taken by radar. A visual bearing was always more reliable than a radar bearing, but that's all we had. The plotters were anxiously awaiting the word that the track was stable, the computer was satisfied, and the guns were finally loaded. We then settled into the familiar and almost comforting routine of clipped code words exchanged in the arcane dialect of naval gunfire support. Soon the fourteen-inch guns were shaking the ship as *Nevada* joined in on whatever hell was in progress ashore on Iwo Jima.

We kept three shore fire-control party frequencies up on speakers in Plot. We could clearly hear machine gun fire and even screams in the background when they called in a mission. The contrast between the calm, air-conditioned, and almost clinical sounds of Main Battery Plot and what was bleeding through the radio transmissions was stark. None of us wanted to even *think* about what it must be like on that wretched beach. Ten minutes before, Willson had waved an unlit cigarette at the plotting table, and fifteen guys had lit up simultaneously. Technically, there was no smoking at GQ, but the nicotine addicts, including our boss, had begun to visibly twitch. I sort of wanted one, but there was enough smoke in the air that I didn't need one.

Willson again asked the director officer if he could see anything. I glanced at my watch. It was getting late in the day. A dark thought hit me: Time flies, when you're having fun.

"The end of the world," Marty said. "And I swear to God: it's getting worse."

Half of us broke for chow at 1830, keeping the other half of the shore-bomb team on station. There was no diminution of the battle ashore as the sun set. If anything, Marty was right. We'd been at Tarawa and Saipan, and it did indeed sound like the battle was increasing in ferocity, with far too many calls for fire just about on top of the spotter's position, meaning they were being overrun. Some of us didn't want to leave, but Commander Willson was adamant.

"We'll be here all night if not for the next forty-eight hours," he declared. "Get fed, get back. We have to pace ourselves, boys and girls, and we have to *not* get so tired that we start making math errors when they're calling in danger-close missions like this."

We acknowledged his point. A danger-close mission was one in which the target was really close to friendly positions.

Dinner was punctuated by the double blams of the five-inch mounts shaking the crockery cabinets in the wardroom. Not all missions called for the big guns, so our secondary battery of twin five-inch .38 caliber guns were in the thick of the fire-support action. The word going around the wardroom was that we, ourselves, had lost thirteen, killed in the early afternoon's counterbattery. It had been a direct hit on one of the lightly armored five-inch mounts, and only the fire-stop doors to the magazines below had prevented a much bigger explosion. I knew a lot of the five-inch gun crew people; this was a sad night for the Gunnery Department.

The rumors from Iwo Jima were getting worse by the hour: thousands, not hundreds, of casualties, almost no progress in getting inland, and apparently all of our pre-invasion bombardment had done little more than move small mountains of volcanic sand around. Some of the rumors were pretty colorful—this was the junior-officer wardroom, where imagination always trumped facts. There was, however, no disguising the fact that the Marines were in deep shit over there on this disgusting little island called Iwo Goddamned Jima.

We ate as quickly as we could and then headed back down to Plot. There was none of the usual chatter as we hurried down through the scuttle hatches embedded in the main companionway hatches. The scuttle was a steel hole wide enough to let a human body through, over which a circular hatch hung upright. The main hatch was a ten-by-six armored slab that weighed more than a ton and had to be hydraulically lifted and sealed. It remained shut when the ship was in action of any kind.

It wasn't as if we were afraid—we were as safe as safe gets in amphibious warfare, locked within the armored steel hide of a battleship. Definitely not scared, but maybe just a little bit embarrassed, especially when we resumed listening to those radio speakers again. Willson finally turned them off. It wasn't the actual transmissions that were bothering everybody. It was all the screaming and gunfire in the background, and the way transmissions just suddenly cut right off in mid-sentence.

SIX

The entire GQ team spent the night in Plot, with some guys
being instructed to go flop along the bulkheads when they began making too many math errors while plotting fire missions. It
started to slow down a little around midnight, but apparently the
Japanese never quit coming. We'd moved back in to twelve thousand yards, so there were many more missions for the five-inch now,
which made sense—you didn't chase machine gun pillboxes with
fourteen-inch shells. Unbeknownst to us, Commander Willson had
switched the tactical circuit to a set of headphones, so he was still
able to eavesdrop on the horror-show ashore. He told us the biggest
problem was mobility, based on what he was hearing over the tactical radio. The Marine bosses were screaming at the troops to get off
the beach, on which the Japs had zeroed in with their artillery. The
replies never changed—we can't move. It wasn't that the machinery
couldn't move—and it couldn't—but that the men themselves were

sinking up to their knees in this viscous, black, volcanic sand-ash-pumice mixture. The Marines simply couldn't move, and some of the wounded, thrashing around on their stretchers, were subsiding into it and actually burying themselves alive. If a tracked vehicle tried to go forward, its treads simply buried the tank up to its turret. Worse, what had looked like normal tideline terraces turned out to be a *series* of terraces, ten feet high, the accumulated accretion of a century of eruptions. And then it rained.

The call went out for Marston matting, those great big, hinged sheets of perforated metal that once unrolled, provided a temporary surface that allowed aircraft operations to resume on a cratered airfield. Some ships offshore had some matting, and once that was brought to the beach the Marines could finally get out of the trap the enemy had set for them. The Navy couldn't help—shells of whatever caliber also mostly just moved this muck around. If the whole island was like this, our own bombardment of *Suribachi* had been a waste of time. We did get reports that enemy artillery was still raining down on the landing beaches, so the captain ordered us to lay down another area bombardment of the volcano's slopes. It wasn't exactly well-directed fire without spotters at night, but I think it made the captain feel better and it certainly made the poor bastard Marines feel better to see those huge explosions tearing up the mountain throughout the night.

The admiral finally called over and told us to knock it off; we'd need the ammo when daylight returned. That was certainly true, and Willson was already becoming concerned about inventory. If we ran out, we'd have to go all the way back to Guam, some eight hundred miles, one way, to rearm, since the underway replenishment ships couldn't handle our Main-Battery ammo. That would mean one less dragon on the line for almost eight days.

Our view of the landing beaches remained obscured at sunrise, but the radio nets revealed the true scope of the disaster. It is the nature of an amphibious invasion that you send wave after wave of troops ashore, trying to achieve a solid numerical superiority against the defenders as quickly as possible. The primary assumption behind that plan was that the troops who'd already landed were able to get out of the arriving troops' way. By L+2, that was only partially true. Some troops had broken out and were spreading out onto the airfield right in front of them, but more, far too many more, were still trying to extricate themselves from the actual beachheads. Based on what we were hearing there was a line of small but deeply buried gun-and-mortar emplacements between the airfield and the beach that had the whole operation pinned down. Lines of nasty rainsqualls in the area meant that our supporting carrier air couldn't make strafing and bombing runs, and if one believed the reports, the ground terrain was getting even worse.

Commander Willson finally got on one of the spotter nets. In plain language he recommended *Nevada* fire Main Battery, danger close, all along the beachhead front line for ten minutes, which might give the infantry a chance to bolt off the beach and onto the harder airfield perimeter, opening up the beachhead to reinforcements. Using plain language meant that Japanese intercept stations would hear him, but by that time the situation was so bad that there was no point to using codes. At first there was no reply, and I half expected a sharp reprimand from the admiral controlling the gunline. Then an extremely agitated voice came up on the net and said: "Jesus *God*, *Nevada*, do it, do it, *do it*. Five hundred yards from the water line! We'll recall the people in the gap."

I personally set the plot and then ordered up Main Battery, full salvos, high-cap, danger close, *commence firing!*

The big dogs let fly and I could only hope and pray we weren't dropping thousands of pounds of high explosive on our own guys' heads. I glanced across at Willson, who'd been getting fall-of-shot reports from the Main-Battery director officer. He suddenly nodded his head vigorously. Go on, he mouthed. Go on. "Go on" was spotter language for: keep shooting—you're right on target.

Dear God, I hope so, I thought. I brought the gun target line to the right two degrees after each ten-gun salvo until we'd traversed the entire one-mile-long landing zone. I was about to reverse the line of fire when Willson put up a hand and I ordered a check-fire. In my excitement I'd forgotten to listen to the radio nets. Apparently that entire Gordian knot of over three *thousand* Marines and their machines had finally been able to go over the top and were running *en masse* out onto the airfield and into new positions. Without opposition.

For about one minute.

We knew the lull wouldn't last long—the Japanese recovered and opened back up from yet other artillery positions, but we'd broken up that lethal logjam down on the beach for just long enough.

And so it went, for the next ten hours. By dusk, the amphibious commander, aware now that anything sent into the beach was going to get stuck, closed the landing beaches. This slowed the slaughter, but it also shut off the flow of ammo and water to the Marines desperately trying to move forward out of that lethally designed killing zone. A frantic-sounding Marine spotter came up and said he could still see artillery gun flashes on *Suribachi*, about halfway up the slopes. Commander Willson jumped to the plot and drew a box on the eastern slopes of the volcano that contained the middle third of the mountain accessible to our guns.

"Saturation fires, " Willson ordered. "Clean 'em out."

We never heard back from that spotter, but that wasn't unusual— we'd learned that the spotters' life expectancy could be really short if the Japanese were anywhere close to them. Sometimes they could make a call-for-fire, sometimes they had to just freeze in place. I felt that as long as we were punching fourteen-inch shells into *Suribachi* and all those caves and tunnels, we *had* to be doing some good. I finally had to just sit down; coffee could only sustain me for so long. Willson started sending the officers to the wardroom in relays; I made sure I brought a sandwich for him when I came back.

The phone from the bridge chirped. Willson listened and then called for another ammo inventory for the Main Battery. In the meantime, the five-inch guns began pumping illumination rounds out over the island. These would burst at about ten thousand feet, deploy a parachute, and then drift down while a magnesium flare suspended beneath the chute lit up everything within line-of-sight like a welding shop. This would go on all night as each of the fire-support ships, the big boys, the cruisers, and the destroyers, expended their allocated amount of flares. The eye-blistering light would give our Marines a chance to spot movement out in front of friendly front lines as the enemy came out of their spider holes with knives and swords to hunt down Marines in their foxholes and kill them silently.

The ammo report came back. Yes, we needed to go re-arm. The cruisers and destroyers could leave the island and find an ammunition ship offshore, go alongside, pass shells and powder cans by highline, and come right back. We could do that for the five-inch, but not for the big stuff. Once we got to Guam, we would anchor alongside an ammunition ship and use her booms and tackle to move the huge shells and pallets of powder cans from her holds to our main deck. From there they'd be passed down elevators and scuttles to the deep magazines. They had to send three destroyers with us for protection against submarines and even air attack during the transit. During the transfer process in the harbor, where there'd be hundreds of men exposed out on deck, humping massive shells by hand to the magazine elevator hatches, shore-based Army anti-aircraft guns would stand ready to deal with any long-range Japanese bombers. The whole process reminded all of us that to go "just down the road" in the Pacific usually meant a one-thousand-mile trip at twenty knots. Since we'd left station anyway, we took the opportunity to refuel, re-provision, and enjoy some mail while we were there. Two other battleships remained on station, so the Marines never lacked for support.

We got back on L-Day +10. The generals and the admirals had

predicted a quick victory on this tiny island, but it was turning out to be anything but. Ten days into the operation, the Marines were taking such heavy casualties that the outcome was actually in doubt. Even with three light aircraft carriers and two battlewagons in support, daily progress was being measured in feet. Willson reminded us that the Japanese had had a few years to prepare Iwo for invasion, and they had probably honeycombed the entire island with *miles* of tunnels, hundreds of fortified positions, extensive minefields, overlapping fields of artillery fire, and caches of ammo, water, and food. Mount *Suribachi*, as we were learning to our sorrow, rose 550 feet above sea level, and was a porous cinder cone filled like an African termite mound with soldiers, stores, water, guns, and firing positions.

A Marine team came aboard when we got back to give us an update on the situation. Simply put, the Marines were getting nowhere and dying by the hundreds. We resumed our station as the on-call fire-support battleship, while *Colorado* finally departed the line. *Colorado* had been taught a severe lesson three days before the Marines went ashore. She and some of the other offshore fire-support forces had closed in to the island in order to put some point-blank sixteen-inch into the flanks of *Suribachi*. There had been no return fire. We now knew that the Japanese had been just laying low in order not to reveal where their big artillery pieces were. *Colorado* went into 2,500 yards, just over a mile offshore.

Apparently, one of the enemy artillery commanders just couldn't resist and turned loose with three eight-inch casemated guns. The first salvo blew one of the scouting aircraft off its catapult rail on *Colorado*'s port quarter. The second put two eight-inch rounds into her pilothouse, killing the entire bridge crew and the ship's executive officer. The captain survived only because he had elected to step into the armored conning tower, whose sides were six-inch thick steel, to retrieve his personal binoculars seconds before. She took more hits along her armored sides, which bounced off, but others landed in the densely clustered 20mm gun tubs on the 01 level and two even penetrated the ship's sides just above the armor belt, starting fires and killing more crewmen down on the forward mess decks. She was leaving for a fuel stop at Guam, and then all the way back to Pearl for repairs.

Our director officer had called down that he could just make out where the incoming was originating, so *Nevada* had turned her Main Battery loose on those casemates using direct fire, controlled from the Main-Battery director. Marty actually got to see one of the artillery pieces get blown out of its cave into the air and then there had been a truly satisfying secondary explosion when the gun's ready-service ammo went up *inside* the mountain. After that, *Suribachi* went silent. All the wanna-be sightseers maneuvered to open a respectful distance from the volcano. And then some kamikaze aircraft appeared out of nowhere and one of them struck *Colorado*, inflicting even more casualties. She was never in danger of sinking, but so many of her crew had been wounded or killed that she probably wouldn't be back. Another formation of kamikazes had attacked the light-carrier formation, crashed one of them, starting a hangar deck fire that eventually required them to abandon ship. Two of our destroyers had had to torpedo her to finish it.

I went back down to Plot after the Marine briefing, which had been truly sobering. One of the phone talkers waved me over to take a call. He said there was a First Lieutenant Bart Martin, USMC, who'd just been brought aboard from the beach for medical treatment. The corpsman making the call said he was badly injured and was asking for me.

I was bowled over. Bart? Here? Bart Martin had been a classmate and close friend at Georgia Tech. His mother and my mother had been sorority sisters. His daddy had been a peanut farmer's son who'd gotten rich in the farm fuels and chemical business in south Georgia. Their plantation was not too far away from ours. We'd grown up in similar circumstances—in large antebellum houses, hunting, fishing, horses, football, cars, and drinking. Bart had become a serious drinker; I'd tried to keep up with him but failed whiskey drinking, much like I failed cigarette smoking. Bart, on the other hand, had adopted Tech's fight song as his modus operandi while at the university. He was a first-class "rambling wreck from Georgia Tech."

Once I'd graduated, while I was still thinking about going into the Navy, Bart had already signed up with the Marines. Being an engineer, he'd ended up in the artillery branch, just in time for Saipan and then Iwo. He'd been assigned to the Marine Third division, Thirteenth artillery regiment, first as an officer in the JASCO, which stood for Joint Assault Signal Companies, who technically coordinated calls-for-fire from front line Marine and Army spotters with the Navy ships offshore and any close air support ships or units. A second-lieutenant in the field would call in a request for naval gunfire to regimental headquarters via field telephone or radio. The JASCO's job was to assign the fire mission either to organic Marine artillery or to offshore naval gunfire or air support. If the decision was made to assign naval gunfire to the problem, he also had to translate the spotter's actual location and where the target was into coordinates that a ship offshore could use to compute a firing solution.

It was a cumbersome process, and it often meant that the front line spotter's urgent request for artillery support, Marine or naval, was delayed, sometimes for hours. A spotter up on the front lines needed rounds on target *now*, not hours from now. The solution, of course, was to assign each naval gunfire support ship its own dedicated spotter. The problem was that the Marines in the field didn't have many radios that could talk directly to the ships. A naval gunfire support warship, like *Nevada*, had unlimited and stable electric power, air-conditioned plotting rooms, and an entire compartment filled with radios, operators, plotters, computers, and message recorders. The Marine spotter up on the front lines crouched in a stinking hole in the ground, surrounded by the chaos of infantry battle, with one Marine next to him hand-cranking hard on a field portable generator that fed erratic voltage to a radio harnessed to yet another Marine's back, while the spotter himself tried to focus oversized binoculars on the enemy position that desperately needed to die, and all this while knowing that Japanese sniper teams were actively hunting for him. On Saipan, and Peleliu before it, a shavetail lieutenant front line spotter had about a three-day life expectancy unless he was well protected.

And now Bart was here in *Nevada*'s sick bay? I asked Commander Willson if I could go see him, and he quickly gave me permission. The forward battle dressing station was just forward of the senior officer wardroom. I had to go up two decks, through a series of watertight doors, through the wardroom, and only then into the medical station. The first thing that struck me was the smell: it was awful. I realized that it was coming from a pile of blood-soaked Marine uniforms piled up around the three triage tables. The second thing was that the station was *full* of casualties. I hadn't known that Marine wounded were being brought out to warships—I'd seen hospital ships offshore and assumed that's where the wounded would go, once, and *if*, they made it off the beach. I learned that the hospital ships had been overwhelmed after the second day and now any ship with doctors and a decent-sized sick bay, such as cruisers and even some destroyers, had been pressed into emergency medical service.

A harried-looking chief corpsman asked me what I wanted. I told him. He ordered a young petty officer to take me over to the triage holding area. This consisted of six movable beds in one corner of the compartment, where corpsmen were tending to a half-dozen motionless shapes covered in bloody medical drapes. A lieutenant commander, whom I assumed was a doctor, was hands-deep into the wounds of one man, his rubber gloves bright red. I saw Bart on one of the beds. His face was ghastly: pale, almost blue-white, his eyes frantic and his lips moving soundlessly. A young corpsman was wiping his face and giving him tiny sips of ice water, which dribbled down his chin into a soggy mass of bandages on his chest. The rest of the station was a subdued tangle of docs and corpsmen tending to wounds, doing ad hoc surgery, and stabbing ampules of morphine into bloody bodies. The corner in which I was standing was much less active, and that's when I realized these were the cases that the triage docs had deemed beyond saving. I felt sick to my stomach. To make matters worse, Bart already stank of dead flesh. The whole compartment reeked of it. Gangrene must be rampant over here.

Bart focused bloodshot eyes on me and I saw recognition bloom. "Lee-boy," he croaked. "They done got me."

"Y'all be still, Bart," I said. "What the hell happened?"

"I was at the regimental JASCO," he whispered. "Then I had to go out and spot."

To my horror, each time he spoke tiny red bubbles escaped from his bruised lips. One of his eyes kept closing and opening, almost as if it was in time with his heartbeat. If that was the case, it was much too slow. "Knew you were here on this big boy. Even heard your voice sometimes."

"Goddamn, Bart, I'm so sorry. But they'll get you fixed up, I promise. We've got good docs on this ship."

He flashed me a familiar "you've got to be shitting me" look. I pretended not to recognize it.

"Lee-boy," he whispered, "we done stepped *in* it over there on that fucking island. Those bastards were ready and waiting. The gin-rals said it'd be a one, maybe two-week deal. They was wrong, Old Son. They *killin'* us, sure as hell. An' they themselves don't care about dyin'. They *want* to die. Goddamned nightmares rising up out of the dark, with *swords*, for Chrissake, screaming shit, and cuttin' guys' heads off."

He gasped with the effort of speaking. I grabbed one of his hands and told him, easy, easy, catch your breath, Bart, easy, now.

His eyes widened. "You don't know, Lee-boy. Ain't nobody knows what's happening over there. It's—it's—"

"We're trying to help, Bart. We're shooting, day and night. Ran clean out of ammo, even."

"Ain't workin', my brother. You just movin' black sand around.

They's deep. They's in the ground, deep. You gotta start using AP, from a long way away. Make it come straight down, not sideways."

And then he took a breath, or tried to. He couldn't find it. His face contorted as he tried and tried to get that breath, and then a gout of bright red blood erupted noisily out of his mouth and nose while his eyes rolled back up into their sockets and he went rigid before suddenly going limp, his entire body relaxing into the peace of the grave.

The chief corpsman appeared. He closed Bart's eyes. "He's gone, Lieutenant," he said. "He really wanted to see you. Kept insisting you were onboard. There was no chance he was gonna make it. I'm sorry, sir. But I'm damn glad you came."

It was my turn to take a deep breath. Bart was dead. My brother in arms. My hunting buddy. My drinking buddy. My girl-chasing accomplice. Lee-boy, he called me. Just like old times. My teenage soulmate. I was speechless. Unabashed, I wept.

Then I heard the Main Battery cutting loose topside. The fourteen-inch guns were speaking. I wanted to stay there, to hold his hand, to speak comforting words, to remember all those good times, but those colossal thumps told me I was needed elsewhere.

God Dammit. God *Dammit!*

SEVEN

Things had changed when I got back to Plot. First, the ship had moved away from Iwo, all the way out to fifteen miles. Thirty thousand yards, to be precise. Just about maximum effective range for our fourteen-inch guns. Someone on Admiral Oldendorf's staff had pointed out that direct high-cap fire, however impressive, was obviously not penetrating to where the enemy really was—deep underground. The solution to that was twofold: get out to extreme ranges, which meant that our heavy shells would be coming straight down and not just blowing volcanic sand dunes all over the place but going deep. The second part was that we were going to start using armor-piercing ammunition instead of high-cap.

Not for long, I thought. If you stood in the magazine, as I had done many times, the differences between an AP round and a high-cap projectile were obvious. Both projectiles had body diameters of fourteen inches. The high-capacity round weighed about 1,700 pounds and carried half a ton of filler, meaning almost the entire body of the projectile was filled with high explosive. The armor-piercing rounds were even longer than the high-cap rounds, and weighed almost 2,300 pounds, but only about half their length was actual, explosive-filled projectile. The forward half of the round was the so-called cap, made of brittle steel. A high-capacity round went off when both its nose and base fuzes sensed that the projectile had gone from a velocity of 2,600 feet per second to zero in a single microsecond.

The armor-piercing round needed time, measured again in microseconds, to actually smash through the target's armor, get inside to where the good stuff was, and then, and only then, explode. That cap was the key. First, it gave aerodynamic stability to what was basically a squat and much shorter round than the high-cap. Second, the cap, being made of brittle but also exceptionally hard steel, shattered the enemy ship's armor plate, allowing that blunt, also hardened, steel shape behind it, filled with "only" 350 pounds of explosive, to penetrate, and with a time-delay fuze, to go off in one of the target ship's magazines or an engine room.

I understood Admiral Oldendorf's order: The theory was that, using their time-delay fuzes, the plunging AP rounds would actually penetrate ten, perhaps twenty feet underground before going off. If that's where the Japanese tunnels were, then the battleships might actually begin to do some good. We'd moved an awful lot of volcanic sand around on the slopes of Mount *Suribachi*. When we could see where the enemy had actually run out their shore guns, the high-cap could do the job. The problem area, however, was on all that mostly flat land between *Suribachi* and those low hills to the north of the volcano. The guys on the ground were finding out that what looked like empty ground concealed a honeycomb of tunnels, firing pits, bunkers, living quarters, ammo dumps, ops centers, and even hospitals. The destroyers could sweep the flat ground and kill any enemy troops above ground, but it was going to take what the spotters had begun calling the beasts to root out the real problem.

But where to shoot them? Between *Suribachi* and the other end of the island, a distance of a scant three miles, the terrain looked mostly like something out of the deserts of the American Southwest. No trees, barely any bushes, large boulder fields with ancient, solidified lava ridges, and a thousand cracks which could be just fissures in the ground or the entrance to caves filled with Japanese soldiers. There was a bigger problem, however: ever since the older battlewagons had become shore bombardment specialists, their magazines had been filled with high-cap, not armor-piercing as would have been the case, say, during the First World War. Each battleship carried some AP, but nothing when compared to the number of high-cap rounds. It was an 85–15 ratio at most. Perhaps the admiral had forgotten that.

I approached Commander Willson with two questions. The first was about the small number of AP rounds we carried. He sighed and said we'd beefed that up a bit back in Guam, but that, yes, it was gonna be a problem. We currently had about 450 rounds onboard.

The second question centered on an even thornier problem. "We do know where friendly front lines are, don't we, sir?" I asked.

"That's a variable feast, Lee," he said. "They gain ground, then get pushed back. But, yeah, we do as long as the Marines themselves know and the division or regimental JASCO keeps us informed."

I pointed out to him that each Marine Division had its own grid system. A Third Division spotter would be working from a different grid system than, say, a Fourth Division spotter. Each division was supposed to be working its own part of the Iwo battle, so as long as they stayed in their own sectors, there wouldn't be a problem. But now that so many Marines had been killed on Iwo, the Marines were assigning fighting forces according to how many men they had left, not according to which sector they were supposed to operate in. That was creating a lot of confusion, because the grid was the basis for determining where the spotter and the target was on the ground on Iwo.

The grid was vital but simple enough. It was a crosshatched system, with north-south and east-west lines spaced at intervals that represented a known number of yards. Each vertical line and each horizontal line had a number. To specify a position, you called out the number of the vertical line first, then the horizontal line's number. If the position was at an intersection, there would be two sets of numbers, like 26 (the twenty-sixth vertical line from the left side of the grid), and 18 (the eighteenth horizontal line down from the top of the grid). If the target was lurking inside a square, you'd need two more numbers, like 26–3–18–2, to move the target's position to somewhere inside that box. Both the shooter and the spotter would position the grid over a map of the spotter's area, and simply go from there. Because the sector system was falling apart, grids were overlapping, causing dangerous confusion.

"Then why don't we establish a single island-wide grid," I said. "Like a chess board. When friendly front lines are established on *the* grid, conduct an area-fire with AP into the grid just ahead of them, or wherever the worst fire is coming from. Then see if enemy fire slacks off."

Willson considered it. He was tired. Hell, everybody was tired. The first two fingers of his right hand were stained yellow from all the cigarettes. There were bags under the bags beneath his bloodshot eyes. Seeing his face, I wondered how old he was. Prewar, a commander could be in his late forties.

"Okay," he said. "Design a grid. Not too big, so we can keep it flexible. Something simple, so makee-learn spotters can figure it out—*and* talk it. Then write up a message draft proposing your grid. Lemme see it, then take it to the XO. If he likes the idea, you'll go to the captain. He'll then send it on to Admiral Oldendorf and his staff. You're thinking long-range, plunging-fire AP, right?"

"Yes, sir."

"And change your shirt before you go see the XO."

I looked down. Some of Bart's blood had splattered onto my uniform shirt. That explained some of the funny looks I'd been getting since returning from sick bay.

With active fire missions raining in minute by minute there was no way for me to lay out a grid in Plot; both plotting tables were in full use. I went up to the CIC space to use their dead reckoning plotting table. This was principally used to track surface radar contacts that might be potential targets for the Main Battery, but since Japanese battleships were in short supply and all the surface radar contacts were American, the DRT was available. I enlisted the help of the CIC officer and his chief. Pretty quick we had a workable grid, based on a reference position which was *Suribachi*'s summit. The anchor point for the grid had to be visible to spotters all over the island for the system to work. There was no missing *Suribachi*.

What I didn't know while the three of us were doing the math was that the captain had come down to CIC to get a little air-conditioning. Apparently, he'd been sitting in his Captain's chair behind us, taking a nap, probably, when our plotting and scheming woke him up. All of a sudden, he was standing right behind us. Whoops. So much for going up the chain of command.

"What's all this?" he asked.

I was the senior guy at the table, so the other two looked to me to deal with the captain's question. "We're designing a new grid for the spotters ashore," I said. I explained what had prompted the need for a single grid for the whole island. Spotters in the field were calling in fire missions based on their own positions as laid out on their own regiment's grid. Regimental artillery command posts then had to convert what the spotter was asking for to bearings and ranges from ships stationed offshore. This took time, especially if there were lots of calls for fire. If the spotter could simply say: the target is a cave at the island-wide grid position X and Y, any ship could make the conversion on its own and respond immediately, cutting out the regimental and the division's CP's involvement.

The captain studied the grid. "This your idea? And why do you have blood on your shirt?"

Oops number two. I explained about Bart.

He nodded. "The boss told us to move offshore to a much longer range so we could try plunging fire instead of direct fire. But this—" He pointed at the grid. "This solves the other half of that problem. Write it up and bring it directly to me. Brent Willson is onboard with this idea, right, Mister Bishop?"

I was surprised that the captain knew my name. The ship's complement was 2,200 officers, chiefs, and enlisted men. Big ship, big crew. But he did.

"Yessir," I said. "He told me to create the grid, then bring it up the chain of command."

"No time for that," he said. "Having multiple grids is the basic problem here, I think. From an infantry squad to a spotter, from the spotter to his regimental command post, from the regimental CP to division CP, from there out to a ship—seems to me that those guys in the foxholes need help *now,* not an hour from now. Write it up, show it to Brent Willson, then have him bring it straight to me. I'll get it to Jesse Oldendorf."

"Aye, aye, sir," I said. "But the XO . . . ?"

"I'll fill him in. And good work, Lieutenant. Get a clean shirt on. You're scaring the watchstanders, all that blood. Glad to hear it's not yours."

EIGHT

The captain wanted the grid proposal to be brought directly to him because in a shipboard organization of 2,200 people, paperwork creeps. The Iwo Jima invasion force, numbering well over one hundred thousand men, dwarfed that number. There were three Marine divisions—the Third, Fourth, and Fifth—each with a Marine Major General in charge. There was the amphibious task force commander, whom was a Navy Vice Admiral in charge. There was the naval gunfire support group, with a Rear Admiral at the top. Add to that the Service Force—the transports, oilers, hospital ships, stores ships, repair ships, ammo ships—with yet another Rear Admiral in charge. Beyond all that, way beyond—back in Pearl, there were even more headquarters organizations, and their staffs. The captain had once observed that there were as many people in charge as there were actually shooting at the Japanese.

As it turned out, however, my grid proposal became an exception to the ponderous chain of command process. Captain Edwards got the message out to Admiral Oldendorf on the flagship, who, in turn, made the proposal directly to the three Marine division commanders, for the moment bypassing the Navy command structure, although they probably got a copy-to. In a way, that made sense—the Marines were being asked to allow lowly field spotters to talk directly to individual Navy ships. They still had to go "up their tape" as they called it, to get onshore *Marine* artillery support. But this proposal would allow a direct line to naval gunfire support. The fly in the ointment, Commander Willson said, was that this proposal was going to take detailed control of what was going to be raining down just ahead of the front lines out of the generals' and the admirals' hands.

All three Marine division commanders objected immediately. How will you know, or your ships know, where those front lines are? We may have broken through, achieved a salient. Admiral Oldendorf responded: we think any spotter embedded with your front line units will know *precisely* where the front line is in his sector, probably better than you do, because it's shooting at him. Your CP is necessarily several hundred yards behind them, where, I grant you, it has to be, but I think it's the CP who'll be behind the power curve, not the spotters. Second, you will be up on the radio frequencies being used by spotters. Listen hard. When you hear a call, check your plots. If the direct call is going to create a problem or endanger troops, jump in and stop it until you can resolve it. Otherwise, manage by exception. Spotter makes a frantic call. You don't see a problem? You don't say anything. It's not perfect, but it'll get rounds on targets a hell of a lot quicker than what we're managing now and possibly even save Marine lives.

The Marines acknowledged all that, but then pointed out that there was another problem: spotters and junior officers in general were getting killed by Jap sniper teams faster than they could be replaced. You couldn't just take any grunt out of a foxhole, give him a radio, and tell him to call in a fire mission. The spotters who did that were second lieutenants who'd been to school for *weeks* to learn about artillery, ammunition, ballistics, spot conversion, and how to adjust artillery fire. In other words, how to "talk."

That was a problem that did not have an immediate solution, until the commander of the third Marine division made a suggestion. Canvass the naval gunfire support task group unit ships to see if there were any *Navy* officers who would volunteer to come ashore and take over the spotting mission with this new grid idea until the Marines could get replacements in. Fire-control officers. CIC officers. Gunnery officers. Individuals who were already involved in the fire-support mission, who knew the radio language, types of ammunition, the difference between direct and indirect fire. If a ship had more than one, how's about sending your spare guy ashore?

Commander Willson hooted when he heard that proposition.

"Hey, Navy," he said. "Want to play suggestion-box roulette? Here's one for you: come ashore and join the fight, and get up close and personal with these Japanese. Go with us to the front line. Spend a few days and nights in the mud and the blood. Talk about raising the ante! You want us to change our caveman ways? Get some skin in the game, Admiral. Send us some of your guys, how 'bout it."

I still hadn't had a chance to change my shirt. Those bastards had killed my best friend. "I'd go," I said. "I'm exactly what they need."

"You are just what *we* need right here, Lee Bishop," Willson replied. "You're the fire-control officer. This"—he pointed at all the men and machinery sweating through the blizzard of fire missions that were still coming in nonstop—"*This* is your show, Lee. The Marines are just embarrassed they can't handle the job, so they're trying to make it look like the Navy isn't man enough to come ashore and pitch in."

I nodded. "Yes, sir," I said. "I get that. But if the admiral takes them up on this, I'll go. Jackie Beamish can handle Plot."

My boss suddenly realized I wasn't kidding. His changing expression told me that he was not amused. He pulled me over to one corner of Plot.

"You have no idea of what you'd be getting into," he said with a grim face. "Those jungle-bunnies aren't kidding when they talk about getting down into the mud and the blood. Some of that shit over there is hand-to-hand—you good at that? Can you use a bayonet? Stab somebody in the throat with a K-bar? Operate a machine gun, or a mortar? Stay awake for twenty-four hours on no food and less water? I don't think so, *Mister* Bishop. And did you hear what's causing the shortage of artillery spotters? The Japanese have special teams that do nothing but hunt down our spotters. They don't *banzai* or work the big guns like the rest of them—these guys slither through caves, trenches, with long knives and look for the guy who has binocs instead of a rifle. I've been up to sick bay too, by the way. I've talked to the wounded, trying to figure out how we can be more effective. And for your information, I was the guy who told the corpsmen where to find you when your friend showed up, asking for you by name. Your friend went to Iwo because he'd been trained, hard, to do all those things. You go to Iwo, you'll be dead with a samurai sword rammed up your ass and coming out your mouth on the first night."

I just stared at him. I tried to think of something to say. Anything. I couldn't.

"You want to avenge your best friend?" he asked, in a slightly gentler tone. "You stay right here. Perfect your grid. I agree with the concept; even if the Marines don't, because Marines hate change of any kind. Having one island-wide grid should help to get our gunfire support response time down to minutes instead of hours, so every time a grunt even *sees* one of those bastards, we can put a big-ass shell right between his teeth. But you going over there as some kind of a noble gesture? They'd have to assign three veteran Marines just to keep you alive. That's not helping."

He paused to catch his breath. "Now," he said. "You forget this hero-volunteer shit and get back to the plotting table. Go do something you're qualified to do."

I slunk back to the plotting table with a red face. Everyone pretended they hadn't heard a thing and I was cranking away on a call-for-fire solution seconds later. After a long watch of firing at targets with the five-inch guns I finally hit the rack at around 0300.

An all-hands call came over the 1MC at 0730. The captain gave us a quick update on what was happening over on the island. The gist of it was that the Marines were still not gaining ground. The casualty count was reaching an unsustainable number, the specifics of which, by the way, were not revealed. He did say that the reserve division had been committed, and that *five* more hospital ships had arrived or were en route.

I got breakfast and went back down to Main Battery Plot. Commander Willson was asleep in "his" corner on a pile of GQ life jackets. The whole gunnery department was standing extended watches now—twelve hours on, six hours off—but he'd been staying with it continuously except for occasional chow and head calls. *Nevada* had taken herself off the gunline for a few hours in order to move five-inch ammo out of the deep magazines and into the ready-service rooms right beneath the mounts themselves. We'd had to move back in to eighteen thousand yards during the night so that the five-inch guns could reach their targets on the island, none of which were suitable for fourteen-inch fire.

I got the Plot crew to do some cleanup and roust out more plotting supplies—tracing paper, new charts, and most importantly a replacement coffeepot. Ours had burned out its element. Electrician mates came in and replaced light bulbs, and the electronic technicians tended to some complaints being reported by the Mark One-Able's systems monitoring panel.

While all this was going on—quietly so as not to disturb the almost comatose commander—Major Jed Baxter, the CO of *Nevada*'s Marine detachment, showed up. He'd been seriously wounded at Peleliu but had refused to leave the combat theater, which was why he had this relatively cushy job on a battleship instead of being on the island. All Marines were slim and trim, but the major was downright gaunt, with dark circles under his eyes and a halting, hesitant gait. He'd come to see me, which was a surprise. I knew him from the wardroom and from the fact that his shipboard Marine detachment "owned" one of our five-inch gun mounts, as was customary for ships with detachments.

"Mister Bishop," he said. "How you doin'?"

"Tired," I said, "but here and not over there." I nodded my head in the general direction of Iwo.

"Amen to that," he said. He had to catch his breath between sentences. Chest wound, I thought. "I sometimes feel guilty at being here and not there, but the other twenty-three and nine-tenths hours of the day, I thank God I'm not. Which is why I came to see you, actually."

"Okay," I said. "How can I help you?"

He moved over to the other side of the plotting room for privacy. "You heard the skipper this morning—it's not going well on Iwo."

I nodded.

"In fact, it's a whole lot worse than he let on. The Japanese aren't "winning" in the sense that they're pushing us off the island. But they've had time—years—to turn that whole island—above *and* below ground—into one great big killing field. We've already lost almost 2,500 killed and nearly ten thousand wounded and we own less than a quarter of the island."

I whistled. Those were big numbers indeed. "They getting replacements in?" I asked.

He nodded but then went on to tell me the unsettling news that the life expectancy of replacements was less than twenty-four hours. They were mostly fresh out of boot camp, i.e., basic training, and simply weren't sufficiently combat savvy to survive more than a day. The Marine veterans of Peleliu, Saipan, and the first week of fighting on Iwo knew better than to pop their heads up for a quick look at something you heard that might be coming your way. The new guys *would* do that, and take a sniper's bullet in the eye. He told me that some units ashore had actually asked their CPs to *not* send any more replacements, because it took as many as three guys off the line to retrieve and then carry the body back.

"But," he said, "what I wanted to see you about was some scuttle-butt I heard, namely that you volunteered to go ashore and become an artillery spotter?"

I glanced over at the sleeping form of Commander Willson before nodding. "I did, but I got told in no uncertain terms I wasn't going anywhere because I wasn't qualified to get involved in an infantry battle. I know about shore-fire control, but nothing about staying alive in something as tough as what's happening over there. I couldn't really argue."

"Heard that," he said. "Especially since the Japanese have made it a priority to locate and kill *anyone* they think is calling in artillery on them. We started with twenty-five Marine officer spotters. We're down to *three*."

That was indeed a shock. Three? "Damn," I said. "How are you getting all this dope?"

"I go see our wounded down in sick bay. Make sure they know there's Marines aboard and that we're gonna take care of them. Every one of 'em's anxious to tell me how bad it is over there, in case we might be thinking about sending them back. Anyway, you heard about General Smith's suggestion that we get some naval gunfire officers to help us out?"

"I did; my boss, Commander Willson, told us that that was the Marines' way of saying how much they appreciated our suggestions that we create a direct grid for the island, as in, you wanna help? Come on over, if you think you're man enough."

He grinned. "Yeah, there's definitely some of that shit going on. But I don't think they knew how few spotters they had left when they said that. Now General Holland Smith has declared that to be a *great* idea, and he's put in a formal request to Admiral Kelly Turner to do just that—on a volunteer basis, of course. Your boss is right about you not really being qualified or trained for close-quarters infantry work. My guess is, if you do go over to the beach, they'll lock you up at a regimental headquarters command post and never let you out of their sight. But tell me this: word is this new one-island grid was actually your idea?"

"Yup," I said.

"Still willing to go?" he asked. "'Cause someone's gonna have to brief it to the higher-ups ashore, and I think you'd be perfect."

I hesitated, but then told him yes, but that I'd somehow have to square it with Commander Willson, who was definitely not a fan of the whole idea.

"I'm on pretty good terms with the Captain," he said. "You know, as head of the Marine detachment on board. I've heard he likes the new grid idea. Let him calibrate your Commander Willson here."

"Well, okay then," I replied, with some trepidation. "What could go wrong?"

"Good man," he said approvingly. "Assuming this call for volunteers deal gets approved, we'll put a Marine sea-bag together for you. Field utilities, your canteen and ammo belt, boondocks. You do know how to shoot a rifle?"

It was my turn to grin. "Grew up in the country down in the woolly part of Georgia. Been in the woods once or twice."

"Perfect," he said. "Now we just have to get a shrink to give you a quick checkup."

"Huh?"

"You volunteered," he pointed out, laughing quietly. "Only crazy bastards volunteer. Sane guys *never* volunteer. What size boondocks you think you wear?"

PART II

THE REAL DEAL

NINE

I arrived at the Third Marine Division, second regimental command post on Iwo three nights later. Earlier, just after full dark, when the Japanese snipers broke for tea, the coxswain of a small landing craft had driven smartly up into the surf line and opened the front ramp just long enough for me to hop out with my gear and immediately sink up to my shins in that black, sandy goo they called "the beach." I barely got unstuck before he was reversing in a cloud of diesel smoke and turning down the coast toward the nearest ammo dump, leaving me standing alone next to several steel boxes full of gear and drinking water.

A sergeant bawled me out for just standing there on the beach. "You wanna die, dickhead? Get off that fuckin' beach, on the double, 'fore some sniper gives you a third eye! *Jezus*, what a dumbass! Get in that alligator, right fuckin' now, stupid."

I jumped into a squat, seriously ugly, tracked vehicle and off we went, up the terraced sand dunes and then clattering on our way over to the CP. The route took us through more wrecked Marine equipment than I thought the whole Corps even owned.

I was startled by the light overhead once I debarked from the 'Gator. The sky was literally filled with magnesium flares hanging from small parachutes as they drifted down all over the island. They were bright enough to hurt your eyes if you looked directly at them. As each one finally landed, another one would pop overhead, sent in from the destroyers offshore who had flare duty for the island that night. As my ears adjusted to the rumble and crack of artillery and smaller guns coming from all directions, I nearly jumped out of my skin when a nearby battery of Marine 105s let go, four guns, firing as fast as they could load. I couldn't see them, only their muzzle flashes. They were bedded down into large holes in the ground not a hundred feet from the CP tents. Strangely, I saw no Marines standing around in those intermittent yellow flashes. And then the most horrible smell hit me.

I almost puked. The stench of decomposing human flesh was so strong that I reflexively covered my face with my sleeve. It was pungent beyond belief and you couldn't get away from it. What little breeze was blowing on that low hill made it worse. My eyes were literally watering and it was all I could do not to gag. I looked around for the source and saw several puffy mounds out on a sunken road that ran near the CP.

"Somepin', ain't it, Loot," a gravelly voice said from behind me. I turned to see a lone Marine standing there, with a sympathetic if gap-toothed grin in the flare-light. Then a second artillery battery, bigger than the 105s, cut loose, hammering the air hard enough to make my ears hurt. The Marine gestured that I was to follow him. I grabbed my pack and hurried to catch up. He didn't walk in a straight line, but sort of zig-zagged, somewhat hunched over, across the rocks and dead shrubs littering the ground. I tried to match his steps but mostly tripped my way along. It was really awkward and I tried to ignore the echoes of Commander Willson's words—*you're not qualified to go ashore.* He'd stopped speaking to me when my transfer was ap-proved. He was even madder when we found out that I was the only naval officer going ashore. Apparently they wanted me, the designer of the new grid, to go first before they sent any more Navy guys, so I could evaluate if it was going to work.

We went about fifty yards to one of the CP tents. As we got closer three figures arose from a deep trench I hadn't even noticed, their rifles pointed in our direction, and one of them issued the night's challenge. My escort yelled back at him—something to do with what he'd done to the guy's mother just last night. The sentry shook his head and cussed my escort out, saying now he was gonna have to shoot the both of us. My escort laughed at that and then said: "First you gotta load that thing, Jimmy, then you gotta shoot it and actually hit something—which you ain't never done since basic. Hey: I've got the Navy guy. Where's Colonel Bryce?"

The other two sentries had subsided back into their trench once they heard my escort's voice, obviously recognizing him. The man called Jimmy made a disgusted noise and pointed to the larger of the tents right in front of us. The breeze came up again and I think I actually whimpered. Jee-zus! None of the Marines seemed to even notice. My escort stank to high heaven as well. I wasn't sure that I could function in this environment. My eyes were watering again and I had to take tiny breaths to avoid throwing up.

We arrived at the entrance flaps to the larger tent. Another sentry waved us in with the one arm he had left. As we stepped inside the stench of death was overcome by cigarette smoke; I wasn't a real, heavy-duty smoker, but God Almighty, was I grateful for that blue haze. The light inside the tent was actually blue. There were proba-bly twenty Marines in the tent, every one of them intensely involved in talking on radios or field telephones, plotting on charts that were stretched across stacked wooden pallets, or arguing with each other. A few crouched at the edge of the tent, sipping coffee from bat-tered canteen mugs while staring like zombies at nothing at all. The artillery batteries outside were still blasting away, adding to the din inside the tent and making the canvas sides flutter with each blast. In comparison to the tense but quiet atmosphere in Main Battery Plot, this was utter chaos.

Suddenly one of the arguers looked up, squinted, and then yelled *Incoming*! at the top of his lungs. In ten seconds, every man there had gone flying out of the tent, including my escort. I was left just standing there, not knowing what to do or where to go. Then an arm reached in through the tent flaps, grabbed my left arm, and yanked me outside. We both then ran as fast as we could to a low mound of dirt with a slanting, rectangular hole in the front, like a Midwest tornado shelter. My escort pushed me into the hole just as the first rounds of incoming Japanese artillery began to land all around the CP. Pursued by the hot flashes of exploding artillery shells, we flew down the ramp. There were no stairs, just that steep dirt ramp that went a surprisingly long way down. There was a dogleg turn at the bottom, and then another, shorter ramp. We ended up in a dark chamber filled to capacity with huddled Marines as booming thumps outside dislodged dirt from the ceiling down on our heads and steel fragments came whining down the sloping rabbit-hole of the entrance. There was one lantern down there, which illuminated a tightly packed crowd of frightened men breathing hard. No one spoke—there was too much noise coming from topside, accompanied by red and yellow flashes that painted the entrance like an evil strobe light.

What have I done, I thought, remembering the major's joke about volunteering.

Then a part of the bunker's ceiling gave way in one corner after a particularly nasty hit above ground. Tightly packed as we were, several Marines were instantly down on the ground, scrabbling hard to pull the dirt off the guys who'd been momentarily buried by the cave-in. The air in the bunker was starting to get really thick with gun smoke and men began to cover their faces against the eye-stinging atmosphere.

Then the shelling just stopped. I exhaled in relief but the guys nearest the final ramp began pulling back, which is when I realized that many of them now had submachine guns in their hands. A sergeant went to the bunker's entrance, turned around, and began pushing men back, creating a ray-shaped path from the entrance toward the back of the bunker. Four men then began pushing wooden pallets in front of the entrance, creating a wooden barrier three pallets thick. I thought I heard muffled rifle fire topside and then some small, or at least small compared with the artillery shells, explosions.

"Get down!" the big sergeant yelled. "Get down and Turtle up."

My escort spun me around and then forced me down on the floor, my ass in the air and my head in the dirt. Within seconds came three bright yellow flashes from the other side of the pallets, which became suddenly transparent even as they disintegrated. I felt rather than heard pieces of hot metal flying by. A man next to me grunted as he got hit. Then came an angry howl as the men with submachine guns kicked the pallet rubble aside and went charging through the dogleg and back up the ramp, firing as they went. We heard several more explosions, which I finally realized were grenades, and then a pretty noisy firefight erupted topside. After a few minutes it subsided, and then the big sergeant announced that topside was clear. The men in the bunker began to climb the ramp, those with guns going first. My escort held me back until the bunker was almost empty, and then we followed, tail-end Charlies.

Up top was an apocalyptic scene. All but one of the tents were flattened, their ragged remains still flickering with fire. The flares in the sky still hung there, floating down their strange white smoke trails, just as others popped above them, as if totally unconcerned with what had been going on down on the ground. Medic teams were already out and tending to the Marine wounded.

There were *lots* of dead Japanese. Dozens of them. A pair of Marines methodically walked among the corpses, administering a through and through bayonet thrust to each one to make damn sure. My escort told me that, when they realized they were finished, the Japanese would take a grenade off their equipment belt, pull the pin, and then stuff it underneath their body. If they were still alive when someone came to check them out, they'd roll over. Behind the bayonet team, other Marines put twenty-foot-long straps on some of the enemy bodies, then backed away a few steps and tugged on the body to make it roll over. If nothing happened, they'd drag it into a shallow ditch nearby.

Three tanks were grinding their way up the hill in our direction. Two of them had squat bulldozer plows mounted on the front. Off in the distance I could hear rifle and machine gun fire, as well as that low, constant rumble of artillery that seemed to never stop. The air reeked of gunpowder, decaying bodies, and another smell that I later learned was the stink of freshly pooled blood. I could just make out the northern slopes of *Suribachi*, where reddish-hued explosions would flare briefly as American artillery rounds landed. Offshore, what had to be a battleship was lighting up the whole island whenever they let go with their big guns. I wondered if it was *Nevada*.

A tall Marine with a skeletal face walked up to us. My escort stiffened to attention.

"Who's this?" the officer asked, pointing to me with his chin.

"One of the new Navy spotters, Colonel," my escort said.

The colonel stared at me with an expression of disbelief. I thought I could understand why. My utility uniform was too big for me, my hair much too long, my utility belt, which should have been laden with four grenades, a first-aid kit, two canteens, two ammo pouches, and a K-bar knife in a sheath, at a minimum, was bare except for the knife. My Marine utility cap had a pair of bright silver lieutenant's bars pinned on the front, called railroad tracks by enlisted people. The colonel casually reached up and took those "tracks" right off. I had no helmet. And, of course, I didn't have a rifle. My escort, who I later learned was a corporal, seemed to be embarrassed to be caught with me by a full colonel.

"Jesus H. Christ," the colonel whispered, shaking his head. Fifty feet away something exploded, sending bloody body parts flying everywhere and provoking some shouting. "What's your name, Lieutenant?" he asked, ignoring the grenade blast and the flying gore.

I told him.

"What ship?"

"*Nevada*, sir."

He nodded. "Well, then," he said, looking over my shoulder at something that was happening behind us. Now it sounded like one of the tanks had gotten stuck. "You'll know all about naval gunfire. That's good. I assume you can talk?"

I knew what that meant—could I speak the arcane language of naval gunfire support. I nodded. "Yes, sir," I said. "I can also run the Ouija board, do grid-spot conversions in my head, and work two targets at a time."

He blinked. "Well, damn," he said. "I'm Colonel Bryce, artillery branch, and this is the CP of the tenth of the fifth and I can't do that. How about actual spotting—front lines, looking at a buncha bad guys, dodging snipers, estimating their coordinates, and calling it in?"

"Never done that, Colonel," I said. "But give me a grid, and I can lend a hand. Once we have an island-wide grid, that'll get easier—and a lot faster."

My escort stifled a snort.

But the colonel seemed to agree. "Yeah, I think you're right," he said. "Each regiment has its own grid. Takes time to sort that shit out. Too *much* time. We've been hearing that the Navy's proposed a single grid for the entire island. My guys tell me that should work but that Holland Smith doesn't want to let go of the reins. Until he promulgates it, we're stuck with the 1933 version."

"I'm the guy who designed that grid, Colonel," I said. "I can draw one for you."

"No shit," he said, and then finally grinned. Five artillery shells landed in quick succession not three hundred yards away. Even at that distance, all of us could hear pieces of spent metal whacking into the ground amid the remains of the tents. Once again, none of the Marines gave the falling bits the time of day. The colonel looked at his watch, and then saw a couple of officers headed our way. He sighed.

"All we need then is a new CP." He turned to my escort. "Corporal, get this lieutenant squared away with proper gear. Everything. Take him down to the seconds pile at the nearest field hospital. Then bring him to the new CP."

"Yes, sir, Colonel. Where will that be, sir?"

"Hell if I know," the colonel said, waving the officers over. "But I'll bet these guys are gonna tell me. Dismissed."

My escort nodded. They'd been taught not to salute for the same reason officers didn't wear any visible rank insignia. Snipers watched for salutes.

We started down a long hill back in the direction of the beach. The corporal carried his rifle at a loose port-arms and kept a tight watch on our surroundings as we went. I asked him how so many Japanese had gotten into the CP area, which I'd assumed had been established well behind enemy front lines.

"Bastards are everywhere," he replied. "They'll put a whole squad down into a hole ahead of our advance and tell 'em not to come out for two days. By then that hole will be behind our lines. Then they come out at night with fucking swords and slip into our trenches and foxholes—from behind. Ain't no ground secure on fucking Iwo."

"Swords?"

"Yes, sir, swords. That way they can kill Marines without making noise. We've lost so many guys that way that our nighttime positions aren't ten feet apart anymore. Now they can touch each other. One guy's always looking behind the foxhole. All night. They take turns."

We dropped down into a long gully that was maybe twenty feet deep and fifty wide. There we ran into other Marines, coming and going, in small groups. Those going down the hill were usually helping or actually carrying wounded guys on stretchers. Those coming up toted supplies, such as ammo boxes or water cans. For some reason the sound of nearby artillery fire was amplified in the gully. The stench of death was also worse.

At the beach end of the gully stood a collection of tents with large red crosses painted on their sides. The tents were in shadow down on the beach because the flare light was blocked by the nearby rocky slope. I counted six machine gun positions spaced around the hospital tents. Two guys at each position watching; the others asleep. Out to sea everything was darkness until one of the ships offshore fired a salvo, followed a few seconds later by the thumps of their muzzle blasts.

I was surprised when we kept walking past the collection of medical tents, where there seemed to be a lot of people milling about. We went a hundred yards closer to the actual shoreline, a series of descending terraces composed of black volcanic sand. I remembered trying to climb through that stuff. This part of the beach was still a huge pile of wrecked vehicles: stranded and blasted tanks, capsized landing craft, trucks and other tracked vehicles mired to their hatches and extending out of sight down the surf line. Almost every large piece of equipment had been hit by something—mortar shells, artillery shells, or machine guns. There wasn't a single object in the half-mile-long junkyard that hadn't been shot full of holes of various sizes. This landing truly must have been a catastrophe.

Three more large tents, square-sided and totally blacked out, appeared out of the darkness just inshore of the wreckage. A crude handwritten sign nailed to a wrecked box proclaimed this area was "graves registration." Graves? Oh, shit, I thought: was this where the Marines brought their dead?

"That one," my escort said, pointing to the third and smallest of the tents. A voice called to us out of the gloom: password. That's when I saw a sentry standing up in a machine gun nest, his submachine gun pointing generally in our direction. My corporal called out the word "bartender" and the sentry subsided back into his pit. "Passwords have lots of 'R's," he said; "Bastards can't pronounce the letter 'L.'"

We stepped inside the tent, which was lit by four dimmed battle lanterns. It smelled really bad in there. The sergeant in charge saw me make a face. "The uniforms have all been washed in the sea," he told me. "Not perfect, but better than they had been, believe me."

A gunnery sergeant worked at a desk while several other men were tearing down utility belts and taking serviceable gear to their respective tables. My escort went over to explain to the gunny why we were here while I looked around.

I realized that this tent contained the equipment and uniforms recovered from all the Marines who'd died so far and whose bodies had been retrieved and brought down here for registration and temporary burial. Everything was piled on individual pallet-tables—trousers, shirts, helmets, canteens, first-aid kits, pouches, backpacks, boots, skivvies, even socks. The clothes that had been "cleaned" were stacked in neat piles; the rest were piled in one corner, reeking of dried blood and other unpleasant things, waiting for their ocean dip.

Along one wall of the tent were the weapons—rifles, submachine guns, .45 pistols, K-bar knives, bayonets, grenades, and various ammo pouches. Three men were busy stripping the guns down, cleaning them, making repairs, and then reassembling them. A corporal made the final inspection, and then loaded the weapon. One pallet held a heap of parts—bolts, magazines, stocks, even barrels. That corner reeked of gun solvent. There were four five-gallon buckets full of dog tags still on their neck chains. That made me swallow hard.

The gunny approached. "Lieutenant," he said in a gravelly voice. "Let's get you squared away." He walked with a limp, and the side of his face was disfigured by a still-livid scar. I stripped off my shipboard utilities and tried out shirts and trousers until I had a reasonably well-fitting combat uniform. There were plenty of sizes to choose from for everything, although some had bullet holes and large dark stains.

I got a set of well broken-in boots, leggings, a fully loaded utility belt, a submachine gun instead of a rifle, a holstered .45, four ammo packs, and the standard logistical loadout. By the time I put my pack on I could barely move and the gunny gave me a twisted smile. "Think of it like you're going to summer camp," he said. "But with guns. Speaking of guns, you fired one of those before?"

I shook my head. "Rifles, handguns, yes, and shotguns; submachine guns—no."

The gunny took my submachine gun and exchanged it for a darkly blued 12-gauge pump-action shotgun with an extended feed tube.

"One in the chamber, five in the mag," the gunny said. "Wait until he's within ten yards or so, if you can, then aim for his groin. You'll be scared and probably hit him in the face instead, but that'll do it. Double-aught buck all the way."

I was just grateful for the fact that the shotgun was half the weight of that big submachine gun. Then the gunny took off my helmet, which had begun to slip down my forehead, and adjusted the cranial straps. Much better. I was conscious of some amused stares from the real Marines in the tent, but no one said a word. We went over to the gunny's desk, where I signed for all the gear and gave them my dog tag numbers.

"Don't wear any rank insignia at any time," the gunny said. "Carry that scattergun at short-port, chambered, red dot, and ready to work at all times. They are everywhere—in spider holes, under rocks, in cracks in the walls—and every one of those fuckers can be a sniper. No area is secure on this island until every one of them is dead. They don't surrender so we don't take prisoners. See one, kill his ass as quickly as you can before he kills you. Expect any so-called "dead" one to have a grenade underneath him. Never, *ever*, poke your head up over whatever you're hiding behind. Their snipers can shoot the eyes out of a mouse from three hundred yards. Every one of them here on Iwo is a battle-hardened veteran who's come here *expecting* to die gloriously for his emperor and they've had years to get this fucking island ready just for you." He paused to catch his breath. "And, finally, just for shits and giggles, why are *you* here, if I may ask?"

I told him who I was on *Nevada*, explained about the gunfire support problems, the grid, and that I was apparently here to set up the island-wide grid so we could speed up getting offshore fire-support.

"You goin' on The Line, Loot?" he asked.

"I don't think so, Gunnery Sergeant," I replied. "Not like I'm qualified, am I."

He stared at me for a few seconds, started to say something, shook his head, and wished me luck. Outside I asked the corporal what the gunny had been about to say. He grinned at me in the darkness. "Gunny thought you sayin' you wouldn't be going up on The Line was funny," he said. "Every swingin' dick on this island is goin' up front eventually, 'cause there ain't enough of us left. And when you do, he don't expect you to last more than twenty-four hours. He didn't come right out and say it, prolly 'cause he didn't want to hurt your feelings. We gotta move out. Daylight's coming."

"Wonderful," I said, readjusting all the gear I was carrying. I had two full canteens on my belt. I hadn't known how heavy they'd be. They felt like small cannonballs.

As we headed back up the ravine, he explained Marine Corps field organization. "At the top is Division; two-star general, commanding as many as twenty thousand men. Next one down is Regiment. There's usually four regiments in each division. Commanded by a senior colonel. After that comes Battalion, then Company, then Platoon, then Squad."

He went on to explain that, because of all their losses, this wall chart organization could change frequently. "You'll hear a guy say he's with Second platoon of K company, Third of the Fifth. That means third battalion of the fifth regiment. Then there's the teams."

I wasn't sure why I wanted or needed to know all this if I was not going to be a front line spotter. He sensed my question. "You gotta be able to say who you are and with what outfit, especially if you're being challenged by a Shaky Jake sentry in the dark. The password is one thing, but the Japs have English-speakers. They listen to our radios. They can get the password, so you gotta be able to give that sentry some more dope if he asks. Else he'll shoot you and ask questions later. Get *down. Now.*"

We dropped to the ground and I actually rolled over on my side from the weight of all that equipment. As I struggled to right myself, I felt a hand on my neck, gripping hard, as in don't move, don't make noise. We were just outside the cone of light from the current crop of flares and almost to the top of the ravine. My escort was in the prone position, his rifle pointed forward as he searched the dark for whatever had spooked him. We'd seen a small group of stretcher-bearers coming toward us, but they'd gone past and were no longer visible. The dull roar coming from the distant front lines sounded louder in the sudden silence. A low gust of wind brought that horrible stench of dead bodies down the ravine. I stopped breathing, hoping it would pass, but it didn't.

Then came an unearthly scream from somewhere to our left and slightly *behind* us. Several indistinct figures came hurtling over the top edge of the ravine, preceded by a small avalanche of rocks and gravel as they came crashing down the sloping sides. They were all screaming now even as my corporal got off his first shots, right past my head. I was dimly aware that there was more rifle fire coming from the stretcher-bearers way behind us, and then I remembered that I had a loaded and chambered 12-gauge in my hands. I swung the barrel, seeking a target, the gunny's words about ten yards flashing across my mind. The Japanese were slightly farther away than that but just like the gunny said, I was scared out of my wits as those tan-uniformed figures ran right at us, waving shiny objects.

I picked out what I thought was the nearest one and let go, aiming for his groin like I'd been told. His head and face dissolved and his momentum gave him one more step before he fell forward. I was about to shoot him again when I remembered I had to pump the slide first. By then two more were getting much too close. The corporal shot one in the stomach and I shot the other, this time in the throat. One of them had stopped two-thirds of the way down the slope and this one had a rifle. I fired anyway and actually saw pellets disturb the fabric of his uniform. The corporal fired twice and the man dropped like a stone, squeezing off one round into the dirt as he went down.

And then there was an eerie silence. The shit stink of corpses was momentarily overwhelmed by the smell of gun smoke. The ribs on my right side hurt where the scattergun had kicked me; I hadn't even managed to get it to my shoulder.

"Not bad for a squid," my escort said, nodding his approval.

"That's squid—*sir*, to you, Corporal," I quipped and he grinned, but I noticed that he was already slapping a new clip into his M-1. We were still in Injun Country.

"Reload, Lieutenant," he said, carefully scanning the desolate terrain around us. "First thing you always do once the noise stops."

It was still dark, so the flares kept coming, sputtering and hissing as they floated down all over the island, painting it in that deathly white glare as I stuffed more shells into my shotgun.

"Eject," my escort snapped. "Then rack one into the chamber, put one more in the tube."

Now there were calls for medics from behind us. We resumed moving forward toward the top of the ravine, stepping carefully. My head was spinning—I'd just killed some enemy soldiers, not from the air-conditioned safety of Main Battery Plot, but up close and personal. There were some dead Japanese from a previous encounter lying around. I jumped when my escort shot one of them in the face. I stared at him.

"He twitched," was all he said. The man's skull quietly fell apart into two pieces as we walked by.

We continued to move forward and stopped twenty feet shy of the top of the ravine. He told me we were going to go left when we got to the top. We had about one foot of protection left above our heads. I could hear the shouts of Marines up ahead, and then there was the nasty rattle of a machine gun. This time I didn't have to be told: I was flat down on the ground in a millisecond, even before the corporal, as a slashing stream of bullets punched dirt and gravel right along the top of the ravine.

A real firefight got underway ahead of us, rifles, machine guns— theirs and ours. Suddenly, I realized I could tell the difference. Then came grenades, then something bigger. I lay on my right side, the shot- gun pointed up the ravine, sharp bits of gravel pressing into my right cheek. Then I realized the gravel wasn't pressing—I was. Had I racked the shotgun? I couldn't remember. I tugged the pump handle back an inch, looked at the ejection port. Shiny brass rim. My escort reached over and grabbed my right arm, as if to say easy there, Loot—not yet.

The racket up at the top of the ravine began to subside, as did my breathing. Suddenly I was really thirsty but unwilling to let go of the shotgun in order to get at my canteen. Once again, I remembered that gunny's look of total bemusement—you *volunteered*?

I asked my escort what his name was.

"Furo," he said. "Frankie Furo. Hackensack, NJ."

"I'm Lee Bishop," I said. "Hancock County, Georgia. Do we get up yet?"

"No, sir," he said. "Best we stay right here until Marines show up. Ours, hopefully."

Fuck it, I thought. I'm dying of thirst here. I put down the shotgun and reached for a canteen, now grateful that there were two. "Why left?"

"'Cause *Suribachi* is down at that end of the island. We got one division's supposed to take it. The others are headed north, to the right, to clear the rest of the island. Gotta secure *Suribachi*, first, though. That's where their big guns are, the ones that can hit anything on the island. Like that CP."

I started to poke my head up to look for the volcano. And get some sense of where we were. Furo grabbed my ankle and pulled me back down into the gully. "Never, *never* do that, Loot," he said in an exasperated voice. "Jap snipers out there can see only rocks and dirt, and then, suddenly, a nice white face. They're already looking through their scopes. They've already got two pounds on a trigger that takes three to make baby go bang. Never, never, *never!*"

"Got it, Corporal," I said, totally embarrassed.

"You better, Loot," he said. "You wanna see the sunrise."

TEN

By mid-morning we'd made it about a half mile after that all-important left turn, sometimes walking, sometimes on our bellies. There'd been a steady stream of Marines coming from and going toward the front, which they referred to as "The Line." A lot of stretcher-bearers—four guys humping their bloodied cargo in a light zig-zag pattern down the trail. Two more grunts with carbines following them, watching for things that moved out there in the weeds. Then we heard an artillery battery go to work up ahead, followed quickly by a second one.

Furo grinned. "Found 'em," he said.

We were about fifty yards away. All the guns were down in a deep crater—three craters, actually, created by what had to have been a sixteen-inch battleship salvo.

Hard to miss 'em, I thought, as about a dozen guns filled the air with ear-whacking noise. I'd thought we could just amble up the trail to find the CP, but just about then came a strange whizzing noise. Metal in the air, I thought. Hit the deck. This time I again beat Furo, but not by much.

"Get down, *way* down," he yelled as he slithered off the trail into a ditch that offered maybe six inches more protection than where we'd been trudging our way forward. I quickly followed, just in time to experience my first mortar barrage. Artillery tears up real estate; mortars, I learned, are a bit more personal. They come fast, unlike artillery, bang, bang, bang, *bang*, and fill the neighborhood with metal flying only a foot or so off the ground. All a mortar crew has to do is open a crate of twenty-four rounds, pull the required number of HE envelopes off the base to achieve the desired range, and then drop them into a steel tube, one after another.

Drop.

Whump.

Drop.

Whump.

Resulting in twenty-four rounds landing on or near you at five-second intervals. Two full minutes of praying to God to help me dig all the way down to China. A whole new definition of eternity. And they weren't shooting at us—they were trying to get rounds down into those craters. Their big guns up on *Suribachi* couldn't hit our big guns because they were fifty feet below ground level, so they'd sent in a mortar team. Off to our left, on the other side of the so-called trail, three-man Marine mortar squads responded with barrages of their own. How they knew what and where to aim at was a mystery to me.

When the enemy mortars stopped shooting, Furo tapped me on my helmet. We got up to a crouch and scuttled toward those huge craters. We slid down the side of one of them like kids on a snowy slope. I was barely able to hold onto my shotgun. I hadn't put the canteen back on my belt correctly and lost it until our two-man avalanche of sand and gravel caught up with us at the bottom of the crater. Some sentries had seen us but recognized we weren't Japanese. Furo pointed at the sorry-looking tents on one side of the crater. One of the sentries waved us on, but first he made me retrieve my lost canteen.

The artillery pieces started up again, painfully hammering our ears now that we were right behind them. They were shooting high-angle, bright yellow lances of flame coming once every fifteen seconds as sweating, shirtless crews pulled ejection handles, spilling smoking hot brass powder cases all over the place while guys on the other side slammed the next round into the shimmering chamber. A team of three Marines sat incongruously behind the line of guns, crouched over radios and yelling adjustments to the gunners. A really big round of something detonated one hundred yards behind the line of guns, showering everybody in an ugly rain of sand and gravel. I never heard shrapnel, but Furo suddenly clutched his stomach and went to his knees. He pointed weakly at the tents of the CP and then coughed up a terrifying amount of bright red blood from his mouth before subsiding onto the ground, his eyes wide open.

I stared in horror, not knowing what to do. Blood pumped through his fingers, which were clenched to his midsection, alternating with the blood pumping out of his mouth. Then his eyes rolled upward and the sickening hemorrhage subsided.

Help him, my brain yelled.

Hopeless, was the reply. Get your ass to the CP. That's why you're here.

I ran.

I ran like I'd never run before, just as another really big shell landed, this time way off the mark. I headed for and then burst into the biggest tent, tripped over a bunch of wires and went sprawling into the command post.

The *empty* command post. Everyone had already made it to the bunker, which was—where? Furo would have known, but Furo was facedown in the dirt on Iwo, like thousands of his buddies. I sat there on the canvas floor trying to gather my wits when three more of those really big shells hit nearby, sending a shock wave through the ground that literally flipped me over onto the canvas. A rain of dirt and sand pelted me from the tent top, and all the battle lanterns went tumbling. Being battle lanterns, they stayed on, but they were now sending flat beams of yellow light across the floor. I was pretty sure my wits were out there somewhere in all those beams.

I relaxed on the canvas and gathered myself into as small a ball as all that gear on my body would allow. If one of those big boys landed *on* the tent it would be quick, I thought. I stifled a horrible suspicion that those were Navy rounds and that someone, somewhere, perhaps even right here at the CP, had made a colossal mistake. They kept coming, huge booming blasts, and in almost simultaneous patterns of three. That was the giveaway.

The shelling suddenly stopped. Over on one side of the tent, whose walls were now fully air-conditioned by shell fragments, there was a bank of radios mounted over a small gasoline generator, which was, incredibly, still rattling away. I could hear chatter from the radios as the clanging in my ears subsided, even though the radios were twenty feet away. A lot of it was pretty frantic, and I could make out the words "emergency" and "cease fire" being repeated. The guy transmitting was clearly hysterical. The other end of the tent began to subside as a pole or two gave way, so I got up and went over to the radio table, which was right next to a much larger plywood table covered in charts. The plot, I thought. I thought I heard shouts outside, but so far, there was no gunfire. Good deal.

Right next to the big plotting table there was a coffeepot, of all things, swinging from a chain nailed to the tent ridgepole. I picked up a hastily dropped mug and tried my luck. Blessed be—there was coffee in the pot. Hot coffee. It came out in sludgy lumps and smelled like a combination of coffee and hot asphalt. Marine coffee. I sank down to the floor, gratefully closed my eyes, and took a sip. Bite. It was wonderful. My hands were shaking as my adrenaline crashed but I held that mug with a death grip. I leaned back against a table leg. My helmet tilted forward over my face. My wits crawled up my leggings and asked if it was okay to come back aboard.

"Who the *fuck* are you?" a baritone voice yelled. "And that's *my* fucking mug, Shithead!"

I opened one eye and examined the mug, which had the words Big Kahuna emblazoned over the silver eagle badge of a full-bull colonel. I assumed there was a name on the other side.

I pushed my helmet back onto my head and looked up at a pair of knees, my head not being able to tilt any farther back. I became aware that other people were returning to the CP.

"I'm Lieutenant Bishop, USN," I said. "I'm one of the Navy guys sent over here to set up an island-wide shore-bomb grid so stupid shit like this will never, *ever* happen again," I said. "Sir."

The colonel squatted down. He was huge, with a face that seemed familiar, and then I remembered a portrait of Sitting Bull I'd seen in *Life* magazine. This guy was his twin. "What did you just say, Lieutenant? What stupid shit?"

"*Big* craters out there, Colonel? Really big craters? Three-packs? I haven't seen 'em but I felt 'em and I'll bet those were at least cruiser rounds—unless the Japanese have eight-, fourteen-, and sixteen-inch stuff here?"

His eyes widened a tiny bit. "That was friendly fire?" he whispered. "That was *Navy* stuff?"

"Friendly's not the word I'd use, Colonel, but I suspect somebody fucked up and drew the attention of one of those thirty-thousand-ton beasts out there."

He closed those black eyes of his for a brief moment and then offered a hand to pull me up. My knees were still a bit wobbly, either from fright or just fatigue. This Marine shit was much harder than I'd expected. I became aware that several real Marines were staring at me, but others were already re-manning the plotting table, reinforcing the drooping folds of canvas, and trying to pacify the poor bastards who were still screaming on the radio. The colonel was even bigger than I'd thought as he put a giant paw on my shoulder to steady me.

"Listen up," he bellowed. "This right here is Lieutenant—" He looked down at me. "Bishop," I said. "From the *Nevada.*"

"This here is Lieutenant Bishop, USN, from the battlewagon *Nevada*, and he's here to set up that new island-wide grid we've been hearing about. How he got here I have no fucking idea. But he needs a coffee mug, 'cause right now he's holding mine, which means I gotta kill him."

I saw a flash of grins around the table and then a hand pushed an empty coffee cup into my other hand. I reluctantly relinquished the colonel's mug. That had been some really good Joe. For the first time on Iwo, I began to feel a little bit safer.

Outside, the deeply menacing rumble and racket that was Iwo Jima resumed. In the absence of the full CP crew that dead-meat stench had slipped back into the tent, but there were enough cigarettes going now to cure that. The colonel looked into his mug and frowned. The final layer was still attached to the bottom; lacking a fork, I hadn't been able to finish it. A Marine came over and introduced himself.

"I'm Major Pete Murphy," he said. "Colonel Nicholas's acting exec. You bring any paperwork?"

"I did, but I lost it in a gully when some enemy jumped us."

I could tell from his expression what he was thinking: well, what good are you?

"I designed the grid," I said. "Gimme some fresh charts, and I'll lay it down for you."

"No shit?" the major said, obviously surprised.

"Not one pound, Major," I said. "I'm the fire-control officer on *Nevada*. My watch station is in Main Battery Plot, where we control our ten fourteen-inch guns. I can plot *and* I can talk. Let's get to it before I start crying."

The artillery section outside had re-manned their guns and there were missions in progress as I explained what this was all about to their version of our Main Battery Plot team, which I felt couldn't be a whole lot different from ours. CP radio talkers received the mission calls from The Line. They announced the spotter's identification and position, using the unique grid issued by that CP's regiment. Then the spotter called an estimated range and an actual bearing from his position to the target's position. A sergeant at the table worked a grid-spot converter, a white plastic contraption known lovingly as the Ouija board, which converted the spotter's numbers and bearings to range and bearing from *our* artillery guns' position to that target's location.

A second talker then called the mission to the actual artillery guys, who set up their tubes. The guns would then fire an initial round or two; the spotter would observe the fall of shot and then call back corrections, or "spots"—right, two degrees, up, fifty feet, add, or drop, two hundred yards. Always in the same order: deflection (right or left), elevation (up, or down, in feet), and range, or distance, in yards—add or drop. But since these spots were relative to where the spotter was, not the guns, the CP plotter would have to work the Ouija board again and then call the spots to the gunners—once again in numbers that matched the target's actual position in relation to where the *guns* were, not the spotter out there in the weeds.

I'd always thought that this process was unnecessarily clumsy: too many layers, talkers, and too many opportunities for introducing math errors. But if there was a single island-wide grid, then we could give each spotter his portion of *the* grid, and connect him by radio directly to the guns, and thereby the actual gunners, who would also have *the* grid. They could then use their own Ouija board to convert the spotters' "spots" to revised gun orders, cutting out the CP. Just like the ships could. The CP folks could listen in, plot a duplicate of the mission on their own plot table, and intervene only if they saw a problem, such as an unplanned troop movement, unknown to the spotter, that the developing fire-mission might endanger.

Sitting Bull, whose name was actually Colonel Sam Nicholas, listened as I explained all this yet again. As I was talking, though, I remembered the bigger, two-part problem lurking out there. Captain Henderson had explained to me that there might be opposition to this concept, because the Marines, and even more so, the Army, wanted to control every step of the process, hence all those command posts—company, battalion, regimental, division.

The second part of the problem was that all the guys out there: the spotters, the platoon sergeants, the company commanders, the battalion commanders—in other words, *everyone*—had been trained the same way. This was going to be a *big* change. How did you get the word out when thousands of battle-hardened Japanese were trying their best to kill every Marine out there, shooters and spotters alike?

I had to remind them of one of their own expressions: it's difficult to remember that the mission was to drain the swamp when you're up to your ass in alligators.

I told the colonel all this and he grinned. "Ain't no biggie," he rumbled. "You got this new grid laid out on the *Nevada*?"

"Yes, sir," I said.

"Okay then," he said. "We'll lay one out here, send a shrunk-down copy to one of our spotters whose grunts are in deeper shit than most. Then I'll put you on *my* plotting table and give you two radios. One circuit to your guy out there in the boonies, the other to your plotters on *Nevada*. He calls in with his grid position, and the grid position of the problem child. You convert, and then you call it to *Nevada* and they shoot. Once they shoot, we tell our spotter to deal direct with *Nevada*."

"But by having one master grid for the entire island, the spotter can call the mission direct to *Nevada* in the first place," I protested. "That's the whole purpose. Cut down the time between help-help and rounds on target."

He gave me what I'm sure he considered was a gentle pat on the shoulder, causing me to almost drop my new coffee mug. "One step at a time, Sonny," he said. "I wanna hear and I wanna see how this goes."

I was about to keep arguing when a hollow-eyed Marine standing behind Sitting Bull shook his head vigorously. I swallowed my protest and went to work with their plotting team, which resembled my team on the ship. They were all enlisted and pretty sharp. There was one exception, a young-looking individual with utilities that didn't fit him. He mostly stared straight ahead and didn't say anything or join the plotting session. There was a sergeant in charge of the team and he showed me around the table and the comms.

Or tried to, because at first nothing worked. The radios were filled with static; I later learned the Japanese were jamming every frequency they detected. Then we had to break and run when another thunderstorm of incoming artillery crumped into a nearby hillside and then began to unmistakably walk down that hill toward the CP.

Japanese had spotters, too? *Shee-it!*

The nearby Marine guns erupted into counter-battery fire as we fled for the bunkers, pursued by a whirlwind of humming metal shards. Apparently, someone up on the crater's rim had seen where that latest incoming was coming from.

This bunker was much like the last one, only smaller and not as deep. I flopped down against some sandbags along the back wall and tried to catch my breath. I was suddenly hungry—what time was it? I looked at my wristwatch, whose face, I discovered, was shattered. I shook it and one of the hands fell out.

Right. Why the hell not.

Then came a booming thump close aboard that bounced every man in the bunker a foot off the floor, followed by the partial collapse of the dirt and plank "ceiling." I gagged on a mouthful of dirt and then tried to breathe through the sandstorm of dust enveloping my face as the weight of dirt and sand increased on my chest. I was buried alive and panicked appropriately, trying with all my strength to move and discovering that only my right arm followed orders. The rest of me was being pressed down into the earth by an incredible weight of black stuff. I blew out a long breath to clear my nose and face and tried to open my eyes. They are open, I realized, but they were gazing into the darkness of the grave.

You volunteered, my vengeful brain reminded me as I tried, unsuccessfully, to draw a decent breath. I had to mentally stamp hard on the urge to breathe harder and ordered my mouth not to open. The darkness scared me the most—it was absolute, the degree of absolute you only see in nightmares.

Hey! I croaked to myself. You're not dead. Yet. Shut up, Brain. What *can* you move?

My right arm. Okay, clear your face.

I did, scrabbling feebly at all the stuff that was in my face, my knuckles scraping against wood, one of the planks, pressing painfully against my forehead. I tried my legs—no joy there. I tried to roll, sit up, bend my neck, kick. Nope. Nothing.

And yet, there was air, right in front of my face. Dusty, chewy, warm air, but still—it was air.

So: stop with all the exertions. Conserve air. Your hand works—start moving stuff out of your face. Make the cavity bigger. There'll be a hundred Marines topside digging like terriers to get everybody out.

Breathe—slowly. Wait. Listen.

And then, yes, after a few uncomfortable minutes that seemed more like hours, I could hear shouting. Muffled, sounding like it was a long way away, but I knew it wasn't. Relax, I told myself. Slow that breathing down. They're coming. You're not bleeding. Nothing's broken. Still, I desperately needed to take one long, deep breath. I *had* to. Then, discipline reasserted itself. Small inhales, exhales. Stop fighting all that weight. Go slack. Get thinner. Like a Marine.

I did all that and then realized that the dirt wasn't playing fair. As

I relaxed it filled in along my body, creepy shit that it was, like some damned boa constrictor. Inhale, it waits, exhales, it constricts. I had no idea how large the air cavity was around my head and face, but I did know there was no resupply coming in.

It's okay, I told myself. They're coming. I know they are. Relax. Doze. Wait. Sleep, maybe.

No, no, no—don't do that! That's CO_2 talking. Squirm. Move. Yell!

I yelled. Somebody yelled back. Over here, over *here*!

A moment later something sharp and hard hit my right shin and I yelled again, this time in pain. Then there were hands scrabbling the dirt away from my face and other hands pulling me up out of the rubble. I took a really deep breath and tried to help, but a face that wasn't quite in focus said: "Stop it, let us do it." I think that's when I fainted.

I came to back up on the "surface." The first thing I heard was that section of nearby artillery going hell for leather. "Get 'em," I mumbled. Get those motherfuckers.

"*Hell*, yes, Loot," a voice said. "You okay?"

I opened my eyes. I was outside. Unlimited air. It was still daylight. I lay on my back, and a Marine leaned over me. His helmet sported a red cross: a medic.

"Yeah, I think so," I said. "I guess I am risen."

"You and Jesus," he said with a grin. "Other guys are hurt—so you stay here; catch your breath. I'll tell the docs you're okay. Here's some water."

"I gotta get back to the CP," I said. "Gotta work the grid."

"Yes, sir," he said. "But for now, stay put. Drink that water. The docs'll clear you and then you can go do that grid shit. Okay?"

More artillery pieces nearby opened up, making any further conversation impossible. I saw that the CP we'd been in was still there, although it, too, like the first one, had been air-conditioned by flying metal. Those guns hurt my ears with their insistent blamming. The corpsman attached a white tag to my wrist and wrote the letters

"OK" on it with a grease pencil, made me suck some water down, and then told me to lie back on the ground. He put someone's backpack under my head. My last thought before I drifted off again was: damn, those guns are noisy. But I'd learned something truly important: if you were fighting with Marines, they'd never abandon you. Never.

ELEVEN

A familiar voice roused me from my nap: "All you white tags, get your asses back on The Line. Up and at 'em, ladies; this ain't the fuckin' Navy."

It was, of course, Colonel Sam, who was now sporting a bloody sling on his left arm. He was standing about twenty feet away, surveying the damage—and the casualties. Not everyone had a white tag, I noticed. He'd managed to retain his coffee mug, though, the one I'd "borrowed," although now it was bloodstained. For a Marine, that probably made the coffee taste better. That strange-looking kid was right next to him. I knew he had to be at least eighteen, but he sure didn't look it. The colonel spied me.

"Lieutenant Bishop," he called. "C'mon—we need that grid. You can nap later."

"Aye, aye, sir," I croaked back to him. I tried to get up. All that dirt falling on me had taken some of the roundness out of my lower limbs, so I staggered as I tried to get to my feet. There were other men getting up and I was conscious that several of them were in worse shape than I was. And there were body bags, the ubiquitous body bags. Harvest time on Iwo. Some incoming dropped along the ridge above us, blasting a series of notches at the top that were perfectly spaced, like some kind of giant saw blade.

It was going on evening, with a few orange lines painted in the clouds to the west above the ugly black silhouettes of the gunships out there. As I watched, a dark gray shape that had to be a battleship disappeared in clouds of flame as she fired a full salvo at some deserving enemy emplacements. A gentle breeze had sprung up, bringing the all-too-familiar stink of sulfur and carrion. Smell the dead shit? Now you know *you're* alive.

I staggered over to the CP tent, passing another crop of filled body bags on the way. They were laid out with military precision, about a dozen. Every man who walked by looked at them, but without moving his head. Apparently, it was bad manners to stare. You didn't want to know who was in there. A guy you'd been talking to an hour ago. From the same town you were from. Don't look. Don't ask. Stay sane.

Some of the guys ahead of me were shedding those white tags, as if ashamed to be "OK" in the presence of all those dead Marines. A bulky sergeant standing near the CP asked me where my piece was. I told him I was Navy and didn't have one. I had no idea where that shotgun had gone. He snorted contemptuously and then pointed to a stacked-arms collection of various kinds of rifles that had been assembled near the body bags.

"Git you one, Navy," he grumped. "You cain't be out here without no rifle."

"Yes, Sergeant," I said and walked over to the stack and pulled out a carbine. It had a clip already inserted, and there was a GI can filled with magazine clips right next to the stack. I pulled out two of what I hoped were the right ones, along with a sheathed knife. Then I hurried to get inside the CP tent.

It was almost as if nothing had happened: the cigarette smoke was already turning the air blue, thank God, and the radios were chattering with frantic calls for fire support. There were more lanterns going so I could actually see better than before. There was one difference from the first CP I'd been in—it looked like everyone here, officers and enlisted, had been wounded, and not by that last barrage that had put us in a bunker. Major Murphy gave me the high sign, but he had a radio handset in one hand and a kneepad, so I guessed he was taking in new fire missions. I went to the plotting table, where I discovered three plotters working hard to lay out the new grid over the island chart. I watched what they were doing, made some changes, and then the colonel showed up. His young shadow with that unsettling stare was still with him, as if waiting for orders.

"This thing ready to work?" the colonel asked.

"Yes, sir," I told him. "All we need now is a spotter who has this grid in front of him."

"The whole damn thing?"

"No, sir, just the piece that covers where he is and where there are enemy forces visible to him. Here's what that would look like."

I lay down a piece of tracing paper and drew the major lines nearest where I postulated the spotter's position to be—up on a ridge, back of the front line, The Line, but close enough to see where the enemy were holed up. He didn't have to worry about covering the whole island—just the part in front of him from which his guys, the line units he was supporting, were taking fire.

"Okay, I got that," the colonel said. "How's about this, Navy. You wanna help? You pick a position on this big grid that's in our sector. That big chart right there shows the whole island. I'll get some people to take you there and then stay with you; you set up shop and then call in to the batteries right here on a freq we'll give you. You confirm where you think you are. I'll call the nearest front line unit and tell them where you are and who you are. They'll give you the targets they need hammered. Then we'll talk the talk, okay?"

There it was. "How's about this proposition. You thought this scheme up. Now you go out and play spotter, and we'll see if it works." It made sense, though—they wouldn't have to train a regular Marine spotter over the radio. In a way, I knew I wanted to do it.

"Yes, sir," I said. "I'll try. These people who'll take me there—they artillery people?"

"Um, no, Lieutenant," he said with a strange expression on his huge face. "They're grunts, but they're raiders. They're Old Breed. Specialists who'll try their level best to keep you alive. Do exactly what they say and maybe you'll make it through the next twenty-four hours."

He laughed when he saw the expression on my face.

"SOBs got 'em a hate-on for artillery spotters, Lieutenant," he confided. "They'll send out sniper teams to find you, once they figure out where you are. The guys I'm sending out with you will make you move when they smell trouble coming. Don't argue with 'em. All three were on the 'Canal and Peleliu. Old Breed Marines. They know their business and they know their enemy."

Major Murphy was standing behind the colonel. He asked who exactly they should send out with their brand-new spotter. He had a sympathetic look on his face when he glanced at me.

"Round up Goon's squad," the colonel said. "This here boy's gonna need some experienced help out there."

The strange kid next to him began mumbling numbers that sounded surprisingly like gunfire-mission-control numbers. His eyes stared at the floor, but his hands moved in syncopation with his words, like the conductor of an orchestra. What the hell?

The major told me to sit down on one of the ammo boxes outside right by the entrance to the CP until he got me my new escort. I watched as the activity in the big tent picked up. I'd been right about almost all of them having wounds. You could tell by the way they walked, or tried to use plotting instruments with damaged hands. Some had visible bandages. I guessed that the Japanese were indeed serious about knocking out command and control sites.

I saw the strange guy again. He was now sitting on an overturned and cut down 55-gallon drum. He was watching the plot, and I noticed that his hands were performing a slow-motion washing action and his head bobbing ever so slightly as he stared intently down the length of the table, where several PFCs and corporals manned radio sets on one side, and other Marines, mostly PFCs, sat on the other side, working plotting tools and their Ouija boards.

My escort showed up and introduced himself as Gunny Malone. He gave me a sideways nod and we pushed through the tent flaps and out into the night air. He'd seen me staring at the strange-looking kid.

"That's Wrecked," he said in a soft voice that was barely audible amid the noisy babble coming from inside the CP.

"Wrecked?"

"Yeah," Malone said. "The first day we set up shop we found him down next to a shell crater, just above the beach. All his clothes had been blown right off him. Nekkid as a jaybird. No eyebrows. Nosebleed. Babbling to himself. Limping like his feet hurt. No helmet. No weapon. Shakin' like a leaf. Wringin' his hands like you just saw. Cryin'. We tried to talk to him but he was deaf—couldn't hear shit. Barely can now. But here's the thing: not a mark on him. No real bleeding. No bruises. Our medic—Navy corpsman—said he'd get him down to the medic station.

"But right then the Japanese found our range and big shells started going off. Wrecked screamed and did a swan dive—like into a swimming pool—into that crater. Three of us joined him—it was a deep crater. Probably Navy stuff; maybe even a Beast. He was down there tryin' to dig to China, sayin': not again, not again, not again, about a hundred times a minute. Us three put our heads down and waited it out, saying our prayers. He kept diggin' the whole time, that not-again shit never stopping.

"Finally the incoming stopped—we were getting used to it by then. Probably big stuff from *Suribachi*. By the time we finally put our heads up, the CP was on the move—again. Officers callin' orders everywhere, Sittin' Bull looking like he wanted to eat somebody alive. We look down into the crater and the kid was still digging, eyes closed, his hands bloody now, total panic. The corpsman had disappeared. Major Murphy said we can't just leave him, so the three of us went back down there and pulled him up to the top of the crater and then we took him with us.

"We moved about six hundred yards into a gully and set up shop as fast as we could. Generators, tents, antenna field, sentry posts. We had some KIA and some more wounded, so we three couldn't just sit around with some shell-shocker. I shared a canteen and he just looked at it. I took it back, drank some water, gave it back to him. He drank some water, gave it back to me. I told him to stay right there. He still wouldn't look at me, but he stayed right there. We got set up and then we had to figure out what to do with him. The colonel came out about then, took one look at him, and you'd think he'd seen a ghost. He said what the hell, and we told him. He said 'We can't leave him like that, just like Murphy. Find him some utilities and bring him in the tent.' We did. The colonel kept looking at him when we brought him in. We'd found some utilities that were too big for him, but at least he wasn't naked any more. His hands were still goin'. Looked like some kinda teenage boy scout, playin' Marine. Still scared, but talking now, a little bit, anyway.

"Murphy asked him his name and unit; he couldn't remember. No dog tags, either. What happened to you? Really big bang. Flying. Landed in the sand. Sleep. Woke up, all alone. Dead guys. I ran away. Tripped, hit my head on something. Sleep.

"'How old are you,' one of the other officers asked him. I could see why—he looks like he's maybe sixteen, max. Don't know. By then a lotta shit was coming in on the spotter nets, so we put him in a corner and told him to just rest. Way he was, somebody gave him the name 'Wrecked.' 'Cause that's what he is."

Malone went back inside and then came right back out. He'd been told to get me fitted out. He took me to yet another stash of field gear.

I'd lost a lot of my equipment in the bunker collapse. There seemed to be no shortage of individual equipment collections, which spoke volumes about the number of casualties we were experiencing. This time I selected a holstered 1911 .45 caliber pistol as my individual weapon, figuring I'd need both hands free when I went to work out there. Once I had what would be considered a minimum collection of field gear strapped on, the gunny took me back to the CP, where we plopped down on some ammo crates.

It was almost fully dark by now but the flares hadn't started up yet. Our nearby guns were silent for the moment, visible only as gray shapes in the darkness. There was lots of activity over there, however, as the crews humped ammunition around the emplacement. I asked the gunny where we were going next. He said he didn't know yet; Major Murphy had told him to wait out here until they had a spotting location set up and a copy of the grid fragment I'd need to work. And Goon's squad.

I was pretty tired and a bit sore from my underground experience. I asked the gunny where I could get something to eat. He seemed surprised. I told him I'd been something of an orphan since coming ashore. He told me to stay put and headed back into the main CP tent. He was back five minutes later with a small tin can that was warm to the touch.

"Beans and franks," he announced, proudly. "We warm 'em up on one of the radio equipment cabinets. All those vacuum tubes get hot."

He handed over a plastic spoon that felt suspiciously sticky. He'd also brought out a mug of coffee. The mug had a crack in it; I had to drink it halfway down to make it stop leaking all over my hand. I finished off the C ration in about six bites and felt much better. The gunny had his own coffee mug. He offered me a cigarette.

I was what people called a social smoker—I'd accept a cigarette if someone offered, mostly to be polite. Our guns may have been quiet, but there were plenty of other ones which weren't. The island was flat enough that we could see some of our own artillery blasting away and then the corresponding red and yellow flashes downrange as their shells landed. Then bright yellow flashes as they shot back.

Now that it was dark the rattle of infantry weapons was much reduced. There'd be flashes of gunfire offshore—mostly five-inch from destroyers—which would illuminate the ships in orange-yellow light themselves for a fraction of a second each time they fired, like a photographer's flashbulb. There were patrols starting out from the CP area to set up night defensive positions around "our" hill. Silent forms, bent forward under packs of ammo and water, trudged out into the darkness. Water was crucial. Killing created quite a thirst. I learned there was no fresh water on the island.

"Another two hours, the bastards'll start creeping out of their tunnels," Malone said. "They come out in onesies and twosies and try to sneak up on our front line foxholes and mortar pits. First thing you know, some bad dream flops down into your hole and starts screaming and swinging steel. I wish we had us some war-dogs."

"I'm surprised we don't," I said. "I've read they've got 'em in the ETO, and so do the Germans."

"I heard we did bring some," he said with a sigh. "But word is they ran away with all the incoming and then the Japanese ate 'em. The Navy's had this island buttoned up for weeks now. No supplies gettin' through. You don't mind me askin', Loot—what's this new grid deal?"

"In principle, same as the grid you've been taught all along," I said. "The big difference is that now each division has its own grid which they lay down over *their* area of responsibility. That means all fire support requests have to come up the chain of command—battalion, regiment, sometimes even division CPs. This new grid covers the whole island with one grid. In theory that means that any spotter, no matter where he is, can call in a mission directly to *any* guns he can get comms with."

Gunny nodded. "I get that," he said. "Oughta get rounds on target a whole lot quicker. I'm the chief radio tech in there; I get to listen to those guys out there callin' in for arty. Too many times our GLO goes back to 'em with ready guns and he don't answer up anymore."

He looked at his watch. "Lemme go see how they're comin' in there. We need to get you out on station before it gets too late and the bastards start creepin' around."

"Iwo's *their* ground," I said. "They've had some time to get ready for us."

"Got that right," he said, getting up. "Colonel says this whole island is like a stone sponge and now there's enemy with a knife in each hole of it. Stay put, Loot."

"Yes, Boss," I said. I was a lieutenant; he was a Marine gunnery sergeant. Of course I called him Boss.

He left me out there in the dark, but I was hardly alone. The first set of flares popped while I waited, revealing that there were men moving around the whole CP area—messengers coming in, sentries and scouts headed out, ammo vehicles bringing up more rounds of everything, LVTs grinding back down to the beach with wounded— and, I had to assume, the dead. That awful smell was back, the sulfur and the dead bodies competing to make all the living just want to stop breathing. The only thing I'd ever smelled that came close to it was when one of the swamps about a half mile from the big house at home had turned over.

Malone came back out and told me to hurry up—and wait. He brought more coffee, God bless him. I'd been having withdrawal pains ever since coming ashore. I asked him what was the deal on the "Goon" squad.

"That's Goon's squad," he said, chuckling. "And it's three guys, not a whole squad. The boss man is Corporal Willy Logan and he's a Scout Raider; other two guys are, too. Kinda famous in this regiment. Willy Logan was one of my guys on the 'Canal when I was with the First Marine division. Me and him got close after the big Matanikau River deal."

As Malone told it, Goon's full name was William Thomas Logan, who was a corporal, from up in the Ozark mountains. Malone said I'd understand the nickname once I saw him; he was, apparently, a dead ringer for the archetypical goon depicted in newspaper cartoons everywhere: six one tall and close to the same wide, with a slab belly, no neck, flattened face with the crooked nose of a boxer, pig eyes, upper arms the size of hams, and heavy, flat hands. He walked with a slouch in size 12 boots and was generally quiet and good-humored except when he wasn't, and then: brother, watch out.

He'd grown up in the tiny town of Hector, Arkansas, population around five hundred, where his father, William Brown Logan, had owned the only automobile repair garage/gas station in that part of Pope County. William Brown was known for fair trade and mechanical expertise with cars and engines, and Willy, as Goon was called to differentiate him from his father, learned the trade early on. His grandfather was known locally in Pope County to be a moonshiner who'd been cooking since Prohibition, so Willy's daddy had a discreet but lucrative sideline "fixing" the bootleggers' vehicles. The pure mountain water coming down from the Boston range of the Ozarks was a major factor in the quality of Pope County moonshine, and it became much sought after in the larger towns of Arkansas. Willy, as a kid, had been mainly used to acquire high-quality white corn from farmers along Missouri's southern border who were willing to exchange bags of dried corn for a jug or two, but he graduated to running the actual product once he turned sixteen.

Willy had one younger sister, named Mary Lynn, who'd gone astray at the tender age of fourteen, having matured as a sultry, wild-child bleach-blonde with a figure that belied her adolescence. She took to calling herself Marlene and sported provocative clothes while causing havoc among Hector's teenage boy population. Her father finally had enough of her antics and made her go live with the Methodist preacher and his family of twelve children to be brought up in a strict and respectful fashion on the preacher's hundred-acre apple orchard and small dairy. The preacher and his wife were known for taking in

"God's strays" and reforming them into proper God-fearing citizens. The preacher's wife, whose name was Grizelda, ran the whole operation more like a monastery than a family farm. Prayer several times a day, gardening and preserving for the table, milking the cows at three in the morning, sewing sessions for suitably modest clothes, and lots of bible study in the evenings. Mary Lynn secretly complained she'd been banished to the waiting room for Hell.

Mary Lynn toed the line for the first year or so, courtesy of Grizelda's eagle eye and handiness with a birch rod. At almost seventeen, however, Marlene slithered back into Mary Lynn's consciousness by pointing out to her that the preacher, a tall, full-bearded, and staunch fundamentalist who was forever quoting scripture and standing in aloof judgment of just about everybody, had been casting some unhealthy glances at Mary Lynn's ever-ripening body when he thought no one was looking. Mary Lynn saw a way out of what she considered a prison by ever so slowly conducting a campaign of covert seduction on the preacher, a skill she'd perfected in high school. The preacher didn't stand a chance and inevitably quite a scandal erupted in dear old Hector. But then came the real calamity: Willy's father and his grandfather, Ebeneezer, took matters into their own hands, shot and wounded the preacher, and then hanged him from one of the preacher's larger apple trees.

They were taken to the county seat, put on trial for murder, convicted—they proudly admitted to what they'd done—and sentenced by a sympathetic local jury to a year and a day in prison. By then some relatives of the preacher had begun talking up a blood feud. The judge took Willy aside and told him he'd best leave the county and join the Army or whoever would have him.

Willy went down to Little Rock, found a recruiter, and enlisted. He served one year, until the pre-enlistment physical exam he'd never gotten revealed flat feet, a disqualifying condition for the Army, which lived on its feet. Then Pearl Harbor happened and Willy signed up with the Marines, who asked if he'd had any problems with his flat feet in the Army. Willy shrugged his shoulders and told them he just sort of shuffled along like he'd always done and gotten along fine. The recruiter gave him a waiver, and here he was three and half years later, a corporal and a veteran of the Solomons campaigns and, most recently, Peleliu.

Malone reveled in telling the story. From all that detail I realized he'd told it many times, and the respect in his voice gave me some confidence. I'd be in good hands. And they called the guy Goon. I couldn't wait to meet him.

TWELVE

I was awakened sometime later when "our" 105mm artillery battery went back to work with a blast of noise and muzzle flashes that almost made me bolt. I no longer had a watch so I didn't know how long I'd been sleeping, but that surreal canopy of flares filled the air now and I could hear the rumble and booming of the fighting across the island in between cannon salvos. A breeze had sprung up and now all I could smell was gun smoke from the 105s, a vast improvement over the stagnant reek of far too many corpses. We retrieved our dead. The enemy did not. Could not. Then I saw the gunny waving me back over to the other CP tent. There were two Marines standing to one side of the entrance, one of whom was a really big guy. I couldn't see their faces, but they bristled with infantry gear. The gunny handed me a small canvas bag, shaped like a gym bag, and a full canteen.

"This here's your escort detail," the gunny said. He nodded toward the big guy. "Corporal Logan here's in charge. There's a platoon up on the edge of a place we're calling the Quarry that's getting hammered from the other side of the hole. Your radio operator's already there; the grid's in the bag, along with the comms plan. You'll be spotting for one of the battlewagons, don't know which one. The password for tonight is Jelly Belly. The Quarry's up toward the other end of the island, about two thousand yards from here, across airfield number two. It's a hornet's nest of tunnels and bunkers. Colonel says good luck."

I took the bag and hurried after my escort team, who were already walking into the darkness. I'd expected introductions and a quick briefing from the corporal, but they were moving quickly down the hill. I was surprised that we were going fast but I sure as hell wasn't going to be left behind. Then I became aware of another Marine bringing up the rear, a diminutive figure who moved silently over the loose scree littering the hillside, soundlessly urging me to keep up by walking close behind me. Our group slowed down when we got to the edge of what looked like a disused runway. The concrete was heavily cratered by various sizes of artillery, ranging from bomb craters that stretched fifty feet across and twenty deep to what looked like small pits, probably caused by mortars. The edges of the runway were marked by high banks of earth and stones, most likely the work of bulldozers scraping the area flat.

We stopped next to a really big crater that covered the edge of the runway, and which had cut into that earthen bank. The corporal sent the second, smaller Marine, whom he had introduced as Monster, down into the crater, but not all the way down. Monster slid down through the loose volcanic soil just low enough that he would be out of sight from watching eyes on the other side of the runway. We joined him in a slow avalanche of dirt and rocks. I was surprised to feel heat coming up from the sides of the crater, and the smell of sulfur became much more pronounced. The corporal made further introductions.

"I'm Corporal 'Willy' Logan," he rumbled. "This here is PFC

'Monster' Guidry, and that's PFC 'Twitch' Chantagras over there. And you are—?"

"I'm Lieutenant Lee Bishop, USN, from the *Nevada*," I said. "I'm a replacement spotter."

There were what looked like sympathetic nods all around.

"Colonel Sam told me I was to take you up to the Quarry so you could set up and start working the big bunkers on the north wall," Logan said. "Said we were to stay with you and keep you alive for as long as possible. If we could."

"That would be much appreciated," I said. "Is this group what I heard the colonel call the 'goon squad'?"

The big guy grinned. "Goon's squad. That's me. 'Goon' Logan. Sir. We're all Old Breed Marines."

I had heard of that distinction. Marines calling themselves Old Breed had been fighting since the Solomons campaign in late 1942. They were greatly respected by all the "new" guys coming in since early 1944.

Logan went on to tell me about how and where we had to go in order to get across the blasted airfield and then on up the east coast to the Quarry, which apparently was one of the places where the Japanese garrison had chosen to make a stand as the Marines closed in. He said we were going to have to spread out a bit and move in a zig-zag pattern along the piled-up dirt berms around the heavily fractured concrete. Out in the open all those flares became a double-edged sword; they let us and the enemy snipers see.

We would eventually run the black sand terraces nearest the beach to the Quarry itself, and then make contact with the stranded Marine outfits assaulting the big open pit and all its fortifications. The area just inland of the eastern landing beaches was relatively secure, but nowhere on Iwo could be considered completely free of enemy soldiers because of all the underground bunkers, gun and mortar pits, and tunnels. Enemy soldiers had popped up out of invisible holes in the middle of so-called secure areas, spraying machine gun fire in all directions at stunned Marines who'd thought they were safe enough to take a load off and eat and rest. The surprise shooter would get shot, but not before killing or wounding a dozen Marines.

Logan told all of us to eat something from our C ration packs and to drink some water. There'd be some food, ammo, and water re-supply points down on the actual seashore just before we got to the Quarry, as long as Japanese artillery hadn't found them.

It took us an hour and a half to get to the designated rendezvous point, where a gunnery sergeant from one of the beleaguered platoons appeared out of the darkness. He had two privates with him who im-mediately took up defensive sentry positions, seeking cover and set-ting up their rifles. We met in a shell hole, where the first question the gunny asked was whether or not we had any extra water. His appear-ance was frightening. He was thin, almost to the point of emaciation. He had bandages on his neck, arms, and head, and they were filthy. He carried a battered-looking carbine that had been clipped vertically to his right hip. His voice was raspy as he explained their situation. Logan offered him one of his two canteens. He drank half of it in one huge gulp and then started choking.

"We can't move," he gasped, finally. "We can't go forward, we can't get out. They know where we are. The only things saving us is the shape of the Quarry's rim and the fact that I think they're shorter on ammo than we are, and we're about flat out. We started with a hundred eighty guys; we're down to thirty-two, and I'm the senior guy left."

Jesus, I thought. A hundred eighty down to thirty-two? If that was typical, no wonder the Marines were calling the Iwo landings a disaster.

"What fire support have you been getting?" I asked. Everyone jumped when something landed about a hundred yards away. "Dead flare," the guy called Twitch said.

The gunny shook his head. "Past three days, none. We have two working radios, but our radioman got blown to bits by a mortar and we lost the frequency list."

"How far to your hide from here?" Goon asked.

"Four hundred yards through sniper country, then a roll down some sand dunes to where we're holed up. It's a good hide, but we can't move out of it until two big bunkers across the Quarry get taken out. Caves with concrete fronts, and all we've got is sixty-millimeter mortars. Our rounds bounce right off and that's if we get a hit—it's a vertical target. I'd kill for a recoilless rifle or two."

I explained that if he could get me to a position where I could see the emplacements, I could take them out.

"How?" he asked in an exasperated voice. "You gotta go through battalion, then regimental arty. We don't know how to get to them."

"That's why I'm here, Gunny," I said. "I'll need a radio, a set of binocs, and a place where I can draw a bead on them."

Logan looked at his watch. "Been sitting here too long," he said. "Let's go. We didn't bring any extra water, but we can share ours and some C rats. But now we gotta move."

It took us twenty more minutes to get to what was probably the only observation point that looked down into and across the whole Quarry, which was a thousand feet across and fifty or so deep. The sky flares illuminated the bottom and parts of the stone side walls, but left a lot of shadows, too. There was a ramp road from the rim down to the bottom, where several pieces of wrecked earth-moving equipment lay along with some burned-out dump trucks. The far wall was higher than the one we were lying on, and it was pockmarked with caves and dark fissures. The Quarry reeked of sulfur, decaying corpses, and human sewage. The gunny said they'd had to collect dog tags and then push the dead bodies over the wall, since the ground was all stone. They were pretty sure the Japanese had been doing the same thing, especially after the first four days of the Marines trying to dislodge them. The platoon had brought a small portable diesel generator with them, and everybody up there kept a tiny dab of diesel oil smeared under their noses to combat the stench. We immediately followed suit.

"They're always watching our rim," the gunny said. "You can't stick your head up over the rim, ever. Their snipers are good, *damned* good. They can part your hair at two hundred yards. We pickaxed a slot through the rock for observation and hung a blanket soaked in used engine oil over it; you're gonna be looking through a crack that's a half-inch wide, and only when the sun's behind you."

"How about at night?" I asked.

"Same deal—one of those sky flares pops just right, they'll see your binocs' lens flash. Takes one guy to say it's safe, light-wise, and another one to take the look—a *quick* look."

"Okay," I said. "Let's get to it. Somebody bring me that radio and some binocs; I'll also need a flashlight to read my grid. Gunny, you'll help me locate the biggest bunker over there and then I'll see what we can do."

"We?" he asked.

"My battleship and I."

He grinned at that thought and then scuttled away to get the stuff I needed. Logan and his Goon's squad followed him down to where the rest of the platoon was. They took my second canteen and half of my C rations with them. I was thirsty, but I certainly understood. Their gunny had drunk two canteens worth at our quick resupply point on the beach, and had been carrying six full canteens on the way back to his men, held together with a length of shoelaces around his neck and shoulders.

It took a full hour to get ready for my first call. The radioman Colonel Sam had promised failed to materialize, so we borrowed one from the resupply point. Radio checks, finding replacement batteries for the radio, locating my observer's position on the grid, then calls back to the CP to confirm I wasn't about to fire at a target that had already been taken and thereby drop ordnance on friendlies in the area, setting up a backup freq in case the Japs started jamming my freq, a test of the authentication tables, and finally, radio checks with the *Nevada*.

I'd half-expected to hear Commander Willson say: Bishop, is that you? But if they recognized my voice, they didn't reveal it. The only thing we'd all forgotten to do was pick *my* radio call sign. The ships had theirs, which they changed at irregular intervals. Each CP at every level of command within all three Marine divisions had theirs. Every spotter had his individual radio call sign assigned according to which division or even regiment they were shooting for. I began to sympathize with front line troops—this was like dealing with a bureaucracy right when you were getting hammered by an enemy mortar crew. I finally decided to call myself Iwo, two-six Charlie, since theoretically I was going to work the entire island, regardless of which division needed help.

The final thing I had to do was actually *see* that big bunker they wanted me to take out. That took a frustratingly long time. The platoon had been able to see it by watching for gun flashes on the opposite wall of the Quarry, but now it was dark and silent. Just as I was straining to differentiate concrete from volcanic rock, a firefight broke out behind me. Logan had told me that we were getting into that time of night when the infiltrators would usually come calling. I went flat until the shouting and the shooting subsided, as did my radioman assistant, an impossibly young-looking private whose name I'd already forgotten. Then more searching until I finally found it, a smudge of lighter gray against darker gray.

The platoon's gunny slid into the sand beside me. "How far away you think that thing is?" I asked him.

He thought for a minute. "We've tried some rifle fire at it," he said. "I'm guessing three hundred yards, based on gunsight adjustments."

"Good enough," I said. I grabbed the radio handset and called the ship, whose call sign had changed to Peacemaker. I began the talk.

"Peacemaker this is Iwo, two-six Charlie: fire mission over."

Nevada responded. "This is Peacemaker, over."

"Target, new grid: four three six one, six eight two five; large concrete bunker. Main Battery, one gun. High cap. At my command, over?"

"Target, new grid: four three six one, six eight two five; large concrete bunker. Main Battery, one gun. High cap. At your command. Peacemaker out."

Then we waited for *Nevada*'s plotters to convert my call to a gun target line and range from their position offshore and then assign one of the ship's Main Battery turrets to the Mark One-Able computer. When they had one of the three guns in that turret loaded, the gun captain would turn the ready switch, which connected that turret and that single gun barrel to the computer. The turret would swing out, that gun alone would elevate to achieve the computed range. All of that should take about ninety seconds.

"This is Peacemaker, over?"

"This is Iwo, two-six Charlie, over?"

"Iwo, two-six Charlie, delay three zero minutes, mechanical, over?"

"Delay, three zero minutes, mechanical, out."

Something had gone tits-up on the *Nevada*—probably the Mark One-Able, since if the problem had been a gun, they had nine more of them to switch the mission to. Either way, we were out of business for the next thirty minutes—at least. Goon brought Monster and Twitch up to my lookout and told them to go wide and quiet, see what was shakin' out there in the weeds. They stacked their rifles, pulled out their K-bar knives, and disappeared without a sound into the menacing darkness.

"Goon," I said.

"Sir?"

"Monster? Twitch?"

Goon cupped and lit a cigarette, handed it to me, then lit one for himself. He settled back against a rock and told me about his partners. We could light up because we were behind ten feet of rock.

"Monster's real name is Aristede Guidry," he began. He was from St. Mary's Parish, Louisiana. I'd already noticed that Monster was short for a Marine. He was wiry, with a gargoyle's face under a full cap of spiky black hair, shorn down to Marine standards. His face reminded me of that vampire character portrayed by Bela Lugosi: hatchet-shaped face, elongated bony nose, dramatically arching eyebrows, black eyes, somewhat pointed ears, and ruddy cheeks which contrasted oddly with the rest of his face, which was china white. He was maybe five seven in his boots but with an oversized chest and slightly bowed legs. His hands were unusually long, almost clawlike, and never quite still. He went around with an expression of barely suppressed, hot-eyed anger that made his eyes bulge a little and hinted at a capacity for sudden violence. His voice was scratchy and rather high pitched; his accent was what Goon assured me was "no shit, real" Cajun. He wore a barely visible necklace that he claimed was made from his mother's own hair, which was something any respectable Voudon priestess would always provide for her children. Every once in a while, he'd tug on that necklace and mutter something, and then expose a one-inch-wide carving of a human skull, complete with glowing red garnet eyes.

Being from Georgia, I'd heard of Cajuns, of course, but this was the first time I'd encountered one. I figured I could understand about a third of what he was saying, not that he talked much. His nickname, Monster, was obviously a play on his small size, especially compared with most of the Marines I'd seen, who were typically six to eight inches taller and twice his bulk. But then Goon explained there was more to that Monster nickname business. He was the team's forward-most scout because he, as well as the third member of the team, Twitch, *liked* to slither soundlessly like a snake out into the darkness, carrying only knives, looking for enemy infiltrators to kill.

Goon told me that one hour before dawn one day on Peleliu, Monster came back to his platoon's front line with three eyeballs threaded onto a bloody boot string. The squad was suitably amused until Monster pulled the plastic and canvas liner out of his steel helmet and began heating up some diesel oil in the helmet over a small chunk of burning C-4 plastic explosive. Once it was heated, he put the eyeballs in the bubbling oil and asked if anyone had some extra salt and pepper in their ration kit. That kind of cleared the camp, Goon said, chuckling. The platoon's gunny sergeant had spoken harshly to Monster, who'd defended his arrangements by pointing out he'd missed breakfast, him.

Later that morning, as the unit advanced under the usual hellish fire, they'd come upon three separate corpses whose faces sported one empty eye socket each, while the other socket revealed the sickly white surface of an eyeball that had been removed but then put back, reversed. Many members of his platoon began giving Monster a wide berth once that story got out; he maintained he knew nothing about such a barbarity, him. When pressed, however, he'd given an evil grin and then 'fess up. Sort of. "Like real chewy aigs, them eyes," he'd said, raising his own eyebrows dramatically. "Cain't scramble 'em, and such, but hard-boiled, or even better, Cajun fried? They's a treat and a whole lot better'n gator eyes, 'cause human eyes ain't as salty, you know. Why I was askin' for some salt." I questioned the diesel oil as a cooking oil, and Goon told me not to go spoiling a good story.

Goon explained that the Japanese spent all day shooting at Marines from their concealed positions and spider holes, but at night they sent out their own version of raider-scouts to terrorize the Marines holed up in their front line foxholes. The Marines had an iron rule: if it moves at night, shoot it. If it calls out into the front lines in English, shoot it. If it cries out like a wounded Marine trying to get back inside friendly front lines, shoot it—everyone had been briefed that if you got wounded and separated from your buddies, however bad off you were, do *not* move or make any sound at night. We'll find you.

Monster, on the other hand, was the exception. He'd go out in front of his squad's position, checking out with the sentries as he crept through the perimeter, and wouldn't come back until false dawn. If the squad later heard screams out there, or the grunting sounds gators made at night, or even strange water-bird calls, where there was, of course, no water, there'd now be murmurs of "Git 'em, Monster" up and down The Line, and they'd grin and nod to one another. Southern-fried eyeballs for breakfast. *Hell*, yes.

He also liked to take along a small harmonica, Goon continued. Now, enemy soldiers prowling the Marine perimeter at night, he assured me, were nothing to take lightly. They'd come out in the dark, leaving their rifles behind and carrying razor-sharp swords or their *hari-kari* belly knives. They were really good at night-crawling and they often managed to creep up on a Marine foxhole, where one would throw a knife into the on-guard Marine's throat, and then the other would roll into the foxhole on top of the sleeping buddy, scream something hideous in Japanese, and then behead the other Marine. They'd quickly throw the head into the nearest foxhole to terrorize the next two Marines, who would instantly start shooting, often hitting other fellow Marines and setting off a general panic. Sometimes the severed head would contain the first casualty's genitals, stuffed into the gaping mouth, something the Japanese enjoyed doing with any Marine dead they came upon. Reportedly, that's what had attracted Monster to the fray.

His routine didn't vary much. He would creep around for a little bit, crawl under a rock like a snake, coil up and take a short nap. Goin' real quiet, he would tell the others. He'd wake up and then smell the air for a few minutes. He claimed he could differentiate between the smell of live enemy and the stink of carrion that pervaded the entire island. And then he'd blow a few notes on that damned harmonica. Any bad guys on the creep out there would freeze at that bizarre sound, and, of course, any foxhole Marines within hearing range would wake their buddies up immediately.

At that point, Monster's favorite tactic was to growl and then shriek like some kind of large cat and then go silent and remain very still again. By this time, he'd slithered close enough to the enemy positions that he'd be able to throw something into their foxholes. His favorite was a supple piece of rubber hose from an AMTRAC's radiator, which, in the darkness, barely illuminated by all those lazily drifting flares, and having been painted to look a lot like a *Mamushi* snake—the Japanese version of a water moccasin—would clear the foxhole, after which the real snake would use his K-bar to stab any bewildered and frightened soldiers who got close enough to him, usually in the groin. He'd then park an armed grenade under each dead soldier, just like they did with our dead. Then he'd go looking for some more foxholes. He'd use one of their own short swords to probe the ground ahead of him to make sure he wasn't about to slither over one of their mines. Why it takes so damn long, don't you see, he'd point out. Good woik takes time, you know, but it's great fun, if you know how to do it.

Or so he claimed, Goon said, although he, himself, admitted to being a believer. Hell, after just seeing Monster's face, *I* was a believer. Especially when I saw every line Marine who encountered Monster step aside—way aside—and avoid direct eye contact. From what I could see, everyone—officers, sergeants, and troops—knew him on sight. Monster, however, wasn't the only one of them who was famous.

"And Twitch?" I asked.

The third guy on my escort team was named Salvos Chantagras, nicknamed Twitch. I figured that was because he had some kind of facial tic, but that was not the case. Goon told me he was of Balkan extraction, but he looked more like every American kid's version of a Plains Indian right out of Central Casting: not all that tall but big through the chest and shoulders, with an angular, wedge-cheeked face, big nose, dark, almost slanted eyes, downward curved mouth, oily black, straight back hair which lay on his head like a wet rug, even after the obligatory Marine Corps high and tight haircut. He, like Monster, exhibited a physical presence that proclaimed: don't mess with me, but less bizarre than our Cajun. There wasn't an ounce of fat on him and his usual physical stance was best described as ready for anything, even when he was squatting down, staring at nothing and silent as a stone. About the only time he did talk was when he had something to offer about their tactical situation. Goon said that if Twitch saw a house on fire, the most you'd get out of him was: Hey—fire.

His nickname had been born the first time he'd gone to the Marine rifle range. Marines were taught the "squeeze" method of firing a rifle. "Pull" the trigger and you pull the rifle off the target; every damn time. They wanted you to grip the rifle hard and then settle the sights on the target before even putting your finger *near* the trigger. Set and lock the perfectly adjusted sight picture, but then don't go disturbing that perfect picture by pulling on the trigger. Squ-e-e-e-ze the trigger, while keeping the sight picture with both eyes open. Let the rifle surprise you while *it* takes care of the business.

Salvos had disagreed. His approach was to set the sight picture just like they told him, but then to place the trigger-finger and just barely twitch. The sergeants weren't having it: twitch, you'll move the whole rifle. Salvos shook his head—I hold the rifle so tight, it can*not* move. Watch. He then proceeded to fire six perfect strings with his trusty Garand at one hundred yards, two hundred yards, and ultimately, at three hundred yards.

The sergeants, baffled by this performance, challenged him to do it again.

All day long, he'd replied, quietly. Even back then, he wasn't much of a talker.

Twitch turned out to be true to his word. Through the weeklong competitions at the end of basic training for expert and then some, Salvos smoked his competitors. Then they handed him a National Match 1903 Springfield with an 8x Unertl sniper scope and a five-round magazine. They ran up head silhouettes at two hundred yards, through which he could put the round wherever they requested it. After that his Marine name was Twitch.

On Guadalcanal, the First Marines' problem hadn't been shooting individual enemy soldiers. It was dealing with *hordes* of them thrashing across rivers and running full tilt up the hill in an angry, noisy swarm, propelled by some kind of stimulant pills, all the while trying to overwhelm entrenched Marines who just happened to be defending themselves with water-cooled, tripod mounted, .50 caliber machine guns. The main problem for the Marines was having enough ammo and keeping their barrels cooled. There were so many damned targets they had to assign a mortar gang to keep constant illume in the air to make sure they got them all.

Twitch's job had been to look behind the screaming, hopped-up berserkers flailing up the slope and locate the colonels and, sometimes, even generals, crouching in their bamboo hides, a radio in each hand and a sword on their hip. He still had that 1903 Springfield rifle with its 8x scope, with which he methodically executed every Japanese officer who appeared in that telescopic sight. By the time the remnants of the assaulting regiment managed to fall back on their own lines, there was not a single officer to welcome them back.

He spent the rest of his time in various hides out around Henderson Field, usually in a wrecked American fighter plane that had been pushed off the runway into the jungle, shooting snipers out of their trees while keeping to the sniper's basic pattern: shoot and then move; always move. There were plenty of plane carcasses out there. The Japanese were perfectly capable of putting a team in the trees— one to attract the Marine sniper's attention, the other to shoot back as the first sniper was falling to the ground with a bullet in his head. If a sniper did something that appeared to be goofy, Twitch would look hard for Number Two; shoot him first, and then go after the decoy.

Twitch's other skill was tracking through cover. He seemed to have a sixth sense when there was something in the jungle, underground, or out among the rocks that didn't belong there. As to underground— Goon swore that Twitch could detect the presence of metal objects underground, such as land mines. Nobody could explain it, but if ever Twitch stopped and put a finger in the air everyone froze until he got down on the ground and crept close enough to point at it. Every replacement platoon leader, company commander, and staff officer was briefed to listen to Twitch; he rarely spoke, they were told, but when he did, act like it's a railroad crossing: stop, look, and listen.

On that disastrous first day of the Iwo landings, Twitch had disappeared. He'd gone over the side from one of the landing boats about a hundred yards offshore. He'd then swum down the coast, all alone, around the southern slopes of the volcano to the westernmost foot of *Suribachi*, and then disappeared into the wet black rocks and tangled kelp beds at the volcano's base. From there he'd climbed almost to the top, hiding at the edge of the open crater for most of the day. As evening approached, he'd circled back around inside the crater until he could sight down into the open backs of the main enemy heavy artillery emplacements, where he'd be relatively safe from naval gunfire. He'd taken explosive-head .30 caliber ammo for his Springfield and used it to set off ammo piles below. All the credit for those secondary explosions had gone to the naval units who'd been firing everything they had at the island once the true scope of the prepared defenses had become clearer.

He stayed up there for two days and a night until he ran out of visible targets, then slithered down the cinder slopes and back into the sea on the second night, when he swam back north to the landing beaches, keeping about a hundred yards offshore. He then calmly walked out of the sea and reported in to the astonished beachmasters. Later he only smiled when those now famous flag-raisers claimed to have "taken" *Suribachi*. He'd eventually rejoined Goon and told him what he'd been up to. Goon then told Colonel Sam. I know, the colonel had said—I sent him up there. Good scout, that one. Hang onto him. Name's Twitch.

We waited some more. I was still trying to get my head around the concept of a three-man special team out among the chaos and out-of-control bloodletting that was Iwo Jima and doing insane things like going up *Suribachi* on L-Day and not getting caught.

"About as crazy as a Navy loo-tenant leaving a nice warm, safe, and dry battleship for the chance to play with us in this shithole," Goon observed with a shrug.

"Um," was about all I could manage as that big mortar started up again and we once again sought cover.

Finally, the *Nevada* came back up and reported ready for the fire mission. I was willing to bet that my replacement down in Plot wouldn't be able to sit down for a week.

"Ready, break—*fire*," I replied. At this range, the ship would give me the warning that the round was about to land in five seconds. That gave me time to get back to my peephole to watch for the impact.

"This is Peacemaker: Shot." A pause. Then, almost immediately: "Stand by, out."

I slid over to my arrow slit just in time to see and hear a colossal explosion erupt behind and above the bunker's entrance. I went back to the radio.

"Peacemaker, this is Iwo, two-six Charlie. Spots: right one hundred, down one five zero feet, drop three hundred."

"Spots: right one hundred, down one five zero feet, drop three hundred." A short pause, then: "Spots applied. Ready, over?"

"Ready, break—*fire*."

Another pause. "Shot." And then another: "Stand by, out."

This time the round hit within the Quarry, but to the left of the target. Plus, it didn't explode. When a five-inch does that, I have to go back to the shooter and call "lost." But a five-inch shell weighs seventy-five pounds. A fourteen-inch high-cap shell weighs 1,700 pounds, so even a dud landing can be both seen and heard. I corrected that shot and called for one more, at which point some big mortar rounds started coming our way as the Japs realized what was going on. Most of the mortars landed behind us and more in the direction of where the platoon was hunkering down. My radioman and I went flat when the first rounds hit, but then I got back up and called in a final spot. We were shooting at a target that was embedded in a sheer rock wall, so I knew it wasn't going to be like hitting a cluster of tanks, which could move. But if I could collapse that rock wall and possibly bury the entrance, it would improve my platoon's circumstances a lot.

The final spotting shell did go off, this time right on the rock wall and about eighty feet directly above the bunker's mouth.

"Peacemaker, this is Iwo, two-six Charlie: *target*. Three rounds, Main Battery, high-cap, fire for effect."

That transmission turned *Nevada* loose to deliver one turret's worth of huge projectiles on or near that bunker's exposed face. After the three rounds completely obscured the target in a flashing cloud of flying rock and dirt, there were no more Type 98 mortars coming in. I heard a quiet cheer from down where the guys were hiding. The remains of the platoon down in the ravine couldn't see anything, of course, but they could surely hear it, which must have been comforting. For the first time since coming ashore, I felt good. Fourteen-inch does that for you. Sixteen-inch is even better.

THIRTEEN

Then I had an idea. Since I had the big stuff at my disposal, I called them back and told them the target was obscured and announced a second fire mission. This time I called for armor-piercing rounds and spotted the impact points back up on the top rim of the Quarry—directly above the bunker, I hoped. I couldn't know how far underground they'd built that bunker, but if I could make the tunnel's roof collapse, they'd be permanently out of business. *Nevada*, using a single turret, fired six more rounds in three-packs, all but one of which landed near or on the overhead line of the tunnel.

One round, the last one, went a bit long, for some odd reason. It took about forty-five seconds between rounds, and I could just envision the turret crew clearing that barrel's gaping maw and then feeding the next shell and its attending powder bags, slapping on the primer pads, and then hydraulically activating the massive breechblock to swing back up, engage, and then rotate to the locked position.

Nothing happened from when these rounds first hit until the

delayed-action fuses fired, by which time I was hoping these even heavier projectiles had penetrated down to where the tunnels and our treacherous enemy lurked. One of those AP rounds apparently found an ammunition storage chamber, because suddenly there came a pillar of flame erupting hundreds of feet into the night air and illuminating the entire middle part of the island with a sustained fiery roar. I knew that if that chamber had been part of the tunnel complex there'd be a similar firestorm pulsing underground throughout every tunnel in that complex that was physically connected to that ammo chamber.

The gunny came scrambling back up the slope to my position with a huge grin on his face. "That mean what I think it means?" he asked me.

"Well, if nothing else, they're gonna be out of ammo," I said. "Where's that other bunker?"

I made a final transmission to *Nevada* indicating the target had been neutralized. I couldn't say destroyed, but the ship would have seen that blast and known they'd done something worthwhile. Hell, everybody on the island had probably seen that eruption, which had illuminated the underside of the clouds. The Japanese started up with another mortar barrage from a different position, which lasted twenty minutes. They couldn't actually hit the platoon's hideout because of the overhang at the top of the Quarry's rim, but they could get close enough to keep all of us pinned to the ground until it stopped.

Goon Logan showed up out of the dark with a big grin on his face. "Nice work, Loot," he said. "It's almost zero four hundred; getting late for infiltrators, but you know they're gonna send a crowd over here later tonight. We need to get what's left of this platoon outta here before first light and back down to the beach. These boys are done."

"I'll get *Nevada* to walk some five-inch rounds around the opposite rim of the Quarry," I said. "We might get lucky, catch some of 'em out in the open." I turned to the gunny. "Have you got comms with your CP?"

He shook his head. "They shift freqs and codes every day. We think there's good guys about five hundred yards due west of here. We sent a couple of runners two nights ago; they never came back. Only positions we *know* about are the ones we can see shooting at us. We flashed an SOS to one of the carrier planes; prolly how you guys got here."

"I've only got a couple of spotter freqs and codes," I said. "I'll get *Nevada* to relay a message to your regimental CP that we're gonna try to extract back to a secure area on the beach. Corporal Logan— when you want to head out?"

"Ten minutes?" he said. "While it's still really dark."

"Okay, then, that's not enough time to go after individual targets. I'll give them an area target instead. I'll get 'em to cover the other side of the Quarry with a time-on-target call. That way the sonsabitches'll be taking cover while we're breaking cover. I'll ask for five-inch this time."

Goon and the gunny acknowledged that, then hurried back down to rouse what was left of the platoon while I got on the radio to *Nevada*. A time-on-target area-fire mission was a box drawn on the grid. It was the shooter's job to cover as much of that area as possible using his fire-control computer by introducing a series of spots manually at the computer. "Time on target" meant that he'd start firing at the time I specified, expending the number of rounds I requested. *Nevada* carried a lot more five-inch rounds than fourteen-inch, so if the objective was to drive the enemy into his foxholes rather than destroy a specific structure or emplacement, five-inch shells would accomplish that. Once I gave them the mission and they rogered for it, I was free to move.

Thirty minutes later, not ten, we moved out on the same path we'd taken in. The platoon's gunny was technically in charge, being the senior enlisted man present, but it was Goon Logan leading the way. Monster had been sent out ahead, with Twitch acting as his wingman. Gunny Malone had told me that my bodyguards were officially designated Marine Raider/Scouts, specialists in small team reconnaissance, behind-the-enemy-lines sabotage and sniping, and what the Marines called pathfinding. If a regular unit was preparing to advance, the raiders would go in ahead of them, usually at night, to reconnoiter what the larger unit might be facing. Our objective was to get away from the Quarry and its surrounding ravines, low ridges, and subterranean enemy. I was the only officer, but I was mostly along for the ride, being "only" a naval lieutenant.

It was nothing like moving through a jungle, which, of course, I had only seen in the movies. The entire island of Iwo Jima was the tip of a submerged, active, oceanic volcano, rising from the sea floor some six thousand feet down. Mount *Suribachi* was only the most recent, in geological terms, vent. The so-called soil was a mixture of shattered lava, pumice, packed sulfur, and ash. Nothing grew right now on Iwo, after months of preparatory Navy shelling and Army Air Forces bombing. The Japanese who'd been living here before the war had mined sulfur. They'd lived on rainwater, rice brought in from the home islands, marine vegetation such as kelp, and locally caught fish. *Iwo Jima*, translated into English, roughly meant Sulfur Island.

Five of the platoon's remaining men were stretcher cases, so men took turns humping them over the ankle-twisting terrain. Everyone else was spread out, ten feet apart, rifles and submachine guns at the ready, and trying to walk in the zig-zag footsteps of Goon Logan. Each man could see only the man in front of him in the gloom. The theory was, if Goon didn't step on a mine, chances were they wouldn't either. Monster and Twitch were still out on the wings ahead, watching for trouble. It was slow going, no more than ten feet per minute at best. I was counting the minutes until dawn broke. I think we all were.

I'd liberated a battered carbine and one spare clip. We'd burned the contents of my gym bag before leaving, destroyed the second radio, and left grenade booby traps under any still-serviceable gear.

Everyone was hungry and very thirsty. The gunny's shirt pocket was bulging with the dog tags of the guys they'd lost. The platoon was upset at the fact that we'd had to leave Marine bodies behind. Marines always brought in their dead comrades.

Nevada's area barrage cranked up when we were maybe three hundred yards out of the Quarry area and slogging through some nasty dunes of black sand. I wasn't sure my fire mission was doing any actual damage, but I thought it might convince the Japanese that the platoon and its accursed spotter were still hiding out under the Quarry's opposite rim.

All of a sudden, Monster yelled and then threw himself flat on the ground while opening fire on something—I couldn't see what because I, too, was getting flat and struggling to unlimber my carbine. A roar of incoming machine gun fire erupted in our direction, with bullets humming and snapping much too close for comfort. In a panic, I wondered: had I charged it? I dared to look up into the darkness, where what looked like a thousand points of red light flashed at us from somewhere ahead. The Marines behind and around me returned fire, convincing me to become one with the earth as a storm of lead flew both ways. I could actually *feel* the incoming fire and the returning fire humming a few inches above my head as I lay there with my eyes squeezed shut.

There came a sudden, almost unnatural silence. I could hear rifles being recharged and clips being slammed into receivers all around me. Someone was crying in pain. The darkness was so full of gun smoke that my eyes were watering. I pulled slightly back on the slide of my carbine, being careful to make no noise. The gleam of a brass cartridge case was barely visible in the breech.

Okay, I thought: my weapon was ready.

For what? Where'd they go?

We were flat down on a narrow trail curling through the dunes and the surrounding badly stunted underbrush. The constellation of airborne flares drifted to seaward, revealing a shattered landscape whose shadows danced erratically in the gloom as my eyes adjusted. Where were the Japanese? I crouched in the dirt while trying hard to squirm my way up against a four-inch lip of crusted volcanic ash. Not exactly great cover, but it was something. I kept closing my eyes and then reopening them, looking hard into the gloom.

I thought I heard feet. Somebody running toward me.

There: three indistinct figures, hunched way over, coming right at me, their feet making no noise. Who they were—what they were—I couldn't quite make out, but I remembered Goon's rules about movement in the night. I raised the carbine and shot each one of them, right in their middles. Then I did it again, even though they were down on the ground, half-kneeling, fully flat, or just subsiding down onto their knees. Fortunately, I hadn't put the weapon in full auto, thereby not expending all my ammo in one terrified burst.

Roll, a distantly remembered voice told me: *Roll!*

I rolled, once, twice, and then took up firing position again, pointing out into the dark. A sudden scream erupted behind me and I rolled again just as someone buried a sword into the dirt right next to my head, swinging so hard that he fell down right next to me. Without even thinking I stuck the muzzle of my carbine right into his mouth. I actually felt the barrel tip striking his teeth. I fired, scattering the entire back of his skull into the darkness. As he subsided, I heard *more* footsteps, this time making no effort to be quiet. I saw a smudge of yellowish uniform materializing out of the corner of my eye, rolled to the other side, and fired again, this time shooting my attacker full in the throat, more times than was probably necessary. I wanted this shit to stop.

The carbine was empty. I ejected the clip and then jacked my one spare into the weapon. I had to think for a second: now what? Oh, right. Release the slide. Chamber the fucking thing!

Move, something told me. Move, move, *move!*

But this time it wasn't necessary. Once again, it had gone quiet. My hands were hurting until I realized I needed to relax my grip on the carbine. By now I was contorted into some ridiculous position where it hurt to just stay still.

Goon appeared. That's when I realized it was beginning to get light. I'd been huffing and puffing and trying not to urinate.

"God*damn*, Loot," Goon said, looking around at all the bodies. "Gonna make a real Marine out of you yet. Twitch, Monster, come see what our squid did."

"That's squid *sir* to you," I muttered, keeping the joke going. He chuckled and executed a mock salute. "All right, ladies," he called. "Move out. We got ground to cover."

"Hey, Loot, " Monster called. "You claimin' that sword?"

"Hell, no," I said as I got fully up and began dusting off my uniform. "I don't need any more stuff to carry. Anybody got another clip for this carbine?"

Monster called dibs on the sword. Nobody had an extra clip. I slung the weapon over my shoulder and unsnapped the holster on my .45. We'd lost two of the stretcher-bearers, so I took a turn. The sky was definitely getting lighter to the east and the terrain had begun to descend toward the shore. The flares had stopped, but we no longer really needed them. We were encountering real dunes now, which Goon explained meant the bad guys couldn't dig in and ambush us because of the loose sand. When I first began to hear surf, my thirst became overwhelming. I was reminded of those haunting lines from Coleridge: water, water, everywhere, and not a drop to drink.

Our squid, I thought. Definitely advancing in the world.

FOURTEEN

After another forty-five minutes we came in view of the sea. We were challenged by a perimeter guard consisting of two machine gun nests. It wasn't a vigorous challenge—in the daylight it must have been obvious we were friendlies. Goon went ahead and begged for water. There were only six canteens between the two nests, but that was enough to give everyone two swallows. Fifteen minutes later two battered-looking AMTRACs came clattering up the beach to collect the wounded and deliver more water. The rest of us collapsed at the shoreline at the bottom of the terraces and concentrated on drinking that water.

Behind us, the daily roar of combat rose throughout the interior. There were support ships visible offshore—destroyers, attack cargo ships, a hospital ship with its big red crosses, and several transports. A steady stream of boat traffic churned through the surf about a half mile down the beach. A dozen AMTRACs were clustered at the shore, picking up supplies and dropping off wounded. I watched for a while, and then fell asleep in the growing sunlight.

Goon shook me awake in what seemed like five minutes; it was actually just after noon.

"Regiment has a mission for us," he said.

"Aoomph," I said. "No."

Goon grinned. "C'mon, Loot—you're famous now. Whole fucking island saw that ammo dump go. Now they want you to go work the Meat Grinder."

I sat up and tried to get the sand out of my eyes, literally and figuratively. A cloud of blowflies rose off my utilities; all the rotting corpses had spawned a billion of them, and they weren't choosy as to whether you were alive or dead.

There was frantic activity on both sides of where we'd collapsed. I saw the gunny passing out bandoliers of ammo to the remains of his platoon. Chewed to pieces as they were, they were going back on The Line. Amazing. Someone had started a small fire in the sand, where the platoon was heating something called 10-in-1 rations. Suddenly I was famished.

After eating and then scoring new (and dry!) socks, two full canteens, and a reworked Thompson submachine gun, Goon and I caught an AMTRAC that was headed up to the regimental CP. The wind coming out of the northwest felt wet; I reminded myself to get a poncho before going back up to The Line. There was enough mist and spray out at sea that we couldn't see the gunships anymore. The wind was coming in onshore, so for once the horrible smell abated.

We made our way back up through the dunes to the regimental CP, which had moved north to be closer to what was developing into what looked like, we hoped, the last stand on the eastern end of their main line of defense. This was on the other end of the island from *Suribachi*, in a sector where the Japanese had reportedly been extra busy building out their positions. *Suribachi* was a natural defensive position, seriously high ground concealing a honeycomb of caves, lava tubes, and huge cracks in solidified lava formations. We'd been told that the northeastern end of the island, being relatively flat, had extensive, concrete-lined tunnels throughout the sector. Real subterranean caves were linked by man-made tunnels to artificial, concrete caves through interconnecting passageways designed so that their entire defensive force would be able to deliver quick, mutual support to any unit, pretty much anywhere. Add to that a few hundred individual hides and superbly concealed rifle positions from which a single soldier was expected to kill ten Americans for every one of their soldiers lost. Including himself. Now that was motivation on a serious scale.

We were surprised to find Colonel Nicholas in charge at the regimental headquarters CP—previously, he'd been a staff officer at the division level assigned to run their gunfire support CP. He was now the regimental commander due to his predecessor being killed by a mortar round, along with four members of his staff. This hadn't been just any mortar round—this loss had been caused by one of the fearsome Type 98 mortars, which fired a 265-pound, one-foot-diameter shell, as contrasted with standard infantry mortars whose diameter was measured in mere inches and millimeters. Our favorite colonel now sported an oversized eye patch. Bastards had hit him in the head, Goon observed; they shoulda known that wouldn't hurt a full bull in *this* man's Marine Corps.

"Hurt my eye, though," the colonel said. "Damn Navy doc took it out when I wasn't looking, squeezed it into a test tube with some alcohol, and sealed it up."

"So it wouldn't rot?" Goon asked, innocently.

"No, dumbshit, so I wouldn't drink the alcohol."

"Good thing Monster wasn't around," Goon offered, and we all got a laugh at Goon's latest sick joke.

The colonel's face sobered quickly. "We got us a nasty job of work in this place they're calling the Meat Grinder," he continued, taking us over to the big chart. "They designed this whole area right *here* to chew up American infantry formations, one Marine at a time. These bastards all know none of them's *ever* going home, so the whole point of what they're doing here, at least according to the big thinkers back on Guam, is to convince us *not* to invade the home islands. I hafta admit, I am, for one, fully goddamned convinced."

"How many casualties so far?" I asked. Impolitely, as it turned out.

"Lieutenant, you do not want to know those numbers, okay? Instead let's talk about setting you up to work the Meat Grinder with that new grid of yours, meaning I need you and any itinerant battleship to go do some good work for Jesus, one on one, as it were."

"Yes, sir," I said. "Brother Goon here says all we need are freqs, passwords, and a willing shooter."

"And some place to set up shop," the colonel reminded us. "That's the hard part—there are as many of them creepin' around up in the Meat Grinder at night as there are shootin' at us during the day. And once *you* open for business, every one of 'em's gonna be lookin' for you."

"Colonel, I got Goon, Twitch, and Monster. What could go wrong?"

Sitting Bull grinned, a little lopsidedly. He'd lost more than just an eyeball. Half his face muscles were gone. "You were right, Goon." He beamed. "This squid's a keeper. Murphy, take 'em over to the NGFS tent."

The gunfire support CP tent was a hundred yards away from the regimental headquarters. It was a newer and bigger tent, but the interior looked and smelled familiar. The blue haze that hung a third of the way down from the ridgeline was doing its job nullifying the carrion stench from outside, although by now we, like any members of a forward unit, carried it with us wherever we went. There were two plotting tables in action and a lot more radio operators. And, to my amazement, there was young Wreck, sitting on a pile of ammo boxes that allowed him to see the plotters at work, obviously supervising what they and the calculators were doing. I asked Major Murphy what was going on. We'd left Goon and his accomplices outside to go scrounge for more gear.

He just shook his head in obvious wonder. "He's some kind of math freak. You remember how he'd just stare at the table without saying a thing? One day he pointed at one of the guys working a Ouija board and called out: wrong. The guy about fainted: Wreck never spoke. And then the guy got mad. The shell-shocker was telling him he'd done the board wrong? The gunny running the table came over and took a look, and then declared Wreck was correct—the calculation was wrong. The guy went over to Wreck and handed him the board and the coordinates called in by the spotter. Here then, Freak—you do it. Wreck simply said: gun target line is X and the range is Y, only he spoke the actual numbers. That kinda stopped the table—he hadn't worked the board, he'd done the problem in his head. Somebody called Colonel Sam down from HQ, and he came over and made Wreck repeat the miracle on another problem. Wreck still wouldn't look at anybody, although he was real happy to see the colonel. His hands stopped wringing and his face just lit up."

"There something between those two?" I asked.

"Colonel's had him under his wing ever since they brought him in. Makes sure somebody watches over him and never lets him go outside unescorted."

"Wow," I said. "There's gotta be more to this. But, damn, look at him."

Wreck was walking the table, watching the plotters and making occasional corrections using only his hands. Each time the guy being corrected nodded and thanked him. No more getting mad. Wreck had become special; a little scary, perhaps, but special.

Another officer came over and took us to the frequency allocation table. He introduced himself as the Ops Officer. I noticed that most of the men in this group were also sporting bandages and other evidence of wounds or injuries. If you were a whole and uninjured Marine on this island, you were on The Line. One sergeant who was bent over a makeshift desk was bleeding through his shirt. Another had a plotting pencil taped to his fingers because he couldn't hold on to it. There were three men lying on cots at the far end of the tent with IV stands. I asked Murphy why they weren't down at the field hospital. No room, he said. Safer to keep them here at HQ. We have docs with us now.

The two of us followed the ops officer to the comms end of the tent to examine the current FM radio frequency allocations for this regiment. The frequencies were assigned via matrix, and that matrix changed every twenty-four hours and sometimes even more frequently. Compared to Peleliu, the Japanese 109th division was apparently much more proficient at jamming our frequencies. The ops boss said they must have a central comms station somewhere on the island, probably inside *Suribachi*, whose elevation would give them excellent antenna transmit and receive patterns. We would not only need an allocation of separate frequencies, but a plan for which ones to switch to and when, once serious jamming started. We'd also need the challenge and reply code schedule for spotters, radio operators, and sentries, which was different from those assigned to the line units.

"The Meat Grinder is different from working, say, *Suribachi*," the Ops Boss said. "Instead of a dozen big emplacements, that patch has a coupla hundred one- or two-man interconnected positions. One sniper pops up just as our guys think they've advanced our front line a hundred yards, i.e., that they're making progress, pushing them back into their own lines. That lone guy can kill five or six Marines in the space of as many rifle shots and then disappear like a damn periscope. Nobody knows when any place up there can be called secure. That means we're constantly pushing replacements into the Meat Grinder, which just gives them more guys to shoot at."

"I understand," I said. "I think the new grid will speed things up, but I still have to get a shooter on the horn, call the fire mission, let them compute, then shoot, then spot and shoot again. There's no way I'm gonna catch a single sniper who only stays up on the surface for less than a minute. Unless the same guy keeps doing that."

"They don't," said the Ops officer. "They'll pop up, shoot five, six rounds, drop back into their tunnel, run fifty yards down the tunnel to the next pop-up hole, and do it again. Nobody's figured it out yet."

"Well, there's one way," I said. "But I'm gonna need me a dedicated scribe and a second, clean topo chart of this so-called Meat Grinder area."

He stared at me. "You serious? You think you can fix this?"

"Can't promise, Major," I said. "But there is a way. It involves a little statistics and probability work, a good plot at my end, and a really proficient shooter out there."

The faces of the men standing near me went blank when I mentioned statistics and probability, but that was okay. I'd been introduced to that arcane discipline in my third year at Georgia Tech. It wouldn't give me accurate positions for the sniper, but I thought it might get me the tunnels they were using to keep on the move.

FIFTEEN

By early the next morning we were in position to work the dreaded Meat Grinder. My three guard dogs plus a radioman who was going to double as a recorder were my "staff." I was the spotter, so I'd call the actual mission. Goon and his boys would keep us alive once the Japanese realized there was artillery, naval or Marine, dedicated to digging them out with indirect fire. The colonel had also assigned a squad of regular infantry to reinforce our defensive ring. Ordinarily, infantry would be assigned exclusively to advancing friendly front lines all along the regiment's sector, but the colonel realized that the usual regimental push wasn't working. He decided to consolidate the bulk of the regimental forces where they were until I had had time to make a dent. Assuming I could. Colonel Sam was still the original show-me guy.

We hadn't had to walk to this assignment. Four tanks had been assigned to get us up to The Line, where they dropped us off into a sixteen-inch shell's crater at the bottom of a narrow ravine. We were now on the edge of the so-called Meat Grinder rock formation. Our first half hour was spent hurriedly digging in as the Japanese spotted the tanks and called in their own artillery. Fortunately, the crater was somewhat protected by a volcanic rock ridge, so for a change the shelling was noisy but not effective.

Unsettling word came from offshore. Apparently, there was an acute shortage of heavy projectiles. The Navy had just begun experimenting with ship-to-ship at-sea ammunition replenishment for the bigger ships, like cruisers, but the battlewagons still had to go off-station for several days either way. The CP told me I'd have to settle for a heavy cruiser, which fired eight-inch shells. For troops-in-the-open targets, eight-inch shellfire was more than adequate. It was not so effective for those targets that were deep underground. Either way, it wasn't like I could argue about it. Eight-inch would have to do until one of the big gray beasts, fed and rested, returned to the scene. I wondered why somebody wasn't staggering the offline periods for the battleships.

My cruiser was the USS *Baltimore*, one of the newer eight-inch gun ships with radar-controlled main and secondary batteries. Her radio call sign was Anthem, which I thought was pretty elegant for a ship-killer like *Baltimore*. My plan for defeating those sixty-second pop-up snipers who'd managed to hold up any progress into and beyond this sector with the grisly name involved mapping their tunnel network. I sent word out all along the front lines: every time a sniper pops up, try to kill him, but then send me his position in six-digit grid coordinates. Estimate it as best you can—don't worry about precise grid numbers.

After twenty-four hours, I ought to have a lot of contact reports such as: at 1130 this morning, a sniper materialized in or near grid position X and killed two of my people before disappearing again. My scribe would then plot it. The positions wouldn't be perfectly accurate, but after recording and plotting a sufficient number of spider hole incidents and applying a few formulae, we ought to start getting a pretty good idea of where the supporting underground tunnels were. As I'd explained to the comms major: the same advantage that the tunnel network gave the enemy in ambushing our Marines would be their undoing, because, ultimately, the tunnels couldn't move around.

After two days of almost constant concealed rifle fire coming our way, we had more than a hundred penciled-in positions laid down on that topographic chart, and it was pretty clear where at least two of the main tunnels cutting through the Meat Grinder sector lay. I drew a mission box that covered one of them for a distance of six hundred yards and a width of two hundred yards. I then called the cruiser and requested an area-fire mission along the length of that box, using eight-inch armor-piercing. I fixed my binocs on the prominent ridge covering what should be the tunnel's southern end, and then informed the cruiser that I would be walking their area fire down the length of a tunnel by issuing spots. It would be a cumbersome process, but my trusty scribe would be recording fall of shot during the mission. If the snipers kept popping up, I'd adjust the area fire until they stopped that shit. This would take some time, but there was a good probability that we'd eventually close down that tunnel. Then we'd go after the second tunnel, I hoped with a beast this time instead of a cruiser.

My plan gave new meaning to the term "indirect" method of fire support. I couldn't see the target. My spots were all going to be relative to the plotted and calculated tunnel axis, garnered from Marines up and down The Line as they peeked over "hot" rocky ridges. The cruiser, like any offshore shooter, would have to convert my standard three spots—deflection, elevation, and range—to gun target lines from *them* to the target. They'd pump out three rounds in a single salvo, one gun from each gun turret, and then I'd give them a spot. Three more rounds and then another spot. I'd walk the cruiser's fall of shot down the axis of where I *thought* the tunnel was. If I was right, it would kill everyone in the tunnel *and* collapse much of the tunnel. Do that long enough, and our guys could finally move forward. If I saw any evidence that our stuff was actually penetrating down to the tunnel, I'd shift to nine-gun salvos.

That was the theory, anyway, and my Marines were anxious for something to happen to those tunnels. The open question was what would the enemy do once he figured out that the Americans had located their tunnels. Goon just laughed. "As if we don't know," he said.

I rolled my eyes. "Anthem, this is Iwo, two-six Charlie: fire mission, over?"

"This is Anthem: roger, over?"

"Anthem, fire mission follows: troops in a tunnel, area fire within grid boundary as follows." Many numbers followed. "Beginning at start-point new grid." More numbers. "At my command, three guns, Main Battery, armor-piercing, along an axis of zero four five degrees true, one-hundred-yard spotted intervals. Full, nine-gun salvos on standby; smoke every third salvo, for a distance of six hundred yards. Report when ready."

The cruiser's talker repeated back my call, verbatim. Then I got a request to confirm armor-piercing. I wasn't surprised—that stuff was supposed to be used to fight other cruisers. I confirmed what I wanted and that was the last I heard about it.

I then warned the closest friendlies. I wanted to make sure they were expecting the sudden barrage right in front of them. Sixty seconds later the *Baltimore* reported ready. I replied: ready, break, *fire*, which called out the first three-gun salvo. She had nine guns, but I thought iterations of three should do it for starters. I could always ramp it up.

That produced an immediate: "Shot, out," followed seven seconds later by the traditional: "Stand by, out." Three smallish explosions erupted along the beginning of where I thought the tunnels were. I sent back a spot to bring the fall of shot a little farther east. I'm sure the troops weren't all that impressed, because the shells hit, penetrated, and only then went off, sometimes as much as twenty feet underground, resulting only in a series of dull thumps up on the surface. At this distance I couldn't be too precise, so I spotted the next few salvos to cover as much ground as possible while talking the firing line gradually to the east in the direction of the most plotted spider holes. I called in ninety rounds over the next fifteen minutes as dawn slowly bloomed. The Marines could clearly see and hear the incoming shells as I spotted the salvos across the center of the Meat Grinder to its eastern edge, closest to the sea.

Once I was done, I called a second mission against where we thought the other tunnel might be, but then held the firing command until I saw something indicating we'd done some good. Anything at all, please God.

Nothing. No indication we'd hit anything but rock. I figured the Japs would know someone was hunting them, but there was no massive secondary explosion like we'd had the first time. On the other hand, there was no sniper fire, either. Maybe we had their attention, I thought. I said as much to Goon. May not want that kind of attention, he pointed out. Then Twitch called out: smoke!

He was right—there was grayish smoke beginning to lift up out of the gullies and crags out in front of us. Nothing dramatic, but something had to be burning underground, like one of those never-ending coal-mine fires. If that was solid rock, there would have been no smoke. I quickly called up a white phosphorus mission along the area we'd just shelled. Alternating, two armor-piercing followed by two white phosphorus rounds. After five minutes of that, the volume of smoke grew dramatically all along where we thought the first tunnel was lurking. If the tunnel had been breached in more than one place, that white phosphorus would be killing enemy troops in great numbers, especially confined underground like that. I figured when it got bad enough underground, they might even decide to evacuate the tunnels and come on out into the open.

Baltimore had a fix for that situation, too.

Having a heavy cruiser in contact and already zeroed in, I'd call for some of that new radio-fuzed five-inch ammo, called VT Frag, standing for variable-time fragmenting ammunition. It was normally used as an anti-aircraft round—instead of having to actually hit an aircraft maneuvering at high speed in three dimensions to cause the projectile to burst, these things transmitted a cone of radio-frequency energy ahead of themselves. If the receiver in the projectile detected even a hint of a return signal, it meant the projectile was close to an aircraft and it would go bang. It could also be fired at a high vertical angle so that it ended up coming straight down. When that RF receiver detected the ground approaching, it exploded, creating an airburst of shrapnel at sixty to eighty feet, which was perfect when enemy troops were exposed above ground, even if they were dug into foxholes.

I told the *Baltimore* we were seeing secondary fires, and then called in a chapter-two mission, again with eight-inch armor-piercing, to revisit the entire area. If we were on target, and now I thought we were, that should drive any survivors into tunnel number two, which plotted pretty close to the first one with one main intersection.

Then I set up a third mission to work the second tunnel, again alternating AP with WP. The *Baltimore*'s plotting room crew obviously now understood exactly what I was trying to do. After the first few of my spots, they advanced the fall of shot on a straight line all by themselves to the southeast, again, right down to the sea. This time, there was a lot more smoke rising up. Goon sat there, behind our rock, speculating on what it was like to have eight-inch cruiser shells going off down there in their happy little tunnels.

By the middle of the day, there was smoke oozing out of cracks we hadn't known about. And definitely no more sniper fire, I was told. I wondered if the line Marines were going to try to advance. They'd been making so little progress pushing the Japanese back up the island that what little distance they gained each time was called a touchdown. In other words, a hundred yards at a time, with far too much blood being lost on our side. The generals and the admirals had predicted this entire assault would be over in five days, given the size of this island. We were now L+12 days in and had little to show for it except hideous casualty figures and all of the reserves already committed. This *had* to work.

SIXTEEN

A new smell began drifting over the Marine front lines as the sun went down: not just dead meat but roasted dead meat, with chemical sauce. Phosphorus has a distinct odor, and everyone knew we were smelling Willie Peter, the phonetic radio name given to white phosphorus munitions. I didn't think it could get any worse on Iwo, but I was wrong about that. God only knew how many enemy soldiers whose bones we'd managed to sear remained deep underground in all that volcanic sand. All the grunts knew was that the spider holes were finally silent, at least for the moment. But now it was getting dark.

"We need to pull back, boss," Goon said. "Get deeper into friendly front lines. Them bastids are gonna be comin' to find you; Colonel sez that *cain't* happen."

"What would they expect us to do, Goon?" I asked.

He looked at me suspiciously for a minute. His two accomplices pricked up their ears. "Git shuck of these parts," he said.

"Then we should do the opposite," I said. "They're gonna be

sending out war parties, especially if the tunnels have been collapsed. They send enough guys, it's gonna get vicious around here later on tonight. I think we four oughta creep *forward*, find a position ahead of our guys *and* their front lines. Then *we* go to ground. Wait 'em out, then tomorrow, when everyone's laying low, we put up an antenna and start some shit."

"And where do you think this magical hidey-hole is gonna be out there?" Goon asked, clearly thinking I'd gone nuts.

"In the tunnels we just fucked up," I said. "I'm guessing they had to bail out, or at least those who survived the Willie Pete did. But that gas eventually dissipates. When we do poke our noses out, nobody's gonna be expecting us."

"Damn right, Loot, including our guys," Goon replied. "You thought about that? You go stickin' your head up out of a Jap spider hole? The nearest six Marines are gonna shoot it right the fuck off. Sir."

"Yeah, yeah, but we won't do that until I call in a fire mission, depending on what I find down there."

"Goon, boy?" Twitch called. "That ossifer right there is on his own with this crazy shit. Just so's you know." Behind him, Monster was nodding eagerly in full agreement.

"That's okay," I said. "Gimme a radio and one fresh battery. I'll be a spotter *behind* enemy lines. Japs won't expect that."

"Ain't nobody in his right mind would expect that, Loot. God-*dammit*!"

"Think how many of those sonsabitches we'll kill before they catch on there's a spotter behind them."

"Think how quick *you* gonna die when they catch on there's a spotter behind them?"

"Na-ah—by then they'll all be dead. Look—you guys don't have to come along. I know it's crazy. But I got friends in high places—cruisers, destroyers, Marine and Navy air. Battleships, sometimes. Tell

Colonel Sam I ordered you to go back to friendly front lines. If it works, well, shit—good deal. If it doesn't, you tell the colonel you warned me. You know he'll be sympathetic."

"*Fuck* me," Goon wailed. "Why'd you have to go and say that?"

I just grinned at him. He had been well and truly had and he knew it. We also both knew the colonel would think this was a glorious idea. He'd also probably say that we were exceptionally brave, too. Not too bright, mind you, but definitely brave. Marines were all about brave, as they were constantly reminding me. And, if Goon signed on, I knew I'd have the other two. Hell, we might even pull this off.

I endured just a wee bit of bad language for the next hour or so as we got ready, but I was always up for learning some new cusswords. The nearest units were asked to start some shit when we finally jumped off.

We started off around 2100; just the four of us. The radioman had flat refused to go, so we made him the messenger—the guy who had to make his way all the way back to the regimental CP to inform the colonel what we planned to do. What *I* planned to do, Goon reminded me, still sulking. He'd said we had maybe an hour, hour and a half before the vampires began to emerge, seeking vengeance. Once both tunnels were clearly burning, he'd passed the word to the line companies to move out, get as far forward as they could before the night games started, and then settle in for some vicious close-in night fighting. We were going to go as fast as we could and then find a hide. We had fresh water, rations, and ammo. We even had two radios—the lap of tactical luxury.

We trudged rapidly through the gathering darkness, headed north *into* the Meat Grinder sector. Twitch took the lead to keep us from tromping into a minefield. The stink of white phosphorus remained strong along the way with the clear evidence of many dead wafting up out of the shattered tunnels. And then the rain swept in, light at first but then growing to some serious downpours and a sudden drop in temperature. It was late February in the Japanese archipelago; we began to see sleet squalls as a cold front came sweeping off the Korean Peninsula and into the East China Sea. Great cover, I observed. More bad language and general bitching.

We poncho'd up and plunged ahead, pushing north by northeast to get to the other side of the Meat Grinder before going to ground, if possible. I made periodic radio checks with the Navy gunline offshore; I didn't want them to forget about us. *Baltimore* had left the gunline to get more ammo; we'd about run them empty. Monster and Twitch sought out a suitable hide while Goon stayed close in case some enemy got at us unexpectedly. They'd taken one of the radios. It was miserable trying to cover any ground in the downpour, but the drumming racket of the rain had to give us some protection from listening sentries. The moon occasionally flared between ragged rainclouds, providing the only light; the weather had made the usual flare-dropping impossible.

As it turned out, Goon and I found a spot right after 2200. We'd taken a break in the dark to wait for the team to reassemble, pushing into a large collection of shattered rocks that was piled up against an almost vertical hillside. It looked like the tailings pile at the edge of an old-time gold mine, with a stationary avalanche of boulders and lava rocks spewing silently down the hillside from what looked like the crater of a large caliber shore-bomb shell, possibly even a battleship's. Except right at the base of the crater, almost buried in rocky debris, there was a cave entrance. Or maybe the entrance to a mine tunnel after all. It was no more than four feet high and maybe three wide.

Goon decided to wait for Monster to rejoin; he would be able to get into that entrance—and back out again quickly if he had to. I thought there was some smoke coiling out of it, but it was hard to tell in all this blowing mist. There was a rock ledge way up that blocked most of the rain from falling directly on us, for which we were duly grateful. I was wearing earphones, so when Monster finally called in asking for our position, I described our hideout and gave him some landmarks, based on the topo map. This big crater wasn't on the map, of course, but fortunately that old mine was. I was kind of surprised that it was even here because the only thing they'd ever mined here on Iwo was sulfur, and that was pretty much an open-pit operation. The other two rejoined in about fifteen minutes and we held a quick planning conference.

Goon told Twitch and me to take our Thompson submachine guns. The Marines fondly called their Thompsons Chi-town typewriters in honor of all the Prohibition days Chicago mobsters, and Goon set a lookout watch at the edge of the rockpile while he and Monster rooted around in their packs for some food and water. Then we switched positions and Twitch and I did the same. The other two set off to make their way back to friendly front lines to make sure the good guys knew where we planned to go to ground. I didn't want to put that information out on the air. Our smokers knew better than to light up a cigarette out here. I even wanted one, given the cold rain and menacing darkness.

An hour later, a rattle of small-arms fire erupted from back in the direction from which we'd come, punctuated by grenades, probably as the first of the night's samurai scouts rose up and began creeping their way into Marine foxholes out there in the dark. It was scary every time I heard it. It was one thing to talk about "the enemy" in the cold, detached tones of military analysis at the CP or down in Main Battery Plot. It was quite another to hear evidence that some suicidal soldier, who'd told his buddies that tonight was *the* night he planned to rejoin his ancestors in a blaze of *bushido* honor, was fulfilling his insane destiny. I could just imagine them waiting respectfully until their hero stumbled on some terrified PFC down in his foxhole and split the boy's head in two, just as the PFC's foxhole buddy blew the attacker's head clean off.

It took a few minutes for the small-arms fire to die down, but not without our having to endure the screams of men fighting and dying in hand-to-hand combat in the darkness. I thought we'd gone farther from the front lines than we obviously had; all this night fighting sounded pretty close by. In a way, I could understand why they were doing it. I'd been told back aboard ship that Lieutenant General Tadamichi Kuribayashi, the commander of the Japanese garrison on Iwo, had told his twenty thousand men that if they each could kill ten Americans, the Americans would suffer two hundred thousand casualties and would think long and hard about invading the home islands. The Japanese had to know they couldn't prevail in the traditional sense on Iwo Jima, but they could, by all their bloodthirsty gods, make the Americans bleed on a grand scale. They should have read up on our Civil War. Robert E. Lee had repeatedly bled Useless Grant's forces white in those last months of the war, but that never stopped Grant from pressing south.

Twitch and I settled in to wait for the other two. I took the first watch; Twitch was out like a light in about one minute. I was surprised he could sleep through all the racket going on around us. I realized that I could have too, however, and had to keep moving around to stay awake.

Goon and Monster rejoined almost two hours later, having painstakingly threaded their way through friendly front lines as the night's festivities ramped up. Goon told me his biggest problem was staying focused on the mission, because there were so many enemy raging out there tonight that he thought he'd have done a lot more good for the cause by simply sitting in the rain and killing them with his K-bar. Plus, he added, it would have been much more satisfying. Monster emphatically nodded his agreement.

"I hear you, gentlemen," I said. "But tomorrow, come daylight, we will kill them in their hundreds, not by onesies and twosies. Remember, your one and only Loot brings lots of seriously hostile friends. Now, Monster—go see what's down there, if you please. And remember, we're both behind you, right, Goon?"

"*Way* behind you," Goon offered, helpfully. Monster gave us an enthusiastic finger and disappeared through the smoldering crack in the rock wall. He was back in less than a minute.

"We cain't hide in there," he announced. "The floor is two-foot deep in dead bodies for as far as I could see down the tunnel, most of 'em burned. There's no air. None."

"Shit," Goon muttered.

"Is there any kind of zig-zag?" Twitch asked, suddenly awake. I remembered the CP bunker we'd dived into when I came ashore having a sharp right turn, followed by an equally sharp left turn, to defeat infiltrators from having a straight shot with grenades.

Monster thought for a moment. "Sort of," he said. "It goes straight in maybe ten feet and then zigs left for another six feet or so, I'm thinking, me. Not much room."

"We block that off, make it airtight, we'll have a hide. It's only for the rest of the night, right?"

"Maybe," Goon said. "Depends on what we find on our doorstep in the morning. How do we block it off?"

"Ponchos?" I proposed. "There's bound to be lots of rifles lying around down there. Make a frame, stretch ponchos, dirt, whatever we can to close the tunnel and plug that entrance hole."

"And in the meantime, we sleep," Goon said.

I put a call into the regimental CP, told them we were going off the air until dawn, while the others choked off the putrid entryway after first pulling bodies deeper into the tunnel. We'd wait underground into the morning. When our troops began to press forward and immediately ran into the usual buzz saw, we'd creep out and call down death and destruction on the enemy—from behind. That was the plan. What could go wrong?

Goon snuck back out into the crater and discovered that the rain was getting heavier. He laid out three wire trip lines of hand-grenade booby traps halfway up to the rim of the crater. That way if bad guys came exploring, we'd get some warning. We used our flashlights to light our way in closing off the tunnel. Once that was done, lights were switched off and we all lay down in absolute darkness. Each of us kept a weapon tucked in close in case attackers burst through the tunnel entrance. We'd thought about setting a sentry watch, but quickly realized that we'd have to have two people awake for that to work. It seemed more important to get some sleep. If an enemy platoon figured out we were in there, we'd be fucked anyway, so why not all of us get some rest.

SEVENTEEN

As it turned out, I was the first one to wake up. Based on the bright light coming through the cracks in our makeshift doorway covers, it had to be midmorning. The other three looked like they'd died in their sleep. I was trying to figure out what had awakened me when another big thump shook dust out of the tunnel's ceiling, followed by a steady cadence of artillery outside. My partners in crime rolled awake, reflexively pointing their weapons, which is when I realized I could see them clearly. We hadn't done such a good job sealing the entrance to the cave after all. I listened to the artillery sounds—not rounds landing, but rounds *out*going. I scrabbled over to that shining crack and peeked out. There was a Japanese mortar squad busily servicing a clutch of 81mm mortars. Goon joined me.

"There's only ten of 'em," he said. "We don't need fire support to stop that shit."

I was about to agree with him when we heard some much bigger guns let fly from just outside the crater—real artillery, not mortars.

Behind us. I keyed my radio and called the *Baltimore*. To my great relief, they answered right up. I called in a fire mission for VT frag right on our position. The ship came back and pointed out that fact. I confirmed the grid, called the target as artillery and troops in the open, asked for fifty rounds of five-inch VT frag, centered on our position, and turned them loose without waiting spots. We weren't in any danger—it was going to be frag ammunition, not high-cap. If I had to correct it, I would, but frag went everywhere. I even settled down behind my crack to watch. The other three did the same.

It was glorious. The fire-control team in the cruiser set a center aim point and then made their own spots. Once I saw that the bulk of the incoming was landing about where it should I gave them an immediate follow-up fire mission, adjusting the height of the air-bursts up thirty feet to increase fragment coverage. A Navy five-inch shell is a little bigger (127mm) than an Army 105mm howitzer. If I'd used eight-inch (196mm), one of the biggest artillery cannons in the business, it would have been overkill. Once a hundred of the five-inchers had arrived, there was nothing left alive or even recognizable as man-made in "our" crater. I assumed that the guns which had been positioned above us, probably on the rim of the crater, had also been dealt with.

I passed the word to the two nearest Marine companies that the crater had been neutralized, and then the general advance against the Meat Grinder began in earnest. We withdrew into our little dirt closet, pulling all the new rock debris created by the artillery strike into the entrance, and then flopped down in the tunnel to take a load off. A single flashlight transformed our grimy faces into weird masks underneath our helmets.

"How about them apples?" I asked my crew. There were appreciative nods all around but then I sensed something was bothering them. "What?" I asked.

"Too easy," Goon muttered. "Musta been a hundred or more working them guns. None of 'em got away. No spotting rounds needed—

first rounds on target; after that *Baltimore* was just makin' hash. It was just like the ship's chief gunner was standin' up there on the rim and callin' that shit down on top of 'em, right from the git-go."

"Well, in a sense, that's exactly what I was doing," I said. "For once I could see them, right there, so my first grid call was precisely on target. Wasn't that why we stayed behind? For the first and possibly last time, we're right here."

"That's what's bothering me, Loot," Goon said. "I'm thinkin' they are gonna figger that out—they're gonna realize that the spotter who called that down on them had to be right here somewhere."

"Which one is that?" I asked. "Nobody could have survived that coverage."

"One'a them snakes *always* survives, and that's what's worrying me."

"But if the regiment is on the move, they'll take care of any survivors, won't they? I thought the plan was for us to sit tight until we got orders to move to a new position. How would anyone get to us?"

Twitch had been sharpening his K-bar during our little discussion. "There's always the tunnel," he pointed out. Monster grinned when he saw the look on my face. I'd completely forgotten about the goddamned tunnel, which, filled with dead soldiers as it might be, was still right *there*, and the only thing protecting us from whatever nightmares might be assembling behind us way back underground were some canvas ponchos and a hideous smell.

Goon took charge, as only Goon could. "Loot," he said. "Call the CP. Tell 'em we need extraction. By now there oughta be at least some of our guys who can get here and get our asses back into friendly front lines. Twitch, Monster, light a coupla matches, rub 'em out and stick 'em up your noses; then go through the ponchos and see what's what down in that tunnel. You hear anyone comin', roll some grenades down the tunnel and get back here. If there's nothin' there, go see where the tunnels go and what else is down there."

They grabbed their weapons, made their sulfur nasal suppositories, and disappeared behind the ponchos into the horribly fetid atmosphere of the tunnels. I stuck the antenna of my PRC radio out through all the debris at the entrance and tried to raise the CP. As I did so it became obvious that the Japanese were not going to surrender the area called the Meat Grinder without a fight, if the rising noise level outside was any indication.

My attempts to raise anybody were a total bust. I tried some naval gunfire frequencies, and then some ground-to-air freqs, with no response. I put the radio into self-test and got a shock: the battery had barely enough power to light up the low-voltage light. I dumped that battery and snapped in the spare. Dead. How could that be, I wondered. Unless it had been issued to us that way. I looked at Goon. Comms are gone, I said. He sighed. His expression said it all: about what I expected. What could go wrong? Batteries.

Twitch and Monster eventually pushed clumsily through the ponchos, introducing a smell so bad I almost threw up. Even Goon, used to the ghastly atmosphere of Iwo Jima, swallowed hard. To help matters, our single flashlight began to give out. The stench had probably killed it. Before our two scouts could report, a great commotion erupted out in the crater. It sounded like a gunfight, with both their guns and ours blasting away not twenty feet from where we were hiding. We all wondered the same thing: how had enemy infantry gotten into the crater just in time to start slaughtering our guys? Three quick explosions in a row punched our covering debris pile back into our faces. Goon pointed at the ponchos, and down into the tunnels we ran. The last sounds we heard from the outside were screams.

We tumbled down into the main tunnel, tripping over the rocks and trying to stay upright as we crunched through the already decomposing bodies. The barest light came from our lone dying flashlight behind us, sufficient only to show where the walls and ceiling were. I began to fight the dry heaves, not having the protection of the burnt matches. Goon grabbed me and pushed me forward, farther into the tunnel, which one of the other guys lit up with a flashlight so we could see. I wasn't in control of myself as Goon pushed me along until the floor of the tunnel turned solid. At some point we stopped and I dropped to the floor, my gut still convulsing from the stench.

I realized that it was hot down here. The air now stank more of volcanic sulfur than dead meat, which was almost a relief. The other three were down on the floor, and as I looked around, Twitch shut off the flashlight. The darkness was absolute. I felt a bolt of pure panic. Goon felt me stiffen up, grabbed my right shoulder really hard, and said: steady. I tried to get control of my breathing. It was impossible. Breathe and gag. Don't breathe and faint.

"Hey, girls," Goon announced. "Ain't nobody shootin' at us, so let's relax while the Loot here figures out what we're gonna do and tells us snuffies."

It took a moment for that comment to penetrate and then I started to laugh hysterically. As if *I* would be able to contribute anything useful to our situation. But: to save face, I made an announcement. "All right, you sonsabitches," I growled. "Fall in, by the numbers. Dress right, *dress*! I want some goddamned order in this whorehouse. Short-arm inspection to follow as soon as I can see your sorry asses, and then, by God, stand the fuck by!"

Goon hooted.

Then came a thundering blast wave from somewhere in the tunnel that put all four of us flat on our asses, followed by the unmistakable sound of the tunnel ceiling collapsing not all that far away from us. Except of course we couldn't tell in which direction because of the darkness. Twitch weakly admitted he'd dropped the flashlight so now we were officially in deep shit and blind to boot.

"Got these fuckers right where we want 'em now, don't we, boys," Goon whispered.

Sometimes, I thought, these Marines went a little far with all this flippancy. On the other hand, what were the options? Summon my mommy? I considered it.

"Okay, find the goddamned flashlight," Goon ordered. "Hand over hand."

Monster found it and turned it on with the lens pointing into his face, scaring all of us again. More explosions came rumbling down the tunnel, sounding a lot like an 81mm barrage. I was surprised that I could now recognize the sound.

"Our boys're movin' up," Goon said. "We gotta get topside so's we can get rescued."

"Which way?" Twitch asked.

"Don't want to go back, step in all that nasty shit," Goon said. "So that way. Monster, turn that thing on so's we all get a look, then douse it. We'll creep up twenty feet or so and then do it again. Twitch, you take point. The rest of you lock and load, then hug either side of the tunnel."

We repositioned our gear before shoving off, checked weapons, drank some water, and then started forward to the drumbeat of explosions happening all over the surface above us. I wondered if we weren't safer down here. I asked Twitch to check the radio, but it was still dead. I did not understand—that battery should have been good for more time. The stink of sulfur was getting stronger, if that was possible, as was the noise of the fighting going on over our heads. And the heat: if any of us had forgotten that the whole of Iwo Jima was the top of a volcano, the tunnel walls were reminding us.

We kept tripping over things as we advanced. The flashlight showed bunkbeds, jerrycans, presumably with water, diesel oil, and even gasoline, and boxes of what was probably rice and canned food. We finally arrived at what looked like a central junction. Two big and three smaller tunnels came together: the one we'd come down plus four others of varying size. Monster shone the dying flashlight all around us. Radio gear, more bunks, metal cans of rifle ammo, lots more water cans, even some desks. Goon was consulting a compass in the flashlight's increasingly yellow light. He shook his head.

"Damn thing's just going around and around," he muttered.

Just then what sounded like a hot firefight broke out in one of the other tunnels leading into the junction. It was a much smaller one than the one we'd come down. The dustup wasn't close, but it was definitely serious. We stood there for a moment, trying to figure out what all that racket meant, until we heard rounds beginning to ricochet off the lava walls and then felt a couple slash into the junction area at about face height.

We each executed a pretty spiffy and simultaneous belly flop and rolled toward the sides of the complex we'd discovered. We'd noticed during our trek from the crater that the Japanese had inserted doglegs in the tunnel every twenty feet or so to prevent an enemy from getting into the tunnel and then having a clear line of fire all the way to the junction. Just like in our panic bunkers, I remembered. I'd landed next to Goon, who was unlimbering his submachine gun but also listening carefully to the gunfire, whose volume was definitely rising.

"Boys," he called. "I think our guys are chasing a buncha enemy back toward this junction. We need to get into one of the other tunnels, and when they back into this junction, open up on 'em. On me, ladies."

In less than a minute we were all huddled down on the tunnel floor about six feet back from the main junction. Monster killed the flashlight so we couldn't tell where we were. Once again, we were down on the ground, Goon and Monster on their bellies, Twitch and I behind them, in the rifle-range kneeling position, shifting uneasily because of the hot rock floor. We kept our weapons pointed into the black presence of the junction as we listened to an increasingly violent gunfight. Neither side was shooting large caliber machine guns—this was an individual weapons fight, complete with an occasional death scream. They were exchanging rifle and submachine gun fire in a tunnel, for God's sake. Not exactly many places to hide except for the occasional doglegs, which made any shooting dangerous for both sides.

My knee began to hurt and I wanted to get flat, but if I did, I wouldn't be able to shoot. We were blind in the total darkness of "our" tunnel. The only lights we saw came from the long rounds that were making their way into the junction now, hitting concrete in tiny red sparks and then ricocheting randomly around the central cavern. I wondered for a moment who were these Marines who'd decided to pursue a bunch of Japanese into an unlighted goddamned tunnel and start a gunfight. It made me wonder what they had done to provoke our guys that much. I tried to flatten myself against the tunnel wall and clamped my eyes shut.

Goon nudged me with his boot and said: get ready. For an instant I wondered: for what? I couldn't see a fucking thing. Then I remembered that my eyes were shut. When I opened them, flashes of gunfire were illuminating random patches of the tunnel walls and ceiling. Some of those flashes were projecting split-second images of the backs of helmeted men, hunched over their weapons, as they backed into the junction room, their silhouettes on the ceiling like disjointed black and white nightmares. Them. Right there.

Goon made a low, animal noise, rose up to a crouch, and then opened fire straight ahead. I was vaguely aware that Twitch and Monster had also joined in before realizing that I was holding a fully loaded Thompson submachine gun in my hands. In a split-second muzzle flash, I saw three erect figures backing toward us from about ten feet away. I pulled the trigger and held it, the Thompson making its distinctive sound as it bucked in my rigidly clenched hands, spraying bullets I knew not where, until I felt Goon's hand grip my left harm so hard that I had to release the trigger.

Gun smoke and a humming silence filled the air.

"Breathe, Loot," Goon said softly, and then yelled "Hey, *Rube!*" into the darkness at the top of his voice. "Goon squad, ladies. What took you so fucking long? Anybody got a cigarette?"

A light snapped on, shining right on us. I couldn't see a thing. Except, there were a lot—at least a dozen, if not more—of Japanese sprawled on the floor of the tunnel, every damned one of them shot to pieces. In the back.

"Corporal Williams, Second of the Third, here. Goon Logan, that really you?"

"Yeah, yeah, yeah," Goon said. "We were workin' shore-bomb back in that big crater with the Navy loot—the new grid guy—but we had to bail."

"You the guys that put that cruiser on all those enemy up on the south rim? Fuck me, that was goddamned amazing. You guys ready to get outta here?"

A scream from behind us made us all jump. The squad had deployed a bayonet detail to make sure all those dead enemy in the cavern were indeed dead. One of them hadn't been.

"Yeah, Corp," Goon said. "Any day now. This hide-and-seek shit gets tiresome after a while, you know? Besides, I think we're outta ammo."

EIGHTEEN

Once we got topside it didn't look like much had changed. Satisfying as it was to be back within the Fold, the battle noise hammered on, unabated, and all of us had to keep down to just stay alive. I didn't recognize where we were, not after all that time down in those tunnels, but I had a much better understanding of why our casualties had been so bad—these bastards had truly honeycombed this miserable island from one end to the other. I'd seen little rock niches down the entire length of the tunnel every time the flashlight came on, small holes with crude steps carved into the soft lava rock, leading up toward the surface, where individual snipers could peek through cracks and crevices, take a shot, and then drop back down into the safety of the tunnel while yet another Marine spilled his life out onto the thirsty black sands of God-cursed Iwo fucking Jima.

Monster announced that the radio was working again, and that the brass wanted me back at the CP ASAP. Like: right now would be nice, apparently. I looked at Goon, who nodded. I had the sense that, wherever the CP was now, it would beat being up here on The Line. As if to make that point, a clutch of mortar rounds whistled their way close overhead, necessitating yet another get-flat exercise while white-hot steel fragments hummed over our heads. One young Marine, whose clean utilities proclaimed him to be a replacement, knelt down on the ground and vomited great quantities of bright red blood the way the beer drunks did behind the EM club, except that wasn't beer, before folding in half.

Goon was yelling something at me, but I couldn't catch it. I thought that by then I was half-deaf and understood why all the Marines were constantly shouting at each other. He gestured at me to follow him but to stay low. I stayed right in his tracks as we scuttled like a couple of land crabs in a zig-zag running pattern until he disappeared over a low bank with me in hot pursuit. I felt a tug on my helmet cover as I leapt over the ridge and down into a black sand gully, barely keeping a grip on my Thompson's strap. I'd learned by now that you could lose, drop, forget, or misplace every piece of your equipment when you were running for it—*every* piece—except for your weapon. That you held onto with a death grip.

Monster and Twitch rolled over the bank a second later, pursued by puffs of black sand as the Japanese kept firing. Twitch yelled as he rolled to a stop. A bullet had hit the bottom of his boot. I swear he grinned in appreciation of the accurate shooting. I took off and stared down at my helmet, with its brand-new, bright metallic crease traversing the crown from front to back. Close enough, I thought. Then I realized I'd failed to reload my typewriter. I patted my utilities for an ammo pack, but had none.

At that moment I heard tanks approaching. It was a distinctive sound—big engines straining at top end, their treads clanking and clinking in a cacophony of abused metal, as they came up behind us. I shot a look at Goon: ours, right? He nodded reassuringly, and as they clattered by us in search of targets, he signaled for us to haul ass for the rear of one of them, walking only in the tread tracks to ensure a mine-free getaway.

An hour later we arrived at regimental CP, which was now defended by more than a hundred Marines in a much more elaborate set of perimeter checkpoints, sentry stations, machine gun nests, and underground bunkers than I remembered from the last time. Twitch and Monster collected our utility belts and disappeared in search of water, food, and ammo. Goon sat down at the entrance to the CP tent and said he'd wait. I called him a chicken. He clucked in agreement.

I took a deep breath, pushed through the flaps, and almost collided with Colonel Sam. What was the regimental commander doing at the gunfire support CP? His faithful shadow, Major Murphy, was right behind him.

"Loo-tenant Bishop," the colonel rumbled. "Nice of you to join us. What have you been up to?"

"Slaughtering bad guys," I responded, bravely. "In their hundreds."

He beamed approvingly. "So we have been told, young man," he said. "So we have been told. Statistics and probability—ain't that some fancy shit, though."

There were several officers and senior NCOs swarming around the command post, which was a hubbub of general radio traffic, fire-mission dialogue, frantic radio calls for ammo and water, and wired-communications shouting matches between local headquarters units up at the front and all these staff-puke slackers back here in the relative safety of the CP. Except that, as before, most of these guys had been wounded.

Relative safety was a bit of a misnomer. Relative was the operative word, I discovered—I could hear nearby shell blasts not all that far away as the Japanese probed the Marines' rear lines with artillery, probably from up on some accursed prominence everyone called Hill 360. The plotting table was in its usual frantic chaos. Wreck stood there, doing his magic thing, looking like an adolescent ghost as he examined all the calculations and waved thin, almost emaciated hands to point out errors. Weren't they feeding him? He still looked impossibly young, and there were deep, dark circles under his eyes. Can't pull him away, one of the lieutenants said, when he saw me looking at him. But he's always right. Can't do without him now.

The Marines had planted an American flag up on the top of *Suribachi* days ago, but there was still a lot of heavy caliber fire ranging up and down this bloody island from positions buried on the northern end. The raising-of-the-flag caper had done wonders for morale, though. The hard part was going to be burrowing into the fire-ants' nest *below* the summit, where there were still hundreds of enemy yearning for a suicide mission.

The colonel pointed Murphy and me toward a coffee mess while he conferred with several anxious-looking Marine officers. I poured two paper cups and took one out to Goon, whom I had to wake up. He gave me a bleary-eyed thanks, gripped the cup firmly with both hands in his lap, and went back to sleep. I saw a sergeant nod approvingly as I went back inside. For some reason that made me feel really good. I'd learned that Marines always watched their officers to see what kind of guys they were. Strict obedience was drilled into them every day, but it was easier to take if you actually liked and maybe even respected the guy with the metal insignia. If you didn't like him, you encouraged him to wear that insignia up on The Line.

Murphy told me the colonel had a new mission for our brave little band. He wanted to embark us on a Navy landing craft and then go out to sea a little ways and then all the way around the island to the northern end. There was now an entire Marine division dedicated to clearing the slopes, hills, and then all those interlocking interior fortifications inside and around the jagged north end. Apparently, General Kuribayashi wasn't in the volcano anymore. He and the bulk of his last-stand forces were at the opposite end of Iwo Jima from the volcano, hunkering down among those fuming hills at the northern end of the island.

I suspected that by this point both sides knew how this fight was going to end, but for the Marines, knowing and achieving that result were two very different things. The Japanese, still crouching in their tunnels back down south inside the heavily shelled volcano, would slowly die of starvation, lack of water, and the suffocating, sulfur-infused heat inside the mountain. Flame-throwing tanks, called Zippos, ringed the volcano now. They would deal with any *banzai* forays out onto the slopes of *Suribachi*.

The northern end of the island presented a different problem. It was a featureless jumble of low hills, ugly, jagged lava ridges, and twisting gullies, all surrounded by terraces of black sand at the base of the low cliffs that dropped straight into the sea. The colonel wanted his ace shore-fire-control team to embed themselves somewhere in those jagged ravines and northernmost cliffs of the island, so when the main force of Marines closed in from the south to exterminate the remaining resistance, he had a naval gunfire spotter on scene, technically in the enemy's rear, to create the naval bombardment anvil for the Marines' approaching hammer. The plan made perfect sense, although I wondered if we'd survive it. I also wondered where he'd gotten the idea for such madness. Three guesses, I thought. I dreaded telling Goon about it.

The colonel told one of the majors at the CP to make arrangements. While we were waiting for him, I asked Murphy about Wrecked. He looked a bit embarrassed and indicated we should step out of the tent for a moment. Goon was still out there, sound asleep, but still holding on to that coffee cup. We walked about twenty paces away and Murphy finally came clean.

"I went to Colonel Nicholas and said we needed to get Wrecked to treatment. He said no so loud I almost jumped."

"He looks like he's dying," I said, bluntly.

"I know," Murphy said. "He eats—Colonel makes sure he's supervised and getting food. But what they haven't been telling him is that the kid pukes it all up fifteen minutes later. So I finally confronted the colonel. Thought he was gonna start pounding on me. Then he just sat down. "You know what's gonna happen to that kid if we send him back?" he said. "They'll section eight him and then he's gonna be sent to some funny farm. They'll box him up, put a feeding tube in, and let him rot. That's what. Out here he's doing something. Something really valuable. How I don't know, I really don't. Funny what a six-inch round in the face can do to you, I guess.

"He's starving to death, I told him," Murphy said. "Can't keep food down. I don't understand, Colonel. Why are you doing this?"

"The colonel went silent and then finally told me," Murphy said. "Wrecked is the spitting image of the colonel's son, who was killed at Schofield Barracks on December seventh. The bastards strafed the housing area, remember? Fifteen years old. Hiding with his mother and the two other kids in the house. Hit with one 20mm round in the stomach. He looks at Wrecked, sees his son. Says he can't just let him go back to some box in an asylum. Then when he started lighting up the plotting table, he had an operational excuse. He knows it's wrong, but he can't let go. Won't let go."

"Holy Christ," I said softly.

"Yeah, I know," Murphy said. "But I can't let him starve, though, so I went behind the colonel's back. First time ever. I've called for a Navy doctor to come up to the gunfire CP and take him out of there. Colonel can't order a Navy doc around, so they'll come get him and do what they gotta do."

"Someone may go after the colonel, though," I said.

"I don't think so," Murphy said. "He's been wounded twice, refused to quit the battlefield. The Corps knows him, and they admire the shit out of him. As we all do. If the Navy makes a stink, the Corps has ways to clamp that off. That kid was so close to an exploding round that it blew his dog tags off his neck chain. And his eyebrows. All his clothes. And yet he can stand over the table, catch errors, and fix them, for Chrissakes—in his head. He may not rot, once the docs find that out. There may be a medical way to bring him back, but not if he dies out here in this shithole."

He paused for a moment.

"There's more," he began. "Colonel Sam. I think he's losing it. He's in command now. That changes everything. That eye socket still has metal in it. Has to be truly painful. Won't take pain meds—doesn't want his mind clouded. He has a broken left shoulder, broken elbow. Right hand's starting to tremble. Plus this obsession with Wrecked. He's constantly coming down here from regimental HQ. He's obsessed with gunfire support—and what you guys have been doing, by the way. But there's other spotters. Other missions. He's got the whole regiment now, or what's left of it. This shit has to stop or they'll relieve him, and that'll kill him. I can't let that happen."

"God bless you, Major," I said, quietly. "Right is right, and I think you're doing the absolute right thing, for what it matters from a lowly squid."

He nodded, and then said: "Okay, thanks for that. Let's go."

I had hoped maybe we could get a twenty-four-hour stand-down to recover from our adventures in the tunnels. Apparently not. No one up there on the front lines was getting any downtime unless they'd been shot. None of us had been shot, had we? Any further questions? It wasn't as if the headquarters staff had it easy, either. Half the guys there were sporting bandages, probably because they'd refused to leave the battle for a hospital ship. Colonel Nicholas himself had set the example. I could almost hear Goon saying: nice try, Loot, but it don't work that way in this man's Marnie Corpse.

I was dead tired as we slogged down to the beach to meet the LCVP. There were small blessings—we'd gotten hot chow, full utility belts, real coffee, and replacement weapons. I had a refurbished typewriter, as did Goon. Twitch and Monster each toted new M-1 carbines, and they each had one of the new PRC-25 radios, a much more compact version of the heavier and bulkier sets. The regiment's armorers had been working overtime, recovering rifles, carbines, and Thompsons from the battlefield (and, of course, the graves registration pile), gleaning the most serviceable parts, cleaning and polishing those, and then reassembling them into virtually new weapons. They even *smelled* new, with fresh gun oil, new canvas straps, and a gooey layer of Cosmoline preservative still visible in some of the cracks and crevices. We all knew one thing—none of these weapons were virgins. Beyond that, we didn't want to think too much about where they'd been.

The LCVP, known as a Higgins boat, was backing up and filling with lots of engine exhaust smoke just at the shoreline, trying to stay perpendicular to the beach while keeping its nose plastered on that sticky black sand. There was a coxswain and a gunner at the stern on an elevated platform. A lone boatswain-seaman manned up the front end, tending the ramp. The boat could carry about twenty fully laden troops, so we were going to rattle around in there during our moonlight cruise to the back side of Iwo. No moonlight, for which we were grateful. I asked Goon how we were going to land behind enemy lines—surely the Japs would have patrols out on the beaches at night.

"They've laid on a diversion," he said. "Two destroyers, four Mike boats. This boat is gonna take us out to sea. The two tin cans are gonna lay down a fake pre-invasion bombardment on the northwestern corner. Make it look like we're trying to get behind them for the final push. Then the Mike boats are gonna come in toward the beach. Lotsa noise, lotsa prep fire, only the boats're gonna be mostly empty. The colonel said to put some 81mm mortar squads onboard, and have them shoot the place up as they come in. The tin cans'll close the beach and use their forties and twenties. While all this ruckus is goin' on, this box-boat is gonna close the beach about a mile around the corner, touch down, let us off, and then get the flock outta there. By then a third destroyer is gonna go *past* where we're goin' in and start shooting up the beach. By then the bastards'll think there's some big deal comin' in, which hopefully will give us time to get ashore and go to ground."

"You think they'll go for that?"

"Well, when a battalion or two doesn't show up on the beach I think they'll know it was bullshit, but by then we're gonna be underground somewhere. And the next day there's gonna be a general advance all across the front on the other side, which should mean they'll be too busy to look for anyone in their rear."

"Shit, Goon, they're clever—you know they're gonna send out scouts."

"Then we'll just have to kill those fuckers, right, Loot? Now that you know, what could go wrong?"

NINETEEN

I've gotta admit: when we finally landed, there was a pretty good
show erupting both up *and* down the beach. Mike boats (LCM) are
big amphibious landing craft, capable of carrying a small mechanized
fighting vehicle or up to eighty fully combat loaded troops ashore.
The noise alone would have driven any Japanese patrol out on the
beach running for cover, even if the Mike boats didn't actually land.
They had heavy machine guns and were happily sweeping the beaches
with them. Just offshore, two destroyers added to the din by firing
40mm and 20mm anti-aircraft guns up and down the beaches as well
as up into the nearby dunes and the first row of those low hills.

We jumped out of our LCVP, climbed the black terrace, and hustled up into the dunes behind the actual beach, where we crouched
down into the warm black sand. Goon then signaled for Twitch to
take the lead—there had to be minefields out here. We followed him
inland for a few hundred yards, detouring when he raised his magic
finger, and then turned left toward the northernmost point of the

island, where there was a prominent headland created by a short, sharp ridge maybe forty feet high. We could see as long as the diversion was going on, but when it stopped abruptly the entire area went dark.

We dropped to the ground and waited. Where were the nightly flares, I wondered. Then I remembered that the enemy had been pushed all the way back into the last half mile at the northern end of the island. Goon said that the rest of the island had been declared "secured" for publicity purposes, although every Marine ashore knew that was bullshit. They were resisting so hard that we were still losing dozens of men every hour. Hence our mission: get behind them and then call down sufficiently precise fire that we could break the back of that fanatic, fight-to-the-last-man, die-with-maximum-honor resistance.

I'd made one request to the colonel before we decamped for the beach and our waiting LCVP. Move a battleship *way* offshore, ten, twelve, even fifteen miles, so that her shells would come in as plunging fire. If the northern end of the island was going to be their last line of organized resistance, that had to be because they'd gone really deep, well beyond the reach of offshore destroyers and Marine artillery tubes, and possibly even eight-inch. They'd had twenty thousand shovels available for the last two or three years.

"We need us a cave," Goon told us. "Let's creep along that ridge over there, listen for patrols. If we can catch one in or near their hidey-hole, we'll kill them all and then make it *our* hidey-hole."

By then we were only able to distinguish between empty space and boulders, dunes, and ridges. It was still so dark that we couldn't see much of anything, but we could listen. There was the usual mutter of gunfire and even some artillery to the south of us, but up here, at the northern end, it seemed as if nothing was moving. And for a change, it was cold. Surprisingly cold.

Offshore we saw the ghostly shapes of some wrecked amphibious craft, barely visible in the gloom. One looked like an LCI; the others were unidentifiable. What had they been doing up here, I wondered. We'd gone about a hundred yards, advancing on our bellies through the stinking warm sand, burnt brush, and lava rocks, when we heard indistinct voices. A low ridge cast a black shadow in front of us, featureless in the darkness.

Goon froze, as did we all. Then the voices became more distinct—definitely Japanese, and arguing. Maybe they weren't, I thought. A lot of Japanese dialogue I'd listened to in training sounded like the men talking were about to pull swords and go at it. Again, I tried to remember if I'd charged my new Thompson. Typical squid mistake, I told myself—no Marine would have failed to do that. Ridiculous, after all this. I checked. I had.

I realized that where I was crouching the ground was getting hotter. Not burn-you hot, but enough to make me want to move. I knew better. In the dark, movement meant noise. This was not the time to make noise. The squabbling—if that's what it was—continued. At least the air was cleaner—the close-quarters fighting hadn't reached here yet, so that sickening stench of dead bodies was missing. The sulfurous fumes, however, were still with us. Goon had told me that that was a good thing. To the Japanese, who took baths sometimes twice a day, foreigners always stank, although here on Iwo, I doubted anyone was getting a bath. We were all grateful to get drinking water, never mind a bath. But if the sulfur kept them from detecting that *gaijiin* were nearby, I was all for it.

Goon's helmet was suddenly touching mine. "They're in a cave or a tunnel," he whispered. "We need to take it. The boys'n me're gonna creep up there, throw some grenades. You wait right here. Anyone shows up, you grease 'em, hear? Now—find you a rock."

"Find me a rock, sir," I said.

"What I meant," he said, with an invisible grin.

He melded silently into the gloom before I had a chance to ask any questions, so I made like a snake and went looking for a large rock as quietly as I could. I finally blundered into one and then froze when I heard what sounded like a human voice on the other side, muttering something—in *Japanese*. My blood ran cold—was this a sentry? Was he talking to another sentry, or just grumbling to himself? I could feel the rock, but I couldn't see it, even when my helmet could almost touch it. It felt pretty solid to my bare fingers. My Thompson was slung, barrel down, across my back. I needed to get it ready to work.

I heard the sentry shift his position on the other side of the rock, which I hoped again was a big-ass boulder, not just a rock. I began to unsling my weapon as carefully as I could by dropping one shoulder and tugging silently on the muzzle. The damned thing caught up on anything and everything projecting from my uniform, but I finally had it on the ground and was able to grip it with both sweaty hands. Make sure, I said to myself. I felt for the bolt. Open. I knew the rate-of-fire lever would be in the full auto position. The whole point of the weapon was to put a stream of .45 caliber bullets going many, many feet per second downrange. I put a finger on the muzzle and wiped a little bit of sand and grit off it. I exhaled quietly. C'mon Goon—light 'em up.

Goon must have heard me, as five bright yellow flashes erupted somewhere up ahead followed by the sound of grenades going off in quick succession. I got to my knees and raised my Tommy. I heard an exclamation from the other side of the rock and then a scrambling noise as the sentry came bursting out from behind it. He popped out so quickly that I had to shoot him in the back with a quick burst.

"Remember Pearl Harbor," I muttered as he went flat, only momentarily visible in the gun flashes, his back a mass of blood and exposed, shattered backbone. Then it was dark again and my eyes were truly night-blind. Goon and Twitch were there in an instant. Goon almost tripped over the dead sentry; he snapped on a red-lens flashlight.

"All *right*, Loot," he said. "Where'd this fuck come from?"

"He was hiding behind my rock," I said.

"*Your* rock." Twitch laughed. "Damn right."

"C'mon," Goon said. "We need to clean up *our* tunnel. Nice one, Loot. Nice one."

It didn't feel like a nice one, but I knew it had been necessary. I had finally confirmed to myself that delivering tons of high explosives onto the enemy's heads from the bowels of a battleship was worlds away different from shooting another human being in the back with a Thompson submachine gun and then stepping over the bloody result as if it wasn't even there. Goon would have said simply: don't sweat it, Loot.

TWENTY

We stepped cautiously through the metal door leading into the tunnel. There were two battle lantern–sized red-lensed lights in the tunnel, one of which had miraculously survived the grenades and was still on. It was definitely a man-made tunnel, low-ceilinged, wider than the other ones we'd seen, and more like an anteroom than an actual tunnel. A half-dozen dead soldiers lay in various positions, their bodies viciously flayed by the fragments from five grenades going off practically in their faces within the concrete confines of the room. There was a wall of radio gear on one side, cans of water, and rifles stacked on another wall. It looked like a squad room. The cans of water leaked copiously, as did the former occupants.

We'd been hoping for a cave that wouldn't have been too deep and wouldn't have been connected to anything. That tunnel entrance at the back meant that more soldiers might be already on their way from some underground complex to investigate all the racket. Twitch and Monster dragged the bodies outside, while Goon and I studied the steel door at the back of the tunnel. It looked a lot like a water-tight hatch that had been taken from a ship, frame and all, and then bolted into the concrete.

"Cover me," Goon ordered, and then swung the operating lever up, releasing the locking dogs. The hatch swung open on greased hinges, revealing a long concrete tunnel that disappeared into darkness for at least a hundred feet before making a turn. I lowered the muzzle of my Thompson as we both studied the ceiling of the tunnel. It was made of what looked like railroad ties joined closely together, but not concrete.

"If we could make it look like the tunnel caved in, they probably wouldn't look any further," I said.

"Sorry," Goon said, sniffing the air in the inner tunnel. It smelled of sulfur, damp concrete, and diesel fumes. "We're fresh outta dynamite."

"How's about our C-4 cubes?" Twitch asked from behind us.

Goon looked at me. "Loot, you got one?" he asked. I nodded. I'd never used it to heat rations; I'd always borrowed the remains of someone else's. But now we had freshly packed utility belts. Four cubes of C-4 might just bring down the tunnel roof. We'd need a detonator, though, and none of us carried one of those. Goon started giving orders.

"Twitch, go get a rifle from back in there and Monster's C-4. Loot, you go to the front hatch, step outside, get small, and listen."

It was still dark out there. I could smell the bodies that had been piled up like cordwood. Blood, death excrement, spilled gut contents. If I ever get off this island, I thought, the one thing I'll never forget will be the hideous smells. There was a small breeze stirring so I moved to take advantage of that and sat down with my back to "my" rock. I parked the Thompson across my knees and waited, suddenly fighting the need for sleep. Then I remembered to check the ammo and chamber status of my typewriter. Finally, I was learning.

Moments later my three compadres joined me. Goon was laying

down a piece of wire as he backed out of the outer door, which he left cracked. We repositioned ourselves to where I'd first hidden, and then he tightened the wire. We heard the crack of a rifle shot, followed instantly by a surprisingly powerful high-explosive blast. That in turn was followed by the muted roar of what sounded like an avalanche. We waited for several minutes before going back inside. The anteroom to the main tunnel was unchanged, but the steel hatch leading back into it was bulging outward, its mechanism visibly deformed and probably jammed.

Four little cubes of C-4. I gained a new respect for plastic explosive. Any investigating patrol that came up on the tunnel from the inside would conclude that something big had hit the tunnel anteroom and that there was no point in digging their way through to see what had happened. But at least now we had a "hide." When the big push started as daylight broke, I could get to work. Monster suggested that we should probably leave once our guys started getting close. Great thinking, Goon responded solemnly.

Back inside, we laid out our comms gear and a makeshift grid table. Monster took the first outside sentry watch. We'd debated what to do with the bodies outside: bury them, leave them, or move them? Goon decided to make it look like they'd been blown out of the cave, in case a patrol passed by. Which meant we were going to have to find some "debris" to strew around the front of the cave. Or, I pointed out, I could call in a dozen or so rounds of five- or eight-inch in the vicinity of the tunnel entrance. All three Marines started shaking their heads. Why not, I asked, with as straight a face as possible. They gave me a collective are-you-shitting-me look. I tried to look surprised and offended at the same time.

A real problem materialized at sunrise, when Regiment told us that the big "offensive" had been delayed twenty-four hours until they could get more men up on The Line. The Meat Grinder had lived up to its name and several units were still badly under-strength. That meant the Japanese would have an entire twenty-four additional hours to come investigate why "our" tunnel had gone quiet. We were not in a position to hold off a company of Japanese infantry who suspected there might be *gaijiin* in this hole.

"If you call for fire, will they answer?" Twitch asked. "Seein' that the big push hasn't kicked off yet?"

"Yes, I think so," I replied. "A call for fire is a call for fire. That's why they're out there and I'm here. But, hell, we could always test that theory."

I laid out the grid map, which showed where Goon and Twitch thought we were. Then I set up an area-fire mission which extended five hundred yards on both sides of our hidey-hole's entrance and from the shoreline to about three hundred yards behind and up the slope from where we were hiding. Five-inch, high explosive, time-on-target, but on my command. Then I drew up a second area mission to the south of the first one, to make it look as if the Marines hadn't made up their minds as to where that fake landing was going to land. Nobody was going to land, of course, but area-fire missions would certainly suggest to the enemy that we might. The new radio worked as advertised, and, an hour after sunrise, the bombardment began. I'd plotted the actual position of our tunnel's entrance out of the area-fire box, but that didn't mean a "long" round might not come whistling through the door despite my best efforts.

Monster came rolling smartly through the tunnel entrance once the shells began to land out along the coastal area in front of the cave. If there *had* been a patrol out there, they'd have been scrambling for cover by now, too. What none of us had anticipated was *where* they'd be scrambling to—which of course turned out to be "our" tunnel, pursued by the ear-splitting blasts of five-inch shells going off right out front, their fragments clattering against the steel door.

Thank God Monster still had his Thompson. For one surreal moment, Marines and Japanese stared at each other in total amazement, and then the gunfight at the OK Corral erupted inside the cramped confines of the tunnel's concrete-walled anteroom. Monster and I had gone flat out of pure habit, so most of the ricochets slapped and spanged a few inches over our heads but right back into the faces of the half-dozen Japanese soldiers transfixed by the sudden appearance of Marines in what they thought was sanctuary from the endless shore-bombardment.

"*Cease firing,*" Goon yelled once he realized that all of them were down. The four of us collectively exhaled while fumbling for our zippers. I could still hear that hornets' nest humming noise, from rifles and submachine guns firing simultaneously in a space not much bigger than a colonel's office, even though it was all over. I was amazed to be alive. I think Monster's initial burst had saved us all.

But not my radios. I stared in horror at my brand-new radio sets, which had been hanging on the wall, and whose batteries were dripping some kind of evil mung onto the concrete floor, courtesy of several prominent bullet holes. Holes that size meant that one of the Thompsons had most likely shot the radios. Our only radios. Super.

By then the area-fire barrage had also finished up outside, so things got really quiet.

"Anybody hurt?" Goon inquired. The rest of us patted ourselves down and reported negative. But then I shared the news. "Hurt, no," I said, finally. "Hosed, yes. The radios are toast."

Goon looked at the bleeding radio batteries. His head sank down on his chest. Our moment of misery was rudely interrupted when Twitch leapt up with a frightening shriek and drove his K-bar into the mouth of one of the bodies on the floor. We'd forgotten to make sure that all the dead were, in fact, dead. This one had opened his eyes.

You volunteered, I told myself for the millionth time. Great God Almighty: now what are we going to do?

TWENTY-ONE

Without a radio, I couldn't call fire missions, which meant the colonel's great plan of getting a spotter behind Jap lines in support of the final offensive was moot. Even worse, when Regiment couldn't raise us, they'd assume we'd been rolled up by the Japanese, one of the well-known hazards of going behind enemy lines, so we were most definitely on our own. Naturally, we all looked at Goon to get us out of this mess. Goon's expression fairly screamed: not this time, ladies.

I could sympathize. Goon had carried our whole crew since I'd first joined up. I suspected he was beyond exhaustion. Now the other three were looking at me, the officer in the room. So, I inhaled a deep breath and took my best shot.

"Look," I said. "We're alive and we're uninjured. We have rations, a little water, ammo, and working weapons. I think we should just hole up and wait for this party to be over. Go outside and remove any signs that there's even a tunnel in here. There oughta be craters everywhere out there. Make it look like those SOBs were part of a patrol that got caught in the open. Then get back inside here, post a watch, and wait. And maybe just sleep. You know our guys are gonna win this thing. Wait for 'em to do that, and *then* come out. It isn't like we haven't made a contribution."

I glanced over at Goon. He was sound asleep. QED, I thought. Twitch and Monster nodded. I got up, went to the entrance, and listened. I turned around to get some backup before sticking my nose outside. Monster and Twitch were also out like lights. Okay, that makes it unanimous, I said to myself. But I still thought I ought to take a peek out front. I barely cracked the hatch. It was full daylight, but I hadn't expected pouring rain. A cold wind was blowing in my face, and for once the air wasn't filled with the disgusting stench of battle. The wind came off the sea and mercifully smelled of salt water. All the bodies were still out there, becoming a little less distinct as a freshet of rain water brought sand down from above the entrance. If we'd been just marooned instead of caught behind enemy lines, I'd have been out there collecting some of that fresh water or even trying for a shower. The skies were dark gray and the dark surf thumped purposefully on the shore.

I looked out to sea, but saw nothing but dark gray curtains of rain sweeping past the island. I knew there were ships out there, but I also knew that the smaller ones, the destroyers, would be pitching and rolling and making their crews miserable. The battlewagons wouldn't care. They'd probably have the deck division topside sweeping the salt off the teak weather decks, given an unlimited supply of fresh water.

I realized I missed my ship. I wondered what they must think of me, ashore on this God-forsaken rock. Then, to my absolute horror, I heard an older man's voice shout something in typical military Japanese, sounding as if he were ready to decapitate someone. I tried to push the door but the wind had blown just enough sand into the crack between the door and the hatch frame that I couldn't fully close it. What I could do was drop the steel bar that would normally seal the door shut into the brackets on either side. I had to put my entire body weight up against one side to make the bar drop. By now the wind outside was almost shrieking across the face of our tunnel.

Then came a commotion as the patrol discovered the bodies out front, by now partially buried by the rising gale outside. The angry man I'd heard before became almost hysterical, and then came a clap of thunder that finally silenced him. Two more blasts nearby followed quickly in succession and then there were several rifle butts thumping away against the hatch. That ruckus awakened my sleeping Marines, who rose up as one, weapons ready. I put a finger on my lips to keep them from opening fire. The banging stopped almost as quickly as it had begun, and then the seams of the hatch turned blue-white, etching a perfect rectangle in the gloom of the tunnel, followed by a titanic lightning blast that sounded like it hit right outside, its thunderbolt rumbling outward for what seemed like miles.

Then came truly heavy rain outside, with so much water pouring down that a small flood began to spread a fan of water into the anteroom from under the hatch. The good news was that there were no more signs that the patrol was still trying to get into the tunnel. I wondered if that last lightning stroke hadn't killed them all—it had been that close. Goon gave me a severe look. "Goddamn, Loot—I leave you alone for five minutes and whaddya you do? Invite a patrol in for tea?"

"They were getting their hair all wet, Goon—what was I supposed to do?" I said.

A final lightning bolt fried the dunes out front, again making all of us wince. I backed away from the front hatch and sat down against the back wall of the anteroom. This time all three of my Marines nodded at me in approval.

We began kicking around options for getting back to friendly front lines. We couldn't go out at night, because we'd be killed the moment we even approached The Line. The Japs obviously had patrols out now that it was daylight, so a daytime prison break was out of the question, too. Hunkering down right here until we heard signs that Marines were outside still seemed to be the best option. Or possibly a nighttime foray to the beach and points south.

The tunnel behind us was blocked. The front hatch too. Air was getting in somehow—so: ride it out? I started shaking my head.

"What?" Twitch said.

"What are the Japs gonna do once our big push begins? Dive into their rat holes and make our boys fight for every inch. They discover that the front hatch here is jammed? They'll blow it open. Or they'll come up from the deep bunkers through that tunnel back there. There's a cave-in? They'll dig it out like the ants they are."

"And then, what are our guys gonna do, they see a tunnel entrance. They'll try to break into it, so they can say howdy with a handful of grenades. Door won't open? Bring up a regular tank and blast it open. Can't see what's in there? They'll bring up a Zippo and send burning gasoline into it. No infantry unit's gonna leave an intact enemy cave in their rear."

Monster had an idea. "Maybe come out at night and sneak down to the beach, go out deep enough to be chest deep, maybe even right in the surf line, dog-paddle until we get back into friendly territory."

"Mines," Goon said. "These fucks have known we were comin' for months. They've mined the beaches and the surf line all around this piece-a-shit island. Don't you remember the first landings?"

Goon was right. I'd forgotten the stories I'd heard about L-Day, where the Japanese had collected some of the shore bombardment projectiles that had failed to explode over the previous days of prep fires, substituted pressure fuzes for impact fuzes, and then buried them along the beach and even inland. Everything from 40mm to sixteen-inch. The lead guy in a platoon would step on a rebuilt battleship projectile and the whole platoon would die. Even better, the guys coming behind them would blame the Navy for a short-round.

The Japanese were nothing if not thorough. They'd come out at night and booby-trapped every one of our vehicles—tanks, AM-

TRACs, trucks, jeeps—which had run afoul of mines inland so when advancing Marines came upon one and went to check it out for wounded or to remove bodies, the enemy would get a second helping.

Wrecked vehicles. Suddenly, I had an idea.

"Goon," I said. "Remember that pile of wrecked amphib boats we saw, about a half mile before we found this cave? The Japanese had pre-sighted the most likely landing zones using long guns up on *Suribachi* and then they let all those alligator craft get just offshore, a minute out from landing, before they turned loose that artillery on 'em? They disrupted an entire landing wave? Backed up all the waves behind 'em, which made those guys easier to hit."

"Yeah," he said. "Killed a lotta guys, too. Before they even got ashore."

"Those landing craft're still there, half-submerged and torn all to hell, right offshore. If we could get into that pile of wreckage, hide out there until we *know* The Line's moved past, and *then* show ourselves, we'd be safe. They won't be paying any attention to them now."

I could almost hear the wheels cranking as my beloved comrades thought about it. The Marine Corps had never encouraged its grunts to think—just follow orders and act, smartly and by the numbers. Goon finally nodded.

"Loot's right," he announced. "Why he's a loot. Okay, we'll go out tonight, see if we can get to that junkpile. If we do make it out there, we gotta look hard for booby traps. You know these fucks have been through all those boats, looking for salvage, since none of our guys ever made it ashore. But once the breakout starts, the bad guys won't be payin' any attention to those wrecks. So: we eat and get some sleep. We'll go out around midnight, before the jump-off arty show cranks up."

Everyone seemed to relax now that we had a plan. I knew there were some possibilities that could screw everything up, such as the Japanese coming down that tunnel behind us tonight rather than to-morrow, discovering the fake cave-in, and deciding to break through it. And then there was the matter of those surf line minefields. Those wrecked boats had never made it ashore, so the mines might still be there.

I looked over at Goon as Twitch and Monster rousted out some rations. The worried look on his face told me he'd also thought of all those possibilities. I shrugged my shoulders and mouthed the words: what could go wrong? He grinned and then reached for his C rations. Cold grub tonight—we'd used all our C-4 cubes.

TWENTY-TWO

We left some booby traps of our own in the anteroom, and then wrote the words "booby traps" in English using burned wood on the wall so that any Marine poking his head around the hatch would see them. There were dead men piled up on top of each other outside the hatch, all of them with their eyes bulging and their helmets looking like they were made out of blackened putty. Lightning kills. The rain still sheeted down outside and the offshore wind was even stronger, creating this weird swirl of cold wind blowing over the warm sulfur-infused sand dunes. Our feet were warm, but the rest of us were chilled instantly by all that rain and sea spray. It was also really dark; the thunder and lightning had subsided once the main body of the storm passed overhead, thank God. Thunderstorms in Asia had always seemed twice as scary to me as the ones back home.

Goon had told us we needed to see where the tide was once we got to the beach. The Japanese knew that when Marines came ashore, they wanted to do so on an incoming flood tide. That way the rising tide would eventually float off any boat or craft that ran aground. That also meant the enemy wouldn't plant mines much deeper than the high-tide mark, mostly because they wouldn't stay planted.

Goon explained his plan: Twitch had announced he wasn't sure he could detect metal in sea water, so we'd crawl in a single file through the final band of wet sand, pushing our knives into the sand to see if they hit anything solid. Once we got past the high-tide line, marked by the sea's detritus, we could move out into the surf line, where we'd be able to stand up and swim out to that tangle of wrecked landing craft.

"What do we do if our K-bar connects with something?" Monster asked.

"Change course," Goon replied. "Go around it. Unless it's a clam. Then eat it."

Monster nodded enthusiastically. He'd heard about clams. Of course he would eat it.

When we got past the high-water line, we crawled on all fours out into the breaking waves in an awkward single file. The storm hadn't made the waves any smaller, but the pouring rain had taken some of the zip and vinegar out of them. None of us had stuck our K-bars into a mine or a clam, for which I gave sincere thanks. It took us an hour to crawl, swim, and frog-walk out to the jumble of wrecked landing craft. The LCI looked like the most useful refuge. It had been hit by a large artillery shell and lay partially on its port side, its mast at about a 30-degree angle. The cargo on the well-deck had apparently caught fire, so there were burned-out trucks, cargo pallets, and even two small tanks. There was also a dismal collection of blackened bodies everywhere we looked.

It was hard to see with all this rain and sea mist, but there was no mistaking what we were looking at. Exposed bones made it easier for us to differentiate between equipment and human remains in the darkness. The artillery fire from *Suribachi* had been so intense that no one had been back to claim the dead. It was small comfort to know that the Japanese inside the volcano who'd done this were now most certainly also dead. Monster broke out in vicious cursing when he realized that the small whitish shapes slithering around down in the well-deck were crabs. Goon had to restrain him from jumping down there and stomping them all.

"We need to go aft," he said. "Less damage back there."

Dream on, I thought.

It took us several minutes to get aft in the wrecked LCI, which was much bigger than the typical landing craft. She was 150 feet long and could carry as many as 185 fully equipped combat infantrymen in her well-deck. She had a ramp forward and that side-mounted conning tower on her starboard side. Typically, an LCI would come in after the first wave had hit the beach, drop an anchor from the stern on her way in so she could pull herself off the beach once she'd put the troops ashore, and then run the bow aground. This one had apparently been hit with one or more 155mm artillery shells and had capsized immediately in about ten feet of water, enough to drown all the wounded huddled in the well-deck.

I was surprised to find her here, because they weren't normally sent in until the beach was reasonably "secure." But then again, the Japanese on Iwo had offered little resistance to the initial invasion waves, preferring to wait until there were hundreds if not thousands of Marines crammed onto the landing beaches before unleashing their big guns from positions on and inside Mount *Suribachi*. The volcano was all the way down on the other end of the island, which showed how big these guns must have been.

We had to climb into the flooded well-deck from the rolling surf and then clamber back through all the bodies and wrecked gear to find a hatch that could get us inside the spaces underneath the conning tower. There were a few more bodies inside, flayed to death by the shrapnel from the shells that had blown most of her port side clean off. The stench was familiar; Monster furiously stomping on all the scavenging crabs wasn't helping. It was, however, a good hide as long as we didn't do anything to invite attention once daylight came. We were walking on the interior bulkheads since the LCI lay way over on her port side. We found what had to have been the crew's messing space, which was mostly dry. I took a battle lantern whose lens had been taped down to a narrow slit and went looking for the radio room while the Marines found dry perches in the messing compartment. The wind and rain continued to roar outside, which we blessed as that meant it was much less likely there'd be patrols out on the beach.

The radio room, on one side of the interior passageway, was more like a radio closet. It appeared to be undamaged since it was farther aft, but that did me no good. The radio sets were all hard-wired to an electrical panel, which had been fed from what was by now a completely flooded engine-room generator. I crawled my way back to the messing space and gave Goon the bad news. But then I remembered something: the *Nevada*'s life rafts were equipped with small battery-operated FM radios. I knew that because one of my collateral duties as a junior officer on the battleship had been to inspect and test the batteries. Did LCIs have life rafts?

Wait until daylight, Goon said. We don't dare go showing a light out here at night. But right now, check this out: he handed me a ceramic coffee mug with what smelled like real coffee in it. Cold, oily Navy coffee, salvaged from a badly dented coffee urn in one corner of the messing space, but still: coffee. I literally pinched my nose and tried some. That's Navy coffee, all right, I told myself. Strong enough that not even mold could grow in it. My stomach revolted, threatening to turn over right there and then and create a spectacle. But knowing that the Marines were watching, I quelled the desire to retch and exclaimed: Damn, that's good. This provoked a quiet storm of chuckling in the gloom of this reeking compartment. I almost could imagine the dead sailors joining in.

"There's more, Loot," Monster offered, helpfully.

We slept better that night than at any time since my arrival on Iwo. Rain drumming on the steel hull, the wind howling outside, the wreck moving uneasily in time to the passing swells, plus our own desperate fatigue. Goon collected all our canteens and positioned them outside to catch some of that free God-water, and then we went down. By now my mind had learned to dismiss our grotesque circumstances—the piteous, mutilated bodies, the ravenous crabs, the never-ending stench of death, that uneasy feeling of guilt that we were alive and they—they were gone. I finally realized that a battlefield had its own rules of survival. Even when you were surrounded by death and destruction, if *you* were alive, that would be enough to just about guarantee a good night's sleep, as long as you felt secure from enemy attack. Out here, temporarily entombed in these dismal steel remains and wrapped in strangely comforting darkness, guarded by all those dead Marines and sailors, I felt pretty damned secure.

The absence of noise outside the hull finally woke us. The storm had apparently blown past and there were pale streams of daylight intruding through the many bullet holes, creating projector-like beams all around us. The surf was still up, with vigorous waves slapping against the slanting hull as if to remind us that this ship no longer belonged to us. Then came a welcome sound: the boom of distant and sustained artillery fire. The big push had begun.

"All *right*," Goon pronounced. "About goddamned time."

Twitch became the hero of the morning when he went rooting through the galley supplies and found an unopened can of coffee grounds. The problem was that there was no way to boil water—our usual method of burning chips of C-4 to heat food wasn't available, and we dared not make even a wisp of smoke now that it was daylight.

"Who says it has to be *hot* coffee?" Goon said. Leave it to Goon, I thought. There'd been a moment of silent reverence when he opened that can as the amazing smell of ground coffee momentarily over-whelmed the noxious atmosphere within the LCI. We put an entire handful of grounds into one of the galley pots before emptying a couple of our canteens into it. Each of us opened a tin of a C ration breakfast packet, lit a cigarette with the group's one working Zippo, and waited for the grounds to dissolve. Twitch found a strainer, dumped the horrible coffee pot, and made us some "fresh" coffee. It was wonderful. A bit chewy, but still wonderful.

The sounds of a rising infantry clash grew outside. We had no idea, of course, where the front lines were, but clearly, the Marines were on the move. I decided to go topside and search for life rafts. I crawled through a badly holed hatch to the weather decks astern of the conning tower. The wind was still up and it was colder than it had been the night before. The skies overhead were filled with fly-ing scud, showing patches of bright blue through a carpet of uneasy, dull gray clouds. The dunes ashore were empty; the constant rumble of distant artillery had not yet resulted in explosions directly ashore. I carefully scanned the desolate landscape directly across from us. I could barely make out where the entrance to "our" tunnel was, partly because of the swirling mist created by the rising winds, a mixture of sand and spray that put everything ashore slightly out of focus. Well, I thought: if I can't see them, they can't see me. Besides, the bulk of the ruined conning tower was between me and the beach.

The LCI *did* carry life rafts, although the big shells that had put her down had also shredded most of them. I crawled across the wet slant-ing deck to the first raft and then used my K-bar to cut my way into it. The Marine K-bar knife was a fearsome blade, but cutting into rubber was not one of its design specs. The more I cut, the duller it became. I had to use one hand to support my body on the tilting deck while saw-ing manfully away at the rubber covering. Once I finally succeeded the inner contents popped out in all directions. C rations, water pouches, fishing packs, envelopes of shark-repellant, dye-marker, medical packs, flares—everything but a goddamned radio.

I stopped looking and tried to think. This was survival stuff. Where would they put a radio? The other half of the life raft was just underwater, but I thought I saw the lumpish shape of another supplies pack. As I bent to cut into it, a dramatic line of artillery blasts began to walk its way across the nearby beach. I almost dropped my knife, the booming explosions were so strong. I thought I heard fragments whistling through the air all the way out here. The barrage continued for another five minutes, prompting Goon to come find me. We were a couple hundred yards offshore, but the concussions were strong enough to hammer our ears. Goon slithered up alongside me and asked me what I was looking for.

A radio, I said. Some of these life rafts should have radios. He looked into the slashing cut I'd made into this other raft. Like this? he asked, holding up a small, waterproof bag. I stared at it.

"Just like that," I said.

At that moment some of those long-distance artillery rounds began erupting in the water between us and the beach, compressing the air again and shaking our trusty wreck. He didn't have to say a thing. We both made like wet monkeys getting back inside as whining bits of metal began to slice through the air around the wrecked landing craft and ping off her rusting sides.

TWENTY-THREE

I unpacked the radio set bundle once we got back into the messing space, still jumping every time a fragment from the shore bombardment hit the LCI. There'd been no let-up since it had begun, which ought to tell the Japanese that the Marines' last big offensive was imminent. Goon had told me the story of the time that the high command had finally realized that the Marines' practice of shelling the next objective for a few hours essentially gave the enemy early warning of where we were going to strike out for next. To prove his point, they'd ordered a heavy push against an objective on the island that was proving almost impossible to gain ground on—but without any preparatory shelling. The Marines had been able to take that objective in a few hours, because the Japanese hadn't been ready. My guess was that since this was the last significant pocket of resistance on the island, the generals figured it no longer mattered, so go ahead and pound on 'em for a few hours, if only to make the grunts feel better.

The radio was in the shape of a long brick, with a telescopic antenna at the top, two semicircular meters on the face, one for signal strength, one for battery state, and all painted haze-gray. There was a battery compartment containing four chunky batteries, still wrapped in semi-transparent oilcloth. There was no frequency selector—the frequency was pre-set for five hundred kilocycles, the standard maritime distress frequency. I expected it to work, but then wondered who'd be listening, or guarding, that frequency out here around Iwo Jima. Certainly not the Marines. I'd never been inside *Nevada*'s expansive radio rooms, but I assumed if I made a call it was going to be a warship that answered.

The next problem was going to be whether they would accept my call or immediately suspect communications deception. While I'd still been aboard *Nevada*, which seemed like a hundred years ago, we'd been constantly changing freqs every day and night to frustrate Japanese who were getting into our fire-control nets and pretending to be American units. Some of them were pretty obvious, but others had been damned convincing. They were also really good at jamming our circuits, usually with some hideous-sounding music. I had to be prepared to deal with challenges from whatever station eventually answered up. We no longer had our code books or even a copy of the grid. I was going to have to wing it, big time.

Then there was the grid, or lack of one: how in the hell could I call for fire without the grid? I couldn't even give them my position, much less the position of any worthwhile targets we spotted out here. Goon said I should forget about spotting, and just notify the Navy of where we were holed up and request rescue, but that didn't help—I needed to tell them *where* to go to rescue us. Then I remembered that the LCI would have been operating off a chart when they made their approach to this part of the island. Was the chart still here? The conning tower hadn't been submerged, so maybe, maybe . . . I told Goon what I was thinking. He pointed out that I'd have to climb an *ex*terior ladder to get up to the pilothouse.

"If some SOB's been assigned to watch the beach area around these wrecks, they'll see you. Believe me, they'll have arty that can reach out here."

"So go up at night?" Twitch suggested.

"No," Goon said. "He'll need a light. The rain's gone. Weather's clear. No fucking lights."

"I think I'll just have to take my chances," I said. "There's no point in calling out to the whole Navy and saying: Help, help: I'm here, only to have them come back and ask: Where's here, exactly?"

Monster made a rude noise. "Them?" he offered from his perch on the overturned sofa. "They prolly gonna be listenin' on that freq, don't ya know. 'Sides, I don't tink any of this radio talk is so smart, me. Best ting to do? Lie low, wait for the brethren to kill *all* them mudbugs, and *then* squeak."

That comment produced a moment of thoughtful silence in the badly battered messing room. I tried to marshal some arguments against, but the logic was pretty overwhelming.

"Okay," I announced. "We have a radio. Let's see what happens over there when the big deal actually gets up here. If we can help, we'll call. If we can't, we'll do what Monster's suggesting: keep our heads down and wait. Maybe live a lot longer."

It took about three seconds to gain general approval of our grand strategy. Go, Monster, I thought. We'd brought back rations and water from the lifeboat. We ate and then got some more rest.

As night fell, we decided not to use any lights within the wrecked LCI. One bullet hole could give us away. We figured the general advance would slow up once darkness fell, anyway, in keeping with the pattern of warfare on Iwo since the first rude awakening as to what we were really facing. We had to assume the north end of the island was just as honeycombed with defensive positions as the rest of it. I decided to examine that radio with what little light was left, which is when I discovered why there was no mouthpiece or earpiece.

Oh, shit, I thought with great dismay. It was a CW radio. There was a tiny key embedded in its face, spring loaded, with a small red light showing when you were putting out Morse code on the air. Hardly suitable for complicated spotting dialogue. Just SOS and a lat-lon. I cursed softly. Goon raised an eyebrow and I told him our new problem.

"Okay, then," he said, in a resigned voice. "We're done. Ain't like we didn't do a righteous job of work during our little vacation on Iwo fucking Jima. And I sure as hell don't wanna be the last guy killed on Iwo. We do what Monster suggested. We lay low. When we're pretty damn sure we *know* it's safe, we make contact."

There was no arguing with that, although I felt bad that I couldn't deliver some timely shore bomb if the guys on the beach got their asses in a crack on the final push. I tried to think of some other way to do it.

Some carrier air came over about then and started to work over the beaches where we'd been hiding out the day before. Over and above that racket I could hear the deep booming of one or more of the beasts, back from Guam and freshly rearmed. I stashed the radio up high, out of the way of any intruding water, and found a place to crash. Out of habit, I kept my typewriter handy, not that I expected bad guys to be jumping onboard. The surf outside had settled quite a bit, and it was starting to get really cold inside. The wrecked LCI still moved in tune with the surf, but gently. Sleep, I thought.

"Hey, Goon," I said.

"What? Sir?"

"What could go wrong?"

"It's Iwo, Loot," he said. "Absolutely every-fucking-thing. You armed and dangerous?"

I snorted. "Armed, for damned sure."

Then I had a thought. I needed that chart. Even with a CW radio, I could warn the Marines if I saw something bad cranking up on the nearby beach area.

"Goon," I said. "I need a chart, a nav chart. If there is one, it'll be in the pilothouse. I'm gonna climb out there and get it."

"No," he said. "I'll do it. What's it look like?"

"Like any chart," I said. "It'll be taped down onto a desktop or a table. Unstick it, roll it up into a tight roll to keep it as dry as possible. I can do it."

"You get some sleep, Loot," he said. "If it's there, I'll get it. I don't need you fallin' offa some damn ladder."

I tried. There was more air activity over the next four hours, up and down the near middle coasts of Iwo. The other two Marines slept like logs, but I only dozed; I think I was just more attuned to carrier air than they were. After one of our light carriers had been sunk by kamikazes right at the beginning of the Iwo operation, the Navy had moved a big-deck up from Guam to augment the escort flattops. It hadn't hurt that other big-decks were preparing for the Okinawa invasion, which meant that the Japanese air forces were getting ready to deal with that now that most of Iwo had been lost to them. There hadn't been any doubts lately about our taking Iwo, only how big a butcher's bill we were going to pay and how many Marine divisions were going to be wrecked in the process; from what I'd heard at the CP, it was beginning to look like all three.

It was still bothering me that we were going to sit out the rest of the bloodshed ashore while meekly awaiting rescue. Surely they had plenty of spotter assets teamed up with the advancing Marine forces by now, but none so well positioned as I was. I think my brain had been working on a way to get back into the battle even as I pretended to sleep. It came to me around midnight. I'd been concentrating on the radio gear these landing craft had been equipped with. I'd forgotten the troops they'd been carrying when the three craft had walked into the artillery ambush. Wasn't it possible that some of them had been *Marine* radiomen?

We had swum out to the largest of the landing craft, the LCI. But there were also two LCMs out here—Landing Craft Medium. Both of them were barely awash at high tide, having been hit hard and often. Plus they were open amphibious boats, unlike the LCI, which had both an open well-deck and an enclosed hull. The Mike 8, as it was known, was some seventy-six feet long; the Mike 6 was fifty-six feet. I hadn't paid too much attention to the Mike boats because they'd been so seriously hammered, but it looked like there was both a 6 and an 8 within fifty feet or so. The larger, the 8, had been torn open from stem to stern. The 6 had been blown in half, with the forward piece upside down and mostly underwater. The back half was upright but fully awash. I couldn't be sure because we'd been fixated on getting aboard the remains of the LCI with its distinctive conning tower and round portholes.

But all three would have been carrying Marine infantry—mortar crews, riflemen, hospital corpsmen . . . and radiomen. Field radios were heavy, especially with spare batteries, and required a single man-mule per radio. If I could swim over there and poke around in the well-deck, I might find one; if undamaged it ought to be still waterproof, and those were voice radios, not Continuous Wave. It was pretty dark out now—no moon and just enough wind to produce haze and mist. The big swells had subsided as night fell. As a practical matter, any bodies on the Mike boats had probably been swept away by now.

Goon reappeared, with what looked like a tight roll in his hand. I didn't open it, but felt the paper in the dark. One side was waxed. Yup. I told Goon my idea about the other boats and the possibility there'd be a radio out there.

"Lemme rest a bit. Then we'll go check."

I agreed, but I didn't want to sleep. I wanted that radio. The next question was: go it alone or wake Goon? That was a tough one. Those boys were truly exhausted. They were relatively safe in here, however bad the smell. I was a good swimmer and there were life jackets hanging on bulkheads in the passageway. I could wear one to help me get there and back. I couldn't dare show a light, but if I could get aboard one of those Mike-boat hulks and poke around, there should be at least some equipment in the bottom of the wreckage or, if necessary, scattered around the shallow sea floor. And if I could recover an intact field radio and get it back to the LCI, I might be in business again and able to help with what was coming tomorrow.

I thought some more: if I woke Goon, he'd tell me to wait a while. Goon had brought me the chart. Now it was my turn. Any number of things could happen to reveal our presence on the wrecks, in which case I might get us all killed. But, damn—if I could resurrect a working radio, I could hurt the enemy bad and maybe at least attenuate the wholesale killing of my Marines.

My Marines; boy, that was presumptuous, and yet, that was my duty, wasn't it? Keep as many Marines alive on this cursed island as possible? Screw it, I decided—I'm just gonna tie on a kapok life jacket, slip out of here, hold my nose through the body mash, get down into the water, dog-paddle over there as quietly as I can, and go look.

Five minutes later I found myself sliding into the water back by the stern, on the seaward side, and looking for the Mike boats. Had they been inboard or outboard of us? The small swell was trying to push me back inshore in the darkness; I should have paid closer attention. Three rusting wrecks. All those Godforsaken broken bodies inside. Trapped in a steel shoebox at point blank artillery range. *All* cut to ribbons. Somewhere right out there. My eyes teared up as I looked into the darkness.

"That way," Goon said quietly, from behind me.

I about shit. He planted a big ham hand on my shoulder. I suddenly realized he was probably feeling what I was thinking. "Sir," he amended.

I should have damn known, I thought, exhaling. "I'm trying to find a radio, Goon," I said. "Just one goddamned radio. There *has* to be a radio over there. I—"

"Yeah, that's what I figured you'd do, Loot," he said as we bobbed neck deep in the sea at the edge of the wrecked LCI. The sea was strangely benign that night, almost as if it were inviting us to go look. There had to be at least one radio, please God, I thought. I just need one. Goon, too, had strapped on a kapok. Without further discussion, we set off for the smaller of the two Mike boats.

I chose the smaller boat because it wasn't in as many pieces. Two main pieces, to be precise, with both of them moving up and down independently, like someone was trying to bend a bar of metal to break it in half, up and down, up and down. The hull coaming was above water; the rest submerged. There was nothing for it but for us both to submerge into the well-deck and feel around for gear. We had to take the kapoks off to do that; we tied them to an already rusting cleat.

We felt around and found gear. Lots of gear. Rifles. Packs. Utility belts. Entrenching tools. Mortar stands. Mortar rounds. Water cans. Ammo boxes. A few bodies trapped in jagged shell holes, festooned with belligerent crabs. Three times we burst back onto the surface, our eyes stinging with the salt, moving over a little bit each time. We clung to the jagged metal, breathing hard, and listened for intruders. Two more times down. Utility belts. C ration packs. Empty boon-docks. A radio.

A radio. No mistaking it. Steel, pimply knobs and buttons, heavy, leaden. A stubby whip antenna, barely sticking out of the case. A dangling, bloodied and tangled, carry harness. A complete collarbone assembly and three ribs.

God.

And then, a second one, this one with a big dent. Two radiomen, I thought, sitting together on the benches in the well-deck, as they would. I grabbed one, Goon the other, and we shot back to the surface, our fists embedded in the straps. Just as a flare popped overhead the wreckage. We instinctively ducked, staring at that magnesium light from just below the surface, which was sea green now, and praying there wasn't a scout sitting right there with a *Nambu*, staring us in the face.

We hung that way for a few seconds, surfaced, and then said fuck it in unison. No-one was out there, and somehow we knew it. We put the kapok jackets back on and paddled together to get back to the LCI, where we were greeted by Monster and Twitch, who helped us hump the precious radios onboard. We tumbled back into the mess-room, where it was still totally dark. We hung the dripping radios by their straps in their tangled harnesses. Goon and I flopped down on the tilting mess-table benches and nodded at each other.

Victory. We hoped. It was probably around midnight. So, now we had radios. *Two* radios. One might even work. And then the really hard part would begin. Convincing Regiment or one of the beasts we weren't enemy.

Worry about that tomorrow, I muttered, and fell asleep.

TWENTY-FOUR

"How'm I gonna introduce myself?" I asked my battered brain trust. "Assuming these things are gonna work?"

From the sound of it, Monster was carefully tearing into some canned food supplies in the tiny galley; he'd found a small bottle of McIlhenny's Tabasco and was looking for something to doctor.

"Can you get to *Nevada*?" Goon asked.

"If she's on station, yes, but her call sign will have probably changed by now. Maybe even her NGFS frequency. And I can't authenticate any transmission I make."

"Maybe you should call our JASCO; let them get you a shooter," Goon said.

"That's the drawback to the new grid," I replied. "We haven't been going through a JASCO. I can't think of anybody who'd recognize my voice, assuming it's even recognizable on a field radio. Except maybe Commander Willson, gun boss on the *Nevada*."

We felt a passing strangeness, our disconnected voices holding a strategy conversation in the pitch blackness of a partially sunken LCI. The only light we saw was shining through the many holes in the superstructure, large and small, fed by the flares. We heard Monster gasp once and then begin a slow, choking routine. Twitch asked if he was okay; Monster gasped again and then rasped: Good! or at least that's what it sounded like. Or maybe it had been: Gawd! I'd tried Tabasco once; good cure for sinus problems. How were we going to do this?

Twitch suggested we test the radios first. Yup, I thought. Absolutely right. I unpacked one of them on the seat of a chair that happened to be sitting in the path of a bullet hole in the side. The bullet itself was still embedded in the table. Looked like a 20mm. The outside light would wax and wane as the hulk moved around, but it was enough.

The radio worked—hell, both of them worked. One dim red light, enough to light the frequency dial. Barely light it, but I could read it. But when you backed the squelch down, there was static, which meant it was responding to its controls.

What time is it, I asked. Twitch had the only working watch. It was 0115. "They'll kick off in two, three hours," Goon said. "With or without a pre-bombardment. They'll come out of the Meat Grinder and push 'em all the way down the beach and into the sea."

"Hoid that one before, me," Monster growled. "Remember, them bastids git'em a vote."

"By God they do," I said. "But we need to establish that we're good guys *before* the party starts, so's we can help out if we see something."

It felt like the sea was beginning to rise out there, or at least the swells. What now? Rising swells meant something might be gathering itself way out there. The LCI was even moving around a little, with her battered hull grinding audibly on the bottom. We were sitting just off the north-northwest coast of the island, right in Typhoon Alley. I'd seen a news picture of one of our cruisers with her entire bow ripped right off by a typhoon wave. Iwo was the personification of misery. I couldn't imagine what it would be like if a damn typhoon came. Besides, I thought typhoon season was in the fall, not February. The grinding hull seemed unconvinced.

I got ready to key the transmitter but Goon put up a hand. "Wait 'til it starts," he said. "You come up now, the bad guys have nothing to listen to but you. New guy, on the air, and not that far away? Once the world falls in on 'em, they may not notice you."

He had a point. We didn't know when our guys were gonna turn loose in this sector. The radios worked, apparently. Maybe eat, crap out for an hour, or at least until we heard shit cranking up all along The Line. And—there had to be more artillery spotters out there, firing for all the regiments. The only thing we had to offer was that we were supposedly behind the Jap lines and thus able to see what the rest of the spotters couldn't see—and hit. If nothing of interest materialized, we'd just be spectators and this had all been for nothing. I was ashamed to realize that that would be okay, too.

Twitch had raided the C rats from that lifeboat where we'd gotten the CW radios. He'd also brought back a box of the canned water. It was horrible. Tasted like bleach. But it was wet and clean. We drank all of it, burped for fifteen minutes, then napped for a bit.

I was awakened by being pitched out of my bullet-scarred chair as the LCI jerked suddenly and then began to slide into deeper water. The swells were crashing straight into the well-deck now, from the sounds of it. Instinctively, I grabbed for the radios. Monster had slid all the way across the battered messroom's deck and fetched up against something sharp. He was not a happy Monster. At that moment a wave of artillery opened up to the south as the Marines announced they were coming, once and for all. I waited for a response but it didn't come. Leave it to those bastards to wait until troops were coming *and* in murder range; until then they stayed down in their holes. Surely the big bosses knew that by now. Surely. Twitch said it was 0530.

I wedged myself on the high side of the table with one of the radios and looked at Goon. He nodded. I began the dance.

"Peacemaker, this is Iwo, two-six Charlie. Radio check, over?"

Static. I repeated the call. More static.

Then an impossibly young, midwestern voice came up. "Eat shit and die, you bastard."

"Negative," I said. "Please relay to Peacemaker—this is Lieutenant Lee Bishop from Main Battery Plot. I have no codes, no grid, no freqs, but if you will contact me, I am behind enemy lines."

"Bull-*shit*," the voice spat.

"Relay the message," I said. "That's all you have to do. I can convince them. You want to be the guy who fucks this up and gets a buncha Marines killed? Relay the message!"

"Make me, bastard. We're comin' for you."

"Iwo, two-six Charlie, this is Reading Railroad. How do I know you, over?"

"I swiped the colonel's coffee mug," I said. "Right now I'm with Goon, Monster, and Twitch. I can't tell you where, but our last station was the Meat Grinder. And I can say the letter R all day long."

That produced a moment of silence. Reading Railroad. Lots of Rs. This was probably a CP. Maybe even our regiment. Then I understood the bind we were in. We could have been captured, for all they knew. Kneeling somewhere in a tunnel or a cave, hands on our heads, answering questions with swords at our throats. I looked at that charthouse chart position where the LCI had been headed. There was no naval gunfire support grid on this chart. Just latitude and longitude. I could establish *my* observation position by just asking him to fire two Willie Peter shells at a set latitude and longitude. But if the Japanese were listening, they'd immediately know where we were.

"Let's do this," I said in desperation. "We can't prove who we are, I understand that. And I can't tell you *where* we are until you're fully engaged and in sight. Ask Colonel Sam to keep someone up this net. If we see something cranking up that merits a beast, we'll call. You can either shoot the mission or not; if not, we tried. Over?"

"This is Reading Railroad, roger, deal. We'll see you, one way or another, sometime today."

"Iwo, two-six Charlie, out."

At that moment yet another air strike rolled in along "our" sector of the beach; six planes, two of whom dropped short, which is to say between the clutch of wrecked amphibious craft and the beach. Two more stunning blasts and then, to our horror, the LCI got underway for the final time in its life, sliding down some underwater feature to total submergence. We had about thirty seconds before the messroom flooded to the overhead and flushed all four of us down the passageway and into the open sea. We surfaced into a roil of seawater and leftover fuel oil, gasping and spitting, until the surf started bumping us up against that overturned half of a Mike boat. I grabbed onto a propeller and then banged my head on the rudder, which was bent over at an odd angle along the keel. A pall of explosives smoke hung over our heads and there were a million bright, shiny dead fish coming up everywhere. My three accomplices were thrashing around the other end of the Mike boat, looking about half drowned.

I had the radio I'd been talking on slung crosswise across my chest. I'd managed to grab that kapok life jacket on the way out so all I had to do was hang on to that propeller and the radio. It wouldn't be full daylight for another hour at least. The noise ashore was gathering strength but it still wasn't close. I could just barely see that my guys had now crawled up onto the keel of the other half of the same Mike boat, just enough to get out of the water. I was still half submerged and that wind blowing across the wrecks had dropped twenty degrees in temperature. My hands were getting stiff in the cold but I held onto that radio with a death grip.

Then, to our right, south along the coast, tracer fire erupted, going both ways. The flares stopped coming, but a walking barrage of artillery began to creep its way up the coast, with bigger stuff going off inland in the higher elevations. It was a good distraction from the cold as hundreds if not thousands of Marines came north, and now the Japanese were shooting back. Mortars began flying in both directions, and even those huge Type 98s were in play, based on some of the explosions we were seeing. The airstrikes had stopped, probably because of all the artillery that was flying, but tanks were visible as moving dust clouds, framed by artillery bursts. The Japanese hadn't revealed everything they had yet, but if this was going to be the showdown, they would now.

The advance was coming from south to north across the entire width of the island and had probably launched from the second airfield, at least according to where the enemy artillery was landing. Being in the surf, we couldn't see much in detail except right along the beach between our last refuge and the actual ocean.

"I'll bet those bastids still have some eyes up on *Suribachi*," Goon said. "Their arty is landing just right."

I heard a strange hissing noise behind me and looked back to see a haze-gray inflatable life raft gathering shape on the seaward side of the smaller Mike boat. It sounded dangerously loud right here, but probably not in comparison to all the ordnance flying ashore. Then I realized Monster had gotten tired of freezing to death in the water as I saw him tumble into the fifteen-man inflatable raft. Twitch followed. Goon motioned for me to join them, but I hesitated. I was freezing just like the rest, but I had a perfect vantage point hanging on to my propeller, which was about three feet above sea level. Besides, my arms were so stiff with cold I wasn't sure I could make it over to the raft. Only my life jacket was keeping me warm enough to stay out here on the remaining fragment of the Mike boat.

And then I saw something ashore that made me forget about the cold. There were small trucks coming out of the hillsides—metal cabs with canvas tops stretched over frames covering their back ends. Many of them were towing light artillery pieces on wheels, and each one of them had an even smaller two-wheeled ammo hamper being towed behind that. They were coming from all directions, punching up and out of all those gullies and ravines in the northernmost sectors of the island. I could see them, but I doubted any of our guys could, pinned down just north of the mid-island airfields as they were right now.

Where the hell was our organic air support? If ever there was Corsair meat on the table, this was it. There were *hundreds* of troops massing over there. Then I remembered—Navy air couldn't fly with all that arty going back and forth. Goon popped up next to me in the water.

"Showtime, Loot," he called, pointing at the gathering mass of Jap infantry.

"I think you're right," I replied. "Our guys can't see that shit shapin' up from the other side of the Meat Grinder."

"Come on back to the raft," he suggested. "Drier and warmer."

"I'm gonna do it from here, Goon—I've got a clear view. Go on back to the raft in case somebody on the beach sees me out here."

He started to object but I waved him back. I'd been working in my head on a lat-lon target location from that LCI's coastal chart and thanking God that Navy charts were pretty much waterproof. I had no compass or even anything to write with, so I'd had to memorize the target coordinates, which I centered on that growing crowd of trucks, troops, and stubby little field guns. Then, like Goon said, it was showtime.

"Reading Railroad, this is Iwo, two-six Charlie, calling in the blind. Emergency fire mission: many troops and field guns in the open, over?"

I will say, Colonel Sam had been good to his word—he'd kept an operator listening for me. The swarm of Japanese, their vehicles, and guns was swelling with every moment. It looked like they were gonna throw everything they had at the approaching Marine forces. Weakened by their appalling losses, our guys probably had no idea what they were about to take on.

Regiment answered: This is Reading Railroad. Break, Vesuvius, Vesuvius, contact Iwo, two-six Charlie for emergency fire mission, over?"

Vesuvius—one of the new, ever-changing call signs. Hopefully, Regiment had sent me on to a beast, but any ship with lots of guns and VT frag ammo could deal with this. My spirits soared. An unfamiliar voice answered just as some wild rounds began to erupt near our little collection of wrecked amphibs.

" Iwo, two-six Charlie, this is Vesuvius, ready to copy, over?"

"This is Iwo, two-six Charlie: emergency fire mission, area mission, several *hundred* troops in the open, *many* artillery pieces in the open, no grid available." I gave them the latitude/longitude coordinates, then called for a box size of one thousand yards. "Two hundred rounds, secondary armament, all available guns, victor tango frag, height: eighty feet, report when ready, over?"

They read it back verbatim; if lat-lon versus grid was a problem, it didn't seem to bother Vesuvius. Nor did they seem fazed that I was calling for every five-inch gun they had on the engaged side, and I also wasn't calling for spotting rounds. This was an *emergency* fire mission, meaning just start shooting. By now our guys were probably only a thousand yards away and closing in on what they thought was a near-empty sector.

"Iwo, two-six Charlie, Vesuvius, confirm eight guns, two hundred rounds, over?"

Eight guns—this *was* a beast I was talking to. Maybe even *Nevada*. "Vesuvius, from where I'm floating, it looks like a *banzai* charge is shaping up—fifteen hundred troops or more, supported by twenty, maybe thirty, seventy-five-millimeter towed artillery pieces. Coming from every direction. Looks like they're gonna charge in the direction of the mid-island airfields. Over?"

A familiar voice came up on the net. It was Commander Willson, by God. "What's your sister's name, Lieutenant?" Commander Willson asked.

"Miz Mary, boss, Miz Mary."

"Roger, break, ready, over?"

"Roger, break—fire, fire, fire."

And they did.

TWENTY-FIVE

The entire northwestern end of the island simply disappeared once the barrage began. There was enough light for the *Nevada* to be able to see the point of land I'd described in my call-for-fire. Evidently she'd moved in closer for the showdown. Eight guns meant four twin-barreled five-inch mounts were going to fire fifty rounds each of fragmenting ammunition pretty much continuously, which would explode about eighty feet above over a thousand Japanese soldiers out in the open. Using sixteen-inch would have been simply wasteful, but I could still call for it if a sufficiently hard target presented itself. This, however, was just murder on a grand scale, which was probably exactly what General Kuribayashi wanted. Hell, he was probably out there with 'em.

The common thinking was that the Japanese army had given up on *banzai* attacks, which the Marines had first seen on Guadalcanal back in the fall of 1942. They usually, but not always, resulted in the total slaughter of the attackers as they charged, usually uphill, into massed and entrenched .50 cal machine guns. Being water cooled, those guns could keep firing for long, continuous bursts at around seven hundred rounds per minute. On a couple of occasions, though, on Saipan and Guam, the Japs had achieved surprise, and the sheer numbers of attacking enemy infantry had cost the Americans horrific numbers of dead and wounded. On Iwo, there'd been one smaller version, where the enemy had managed to get into a field medical station and kill just about everybody. But this was the real deal, and, we all hoped, possibly their last gasp.

The area barrage took about eight minutes, after which, even with an offshore wind, it took almost fifteen minutes for the smoke to clear. It was over so quickly that the leading elements of the Marine offensive were still some distance away. The ground that I could make out from sea level had been turned pretty much to black sand. There were no recognizable features remaining along the beach, and certainly no recognizable human forms. A few sporadic Marine artillery rounds came in, but I think once the other spotters had seen what happened along this sector of the northwest coast, they'd simply stopped.

I joined my compadres in the lifeboat. None of us said anything at all. My Marines were too stunned to speak, and my teeth were chattering too hard. Then I remembered I owed Peacemaker—excuse me, Vesuvius—a report. "This is Iwo, two-six Charlie," I said. "Target obliterated. Mission complete, over?"

"This is Peacemaker," came the reply from Commander Willson. "I should hope so."

"Stand by," I replied. "We thought they were done on L-Day, remember, over?"

"So we did, Lieutenant," Willson said. "Vesuvius standing by, though with hot guns, over?"

"Roger, hot guns, out."

The barrels on those five-inch mounts must have been glowing, which, as a practical matter, meant the guns couldn't be loaded again until they cooled down.

"Loot, for Chrissakes, *look!*"

I looked and then swore. There were more Japanese coming out into the open. This time, instead of towed artillery pieces there were odd-looking army tanks, and they were firing at long range over the heads of their own soldiers, which must have been a nasty surprise for all those Marines coming north, thinking it was all over but the shouting. There weren't thousands this time, but there were enough of them to make our guys hit the deck and call for tanks of their own. Regiment called and asked for targets. I could still only give them lat-lon positions out there along the beach and that coastal strip but they got their organic Marine arty into it within one minute. It looked like 105 and even some 155 tubes, and they got on target pretty quick.

Since I could see, I could spot, but first I had to give them my position. By now it wouldn't much matter if the Japanese knew where I was—they'd have problems of their own momentarily. I gave them a bearing and range relative to the starting point of the previous area fire. That was close enough.

I could see pretty well, even from inside the canvas cover that stretched over the open-ocean lifeboat, so I walked them around the neighborhood, wherever I saw groups of enemy headed south. I kept dropping five-hundred-yard down spots on the range calls to keep the Regiment's guns concentrated on those running soldiers, who appeared to be paying no attention to all to the hot steel raining among their screaming ranks. And then I guess some alert bastard figured out how it was that those rounds were staying right with those running troops, because we heard the distinctive sound of mortar rounds hissing our way in between the Marines' salvos.

All four of us bailed out of that life raft in about five seconds and started swimming away from the wrecked amphibs, out toward the open ocean, as sharp cracking mortars started going off when they hit the water, sending hot metal shards spanging off what was left of the amphib hulks and quickly sinking that poor life raft. Reading Railroad called urgently for spots. I went back and said we were swimming for our lives offshore and under mortar attack, and were there any PT boats handy? That stumped them, but those damned Japanese kept the mortars coming, although I didn't think they could actually see us, just the battered hulks where we'd been hiding. We fervently hoped. Again.

And then came a welcome sound. *Nevada* had rejoined the party. No more five-inch. It was time for beast talk.

As the four of us treaded water—really cold water—we heard the authoritative thunder-dragon boom of her fourteen-inchers. Moments later the world ended along that stretch of beach and the open ground behind it. We felt the shock of those enormous shells hitting in our submerged bellies and legs. Once again, the land disappeared in gigantic clouds of sand and shattered rock. We scuttled back toward the beach for the cover of the gunwale of the larger Mike boat to get out from under all the debris raining down into the surf line. I caught a glimpse of more muzzle blasts scorching the morning air farther out to sea, followed by even bigger explosions farther inland. Another of the beasts had joined the fray, probably using *Nevada*'s targeting information. The reconstituted *banzai* waves dissolved into a cloud of black sand, blood, smoke, and fire. When it finally stopped, nothing moved over there on Iwo Jima.

Monster announced that he was going to die from the cold, him. I thought I might join him. Then we saw a wave of Marine tanks pop over the low hills just to the south and come rattling down the dunes until they stopped right about where our tunnel had been located. A second wave crested the higher dunes and swung east, spreading out to complete the containment of the last stand of the 109th division. I half expected another swarm of Japanese to come boiling out of those low hills, but this time it didn't happen. Hundreds of Marines rose up out of the dunes and charged down onto the flat sands, clearly intent on ending this mess once and for all. No one rose to meet them. I forgot the cold as I realized that we might finally, *finally*, have beaten these bastards into submission. *Nevada* had lived up to her prewar call sign: Peacemaker.

"We might as well swim to the shore," Goon said. "If more do show up I'd rather just lay down and die than stay in this fucking water."

There were a lot of surprised faces when the four of us stepped out of the low surf, stiff with cold. The area along the beach still seemed to quiver from that last barrage of fourteen- and sixteen-inch shells, as if the bloody bedrock was still resonating to such a shock. There were hundreds of Marines out there now, every one of them staring at his boots every time he took a step. The ground was a blend of pulverized volcanic rock, wet, bloody sand, and the tiniest bits of human flesh and Japanese uniforms imaginable. There were no bodies in evidence, only a sticky, reddish stain in the coarse sand peppered with flakes of human bone, and the mess was everywhere.

"Goon," a corporal shouted. "Hey, it's Goon! Wouldya look at this shit—the Goon squad."

A low chorus of cheering welled up as comrades from the Fifth Regiment recognized them and then began to converge on us, trying hard to walk through that sand without getting any on them. I heard men calling for Monster and Twitch. I might as well not have even been there, which was fine with me, because I now had hopes of getting back aboard *Nevada*, whose lurking, dark gray bulk was just barely visible in the offshore haze, looking like some steel mountain. High up on her superstructure a bright yellow light was blinking busily away at a distant destroyer or maybe a cruiser. Those monstrous guns were laid flat along her main deck, while tiny figures manhandled the cleaning poles as they scrubbed the barrels. Navy air resumed their search for enemy stragglers now that the artillery had stopped.

Was it really over, I wondered. Not quite, I realized. About a thousand yards up the coast, right at the end of the island, a dark gorge cut a three-hundred-foot-deep notch into the black escarpments overlooking the sea on the northernmost point of the island. The sound of shooting drifted down on the crowds of troops along the beach. Several of the Marine tanks lurched forward to go up there, struggling to grind their way through that disgusting amalgam of blood-soaked sand, pumice, and shattered ground where nearly a thousand Japanese had been hammered into oblivion.

"You Navy Lieutenant Bishop?" a voice asked from behind me.

I turned around to find an impossibly young-looking Marine first lieutenant standing behind me, with a radio handset in his hand. A PFC stood next to him, holding the field radio itself. I nodded. I knew he was a first lieutenant because he had a single gray bar stenciled on his collars. "Colonel Nicholas wants to talk to you," he said. "They need a spotter. There's a buncha holdouts up in that canyon." He handed me the handset.

"This is Iwo, two-six Charlie," I said, my voice just a bit sandy.

"I'm hearing good things about you guys, Lieutenant. You caught a *banzai* attack just in time, apparently. Higher HQ is most appreciative."

"They were right there, Colonel," I said. "The hard part was finding a radio."

"Well, we're damned glad you did. But now I got one final job for you. I hope, anyway. We think Kuribayashi himself is up there in that gorge due north of you with the Last of the Mohicans. Can you and the Goon Squad get up there to where you can see into that canyon and sterilize it for us? It's time to declare Iwo secured."

"Affirmative," I said. "We'll head up that way now, while there's still light."

"Good man," the colonel said. "We sent a company into that canyon this morning to mop up. But then they went quiet. I got a bad feeling about those guys. Some experienced non-coms, but the rest . . ."

But the rest were replacements, I thought. "Could they still be holed up in there?" I asked.

There was a moment of silence. "I need you to do to that canyon what you did to that beach, Lieutenant," he replied, finally. In other words, I thought, I'm not going to answer your question. We need this Iwo Jima operation to end. Today. Tonight. Company or no company.

That's when I discovered that my guys had seen me talking on the radio and had come back to listen in. They were looking at me right now and I knew exactly what they wanted to know.

"Lemme get into a good position, Colonel. Right now, I can only see the front half of that canyon. Are there any serious fortifications up there?"

"Rumors of a big blockhouse. That's why they think Kuribayashi might be up there. But those are just rumors."

"We'll go take a look, Colonel," I said. "In the meantime, ask a beast to go long, twenty-five thousand yards. If there's a real blockhouse in that canyon, I'm gonna need armor-piercing and plunging fire."

"You got it, Lieutenant. Wreck sends his regards. He'll be your Ouija man, by the way. As soon as I can find him. Out."

TWENTY-SIX

Even more Marines were pouring into that long strip of land along the beach while the four of us stood there next to the surf line. I asked the first lieutenant if we could have his radio. I'd had to let go of mine because my arms were so cold. He hesitated. He looked like a replacement, which meant he was worried about not getting it back. He'd probably signed for it.

"Got me a better idea, me," Monster offered, with a friendly smile. "Y'all come with us, you. Learn somethin', no doubt. Up there, with all them. They'll show you some shit, ain't no doubt about that either. Be good for your mo-rale, don't you just know it."

Twitch politely took possession of the radio as the youngster quickly retreated south to attend to some sudden urgent business. Goon rounded up some weapons for us, and Monster went off to scrape up some food and water. There were probably a thousand Marines spreading out along our previously empty quarter. Word must have gotten out that Iwo was about to be declared secured, because there sure hadn't been that many of our people up here a few days ago. I marveled at the push to declare victory coming down from the higher headquarters. Perhaps they were a little embarrassed at the difference between what they had predicted and the bloody disaster that had emerged. Or that, possibly, there was an ever bigger calamity beckoning, called Okinawa.

We moved up the beach for a few hundred yards or so until we were out of the jelly patch and then gathered behind a big rock. Monster returned with some C-4 cubes, four full canteens, and some 10-in-1 rations. We rebuilt our utility belts while Twitch fixed us a hot meal of mystery meat, vegetable mush, hot sauce, and clean water. The sun was headed in the down direction and the air was cooling off even more. Various outfits were setting up night camps behind us, with tanks taking up station here and there. Nothing like the old days, with the expectation of Japanese leaping out of the darkness with flashing swords and terrifying screams. Apparently, these guys thought the battle was over. I said something about that.

"All those bright lights back in Pearl thought this whole thing would take five days," Goon pointed out. "Didn't exactly work out that way, did it."

"Yeah, buddy," Twitch said. "If Sitting Bull wants a battleship to go fuck up that canyon, maybe he knows something about that canyon we don't."

I made a rude noise. "There's nothing *we* don't know about that canyon," I said, trying to keep the bitterness out of my voice. "That canyon will have enemy in it. Lots of 'em. They'll do another suicidal last stand. There'll be caves and spider holes. Mines, too. There'll be mortars nearby." I nodded toward the Marines digging in for the night just behind us. "And half those eager beavers making camp over there'll be casualties by noon tomorrow. Secure, my ass."

Goon laughed. "You catching on, Loot. We lost over three hundred guys after Peleliu was declared 'secure.'"

"I'll wager," I said, "that the generals running this abortion have already declared the island secure just to get Pearl and Washington off their backs."

My trusty Marines stared at their boots. They'd been trained to keep such thoughts to themselves, even if they believed I was right. I switched to what was really bugging me. "Did you hear the Colonel say there's a company of Marines that went into that canyon and didn't come back? A company? What's that—two hundred fifty guys?"

Nods all around.

"He wouldn't answer me when I asked if they might be holed up in there somewhere," I continued. "He just wants us to set up shop, get a good lookout point, and then let a battleship give that canyon a fourteen-inch enema."

My guys began to look uncomfortable, as if embarrassed at what I was pointing out. I pressed on.

"Any bad guys up there are gonna do a last stand; you know they are, whether the island is secure or not. But here's what's bugging me—they got a company of Marines trapped up there. Regiment wants me to set up shop so I can see the whole canyon and then clean house. And now would be nice. Yesterday would be better, whether there's some of our guys up in there or not. Am I right or am I right?"

Goon nodded. "You know you are, Loot."

"Exactly," I said. "I personally can't believe Colonel Sam would just wash his hands of two hundred fifty guys, so somebody's leaning on him or his bosses pretty damn hard. Either way, if anybody's gonna rescue those poor bastards, assuming they're even alive up there, it's gotta be us."

"But how, Loot?" Goon said. "There's no way we can go into that canyon, especially if there's a buncha *kamikaze* wannabes coiled up in there."

"I think there *is* a way," I said. "You see all those tanks parked back there? Bangers *and* Zippos, right? Let's get all or at least some of those bastards to go up in there and push every last swingin' enemy dick back into his hole long enough for any holed-up Marines to escape. Then pull all those tanks back, and *then* I'll work my magic on the whole fucking canyon."

"Regiment ain't gonna go for that, Loot," Goon said. "Not if they've done wrote those grunts off. They got thousands dead and wounded. What's a few more, right?"

"I disagree, Goon," I said. "Generals or no generals, no Marine colonel is gonna write off two hundred fifty Marines."

"Then what the fuck, Loot?"

"I'm sorry to say I think the Navy might be the problem," I said. "If the Marine generals have told Pearl that the island is secured, maybe prematurely, I'll admit, the Navy's gonna remove the shore-bomb assets. Get 'em back to Guam, get 'em ready for Okinawa. And then the main event."

"Them boys is just fucked, then," Twitch said, bitterly.

"Regiment doesn't need to know," I said. "Who's the head honcho of all those tanks back there?"

Goon looked around at the other two; it was obvious they had no idea.

"Go back to the night line," I said. "Find the tanker-clanker CO, ask him to come see me about a rescue mission. And a chance to maybe kill General Kuribayashi himself. You know, sex it up a little."

A major showed up forty-five minutes later with the Goon squad in tow. The sun was a few minutes from disappearing below the western horizon, a deep orange oversized ball framed by thickening gray mist. Goon shot me a warning look as the major walked up. Word that I'd asked for a meet with the tank CO had apparently gotten loose among the tankers. Several of them had come up to listen in.

"I'm Major Grimes," he announced, in a tone of voice that quickly explained Goon's warning look. The major's uniform and gear were far too clean to have seen much combat service. He had the imperious look of an officer who hasn't *ever* stepped into the decomposing mush of a dead Japanese soldier. He was also clearly not pleased at being summoned by a mere lieutenant, and a Navy one at that. "Who wants to see me?"

I stepped forward. "I do, Major. I'm Lieutenant Lee Bishop, USN, and I'm a spotter for Colonel Nicholas."

"Spotters work for the JASCO, *Mister* Bishop," he semi-sneered. "Tank formations work for Regimental Artillery. And we're busy just now. So?"

"There's word that a company of Marine infantry is trapped up in that gorge just to the north. That's where Regiment thinks the real last organized resistance on this island is holed up, including possibly General Kuribayashi himself. I've been tasked to direct battleship fire into that gorge so that all those troops behind me there can go forward and end this mess. Before I do that, I'd like to ask if you and your tank formations could do a reconnaissance-in-force up there and see if you can get them out."

"*You'd* like to ask?" he said. "And who the hell are you? I get my tasking from the regimental CP, at a minimum, and I've had zero tasking having to do with any mysterious missing company. Besides, tanks don't go anywhere without supporting infantry. And all that infantry back there isn't going anywhere until another big barrage happens. So: the answer is not only no, but *hell* no. My orders are to advance with my twenty tanks in support of a general forward movement *after* an area bombardment, and, until then, to hold in readiness within two hundred yards of The Line. That's precisely what I'm gonna do. Bye, now. *Lieutenant.*"

Goon started shaking his head as the pretty major strode away. Then a couple of sergeants and one tank driver ambled over and started inquiring about this missing company. I told them that the Full Bull running the regiment had said a company went in and didn't come back out. The area where they went missing was up in that canyon north of us, and I'd been tasked to call in battlewagon fire in front of it and then on into it. I told them it didn't seem right to just write off two hundred fifty Marines. Yes, they may all be dead. But they might be holed up somewhere, defying the Japanese to come get 'em, and it didn't feel right to blow the place up without at least having a look. The three of them nodded and then said they'd see what they could do about that.

The radio requested my attention. It was Colonel Sam. "When will you be ready?" he asked.

"We're trying to find a place for me to set up without doing it in the area I'm going to work, Colonel. The terrain isn't cooperating."

"By 2100, Lieutenant. Your beasts are being summoned."

"Roger. Understood. Iwo, two-six Charlie, out."

Goon spoke up. "We hafta go up toward that canyon anyway to find you a spotting position; maybe we'll just keep walking until we run into trouble?"

I nodded. "Yeah, that's what I was thinking." I nodded my head in the direction of the Marine eavesdroppers. "You think those guys are gonna help?"

"I *know* those guys are gonna help," he said. "They just gotta get that Major outta the way."

"Okay, tell 'em we're gonna move up. Tell 'em it takes time to check out the best spotting positions, get the comms set up, tie the grid to features I can see. Twitch, get on the horn and ask the CP to confirm flares over this end of the island tonight. Otherwise I won't be able to see."

Twitch took the radio, while Goon, Monster, and I collected some typewriters and extra magazines, along with fresh canteens and first-aid kits. We'd only gotten a hundred yards or so before dark forms began appearing out of the post-sundown gloom to join up with us. Apparently, the word had spread up and down The Line as to what was going on. I'd expected nothing less.

Twitch rejoined and confirmed flares in thirty minutes. I sent Monster and Twitch out ahead to do their scouting work. Mines. Spider holes. Places where I could set up shop. Places where a company of terrified replacements might have gone to ground after running into an ambush. Goon and I slowed down and called in our new friends. I told them what we were trying to do and that we had a time bind. At 2100 two battleships, maybe more, would start working over this whole area in preparation for a general assault at dawn.

"If we don't find and extract those guys before then, I'm gonna have to tell you to bug out, because the world is gonna end up here."

"Where *you* gonna go, Loot?" a voice asked.

"Hell, I don't know," I said. "Wherever Goon here says to go."

That provoked general laughter, but I felt they were with me on this little excursion. Too bad about the tanks, but hell, we were gonna give it a try. "Spread out, stay behind Corporal Twitch up ahead and listen to what he says. He's got a nose for metal in the ground. Corporal Monster is our other scout. Now listen: he finds enemy, he'll wanna cook and eat 'em. You smell barbeque, go the other way."

More laughter, and then we heard tank engines behind us. Those sergeants weren't going to be left behind on this little caper, either. I couldn't tell how many, but if the Japanese discovered us intruding into their final position and opened up, those Shermans would keep us alive. I wondered how they'd distracted that pompous major.

Ahead of us there was darkness and then there was real darkness. We were facing a narrow canyon of volcanic rock, perhaps a hundred yards wide with walls two, possibly even three hundred feet high. We couldn't see anything in the canyon, but the rims were being illuminated by the flares, which had just started to pop over this end of the island. It looked like it went in straight for a couple hundred yards and then bent to the right and out of sight. We couldn't see the sides, either, other than as large panels of black rock, but I knew there'd be the usual collection of cracks, crevices, caves, pits, and, most important of all, that rumored concrete blockhouse at the back of the canyon. I had plans for that blockhouse, but first we had to try to find our orphans.

"Higher would be better," I told Goon.

"That's what I told Monster and Twitch," he replied. "Look for a way up to the rim."

TWENTY-SEVEN

The flares also revealed what was coming up from behind us, which were three conventional Shermans, called bangers to differentiate them from the flamethrower tanks, called Zippos. We headed for the canyon entrance at a noisy crawl, so all the pedestrians moved to get behind a tank, including Goon and me. More tanks seemed to be coming from way behind us, but hearing anything was pretty tough with all those boots crunching through the black gravel. Twitch and Monster had gone ahead, but not too far ahead, to see if they could find any sign of our missing Marines. We came under machine gun fire almost immediately. We hit the deck while the tanks calmly swiveled their main gun from right to left, blasting high velocity 75mm rounds into whichever hole had started to blink at them. One or two would usually silence the machine gun. Then one of those big Type 98 mortars went into action, but they were obviously shooting blind because rounds began to explode all over the place, including the side walls *inside* the canyon. Where everybody suddenly saw American .50 cal tracer fire going straight up into the air.

The rounds were coming from about seventy-five feet up the left side wall in one continuous stream, an obvious signal. Two of the infantrymen who'd come with us responded by standing a fifty on its ass and doing the same thing—firing a steady stream straight up in the air. There was a landslide of rocks and scree piled up against that wall, down through which dark figures began tumbling in a human landslide. All three tanks were now blasting away indiscriminately into the canyon with their main guns, their fifty, and even their two .30 caliber machine guns. Any bad guy who wanted to stick his head out to see what the hell was happening would lose it pretty quick. In the meantime, the crowd of Marines now crouched down on the deck at the foot of that wall had grown to more than a hundred.

C'mon, guys, I thought, watching what was happening on the left wall. Get the hell outta there. But they seemed to be waiting for something. Then a fresh flare popped practically overhead and I saw what it was. There were teams of four trying to wrestle stretchers down all that loose rock and gravel. They weren't making good progress. Some of them actually lost control of their stretchers, spilling the wounded men out onto that hillside of gravel. Every Marine down on the deck behind the tanks got up and went at a run toward that pile of rocky debris and then up that slope, heedless of any enemy fire, and turned the four-man teams to six- and even eight-man teams.

Once they got everybody down, our mob of volunteers started to withdraw while the tanks still had ammo. I finally saw one lone Marine way up there trot to the edge of whatever feature they'd been holed up in and hop over the edge, sitting down on the ensuing landslide and bouncing on his ass all the way down. Two guys ran back, helped him up at the bottom, and took off for the canyon entrance.

"That's their CO, I'll betcha," Goon said proudly. "Monster found a path up to a really good place, Loot. On the other side. He's up there doing some recce."

The tankers must have been watching somehow, and when the last three Marines had everybody, even the stretcher-bearers, in a slow trot in the go-back direction, they pivoted on their tracks and headed after the diminishing crowd. They swiveled their gun barrels to directly behind them and kept up a sporadic fire up into the canyon in case any bad guys got brave. We three hugged the right sidewall of the canyon, got low, and started back in.

We made our moves as each flare burned out and before the next one popped. It was really dark in that canyon, with lots of residual gun smoke. If there were still any defensive nests active, they'd have to be deaf and blind by now. We went a few hundred yards farther in and then Goon nudged me to the right. We started up an inclining path that was about one foot wide, with a sheer drop into darkness on our left side. Twitch went first. He'd sense trouble ahead before Goon or I ever would. There was a light breeze now as we got nearer the canyon rim and we could smell the sea. A sliver of moon flitted in and out of some flying scud. We could only see it between flares, which maybe meant the Japanese couldn't see us except in one-second blinks. We tried to be extra quiet, but we couldn't prevent the occasional rock from going over the side and making a racket down below.

We went down on our bellies once we got just below the rim. I looked over the rim and immediately saw a circular depression perhaps twenty feet wide at the edge of the rim, which would protect us from rifle fire. To the south we couldn't actually see *Suribachi*, but there were dust clouds boiling up not too far away, probably "our" tanks rejoining The Line. I wondered what that major would have to say when he found out what his people had done on their own initiative. Strict obedience to orders was a rule hammered into every Marine's head several times a day. But when the situation called for both bravery and initiative, Marines inevitably went right for it. That's what made them such a formidable fighting force.

Monster's "place" was indeed perfect, because now I got my first look at that blockhouse. It was several times bigger than any pillbox

I'd seen elsewhere on the island, looking more like a concrete headquarters building than a fighting position. I could also see back along
the whole length of the canyon, which narrowed from the point
where we'd gone in looking for the missing guys down to barely
twenty feet right in front of the big blockhouse. The end of the canyon was no more than fifty feet behind the blockhouse and it rose
in a sheer, black wall that slightly overhung the building. Last-stand
position, indeed, I thought. It couldn't be bombed except maybe by
skip-bombing, but a fighter-bomber would have a tough time lining
up because of the narrowness of the canyon and that dogleg turn.

"How you gonna do this, Loot?" Goon asked.

"What time is it?"

"Twenty-forty."

"Where's Monster?" I asked.

"Sniffin' around," Twitch answered from ten feet back of the rim.
Apparently Twitch was not fond of heights.

"Okay, I'm gonna start with a cruiser," I said. "Begin at the head
of the canyon and move inward. Those three tanks did some house-
cleaning up at the front. I'll save that blockhouse for last and use a
beast for that job. I think we're gonna have to watch for enemy coming up here once they realize there's a spotter driving the fire around
the canyon."

"Twitch said there's another path down to the bottom over there,
on the eastern side of this ridge. If they start comin' up that, you may
have to beat feet outta here. We can slow 'em down, but . . ."

"I understand," I said. "Once I switch to the big guns, I'll keep
that cruiser on standby. Use five-inch, VT frag."

"How you gonna git that big box down there, with that overhang
in the way like that?"

"Carve away the overhang," I said with a grin. "With a fourteen-
inch carving knife."

Exactly at 2100 I made my first mission call, while Goon and

Twitch started checking around to see if there were any other approaches to our little bowl on the rim. Monster still hadn't made an appearance and I'd asked Goon about that.

"He'll come in when the shit hits the fan," he said. "Twitch'n me are gonna keep on the move, make sure no bad guys start creepin' up on you. We'll go a little ways down that eastern path, see if there's any good defensive positions."

That sounded fine to me; once I went to work, I'd be focused on the numbers.

The first thing I had to do was get control of a heavy cruiser's eight-inch battery and start walking it up the canyon below. My first shooter for the evening was the USS *Indianapolis*, an eight-inch gun heavy cruiser whose call-sign was Crowbar.

I wanted eight-inch common; no need for armor-piercing until I found a hard or underground target. I had my grid map laid out on a flat stone and I'd correlated grid numbers with some geographic prominences. I called for the first spotting round at the front of the canyon. The ship fired the first round. I saw nothing. I told them to fire again. Still nothing.

"Lost," I said. "Check fire, check solution."

This was embarrassing—for the ship. Their solution was so far off that I, the spotter, never saw where their rounds were landing. I hoped no friendlies had just had an eight-inch round drop into their trenches. The flares continued to pop overhead and I watched carefully to make sure nothing was moving down there in the canyon. I decided to re-call the mission, and checked to make sure I wasn't the problem. They read back the target's grid coordinates, which matched, and we tried again.

Again, lost.

"Crowbar, this is Iwo, two-six Charlie. Name your grid."

"Iwo, two-six Charlie, this is Crowbar. Grid is Mayhem, niner, five eight zero, over?"

"Wrong grid," I replied. "Grid is Backlight, wide-wide zero, over?"

There was a long moment of silence. Then they came back: "Not available, over?"

"This is Iwo, two-six Charlie. Roger, out." In other words, you're of no use to me. Go away.

I called Regiment. They'd obviously been eavesdropping. Right then something crashed onto the rocks no more than twenty feet away. And then ignited. It was a flare whose parachute hadn't deployed. Now it was going to illuminate my little depression with a million or so candlepower for five minutes. I got small. I could feel the heat from the burning magnesium. If there were Japanese watching, the only thing that would save me was the fact that no one could look directly into that blaze without going blind. Regiment called back.

"Iwo, two-six Charlie, stand by for new teammate," they said.

Somehow the cruiser had been assigned to me for a fire mission without having been issued the new island-wide grid. I relaxed down onto the sand and waited for that damned flare to burn out. It sat there like a flaming snake, hissing fiery particles into the air. How many heavy cruisers were out there, I wondered. I didn't want to start the evening's proceedings with a beast. I wanted to save the fourteen-inch to work that big-ass blockhouse.

It took them five minutes to assign a new cruiser, this time the USS *Pensacola*, whose call sign was Nightrider.

"Nightrider, this is Iwo, two-six Charlie. Fire mission, over?"

"This is Nightrider, roger over?"

"Nightrider, this is Iwo, two-six Charlie. Fire mission: target: fixed positions in a canyon, machine gun nests." I spelled out the coordinates. "Main Battery, one gun, one round, common, at my command, over?"

They read it back and it sounded like they knew what they were doing, unlike *Indianapolis*, whose "talk" had been hesitant, if not tentative. This happened—unless a ship did naval gunfire support on a regular basis, we couldn't expect them to be really good at it.

"This is Nightrider, ready over?"

"This is Iwo, two-six Charlie, fire, over?"

"Shot, out." Then: "Stand by, out."

A hot blast erupted just to the right of center in the entrance to the canyon. Much better, I thought. "Left, one hundred, no change, add one hundred, over?"

They read it back, and then reported ready. I told them to fire, and the spots appeared to take effect. Okay, I thought, I've got me a genu-wine shooter.

For the next thirty minutes I walked her shells up and down the canyon, even whacking the sides of the canyon from time to time in case the Japanese had placed some nests up high. The CP had taken the precaution of positioning the cruiser on the long axis of the canyon so she could hit anything inside. I'd asked for the battleship to take station at a much longer range on the same axis.

I assumed *Pensacola* would step aside once a beast got into it. I know I would. I couldn't make out individual targets in the darkness, even with the flares, but I could cover the ground, and *Pensacola* did a fine job of responding to spots. I did wonder from time to time why I still hadn't seen Monster—I'd expected him and the others to rejoin once I started throwing eight-inch into that canyon. Maybe he'd already joined up with the other two as they surveyed the top of the ridge for more paths. The canyon was to my left. It looked like the overall ridge had been split with a giant axe down to a depth of 250 feet.

There was no enemy response down there once the shelling started, which was what I'd expected. You don't come out of your holes until it stops. So I checked fire. For all we knew, the Japanese had withdrawn entirely from the canyon after confronting tanks, although as I surveyed the terrain, I couldn't see where they'd go. I was on the only high ground nearby, with the sea at my back, and with only that windowless concrete building offering any heavy-duty protection if there were Japanese down there running for their lives. But you never knew on Iwo; we hadn't checked the slopes on the other side of my position. There could be a thousand of them embedded down there, for all we knew.

I still hadn't quite figured out how I was going to bend battleship fire around that slight dogleg in the canyon, but from that far away, I'd have some plunging fire to work with. I'd been half joking about carving away that overhang, but I might have to do just that. I continued to watch the canyon's floor. I was a bit anxious being up on the top of this ridge without my bodyguards. What if some enemy scouts took the path that we'd taken to get up here? I'd be easy pickings. A sudden eruption of small-arms fire somewhere to my right answered my question.

Goon and Twitch, and, I hoped, Monster, had obviously run into some trouble on that eastern side path. Maybe that big blockhouse had sent a team out to see if there was a spotter up on the ridge. That's where the shooting was coming from. That path was on the reverse slope, so my cruiser couldn't help. I pulled my submachine gun closer and looked around in the shadows for a firing position if anyone popped up behind me. Maybe that's where Monster had gone—to see if there was a third way to get up here from down below.

The noise from the back slope got louder and then I heard a couple grenades go off, their sharp bangs echoing off the surrounding hill surfaces. I stuffed the grid map into my utility trousers pocket, grabbed my typewriter, and trotted off in the direction of the firefight. I had two grenades and two extra clips for the Thompson. If my guys were in trouble, another submachine gun wouldn't hurt.

Fifty feet on I nearly collided with Goon in the darkness.

"We gotta get you outta here," he said, panting a little bit. "They know you're up here."

"How many?"

"Can't tell in the dark," he said. "But enough. You're gonna have to run for it, same way we came up. Gimme that chattergun and your ammo and then git."

"Fuck that," I said. "I've got a beast ready and waiting. They'll send troops back into the canyon, ready to meet me when I get down there. I'm gonna go back to work. Here's the Thompson and a grenade. too. I'll keep one and I have my .45. Lemme get to it."

He stared at me for a second. His job was to keep me alive, but my job was to smash the supposedly last standing enemy positions. He nodded, took the weapons, and disappeared up the slight slope to rejoin his guys.

I ran back to my observation post. The first thing I did was order the cruiser to repeat the last mission with nine rounds. Maybe I'd catch any enemy starting into the canyon on that side to surround my position. At that moment six Marines appeared at the top of the path we'd taken, lugging two 60mm mortars. They saw me and backed fifty feet behind me and then began to set up shop. Two men attended to the mortar; the third dug in as best he could into the rock and became a sentry. I was no longer alone. I hoped there'd be more coming.

Pensacola put nine more rounds, which represented a salvo of her entire Main Battery, into the canyon in quick succession while I laid out the grid and then called the CP. "I need the duty beast," I said. "Right now."

The beast apparently had been listening. "This is Armageddon," a voice announced on the circuit. I'd used her once before. She was the USS *North Carolina*, with 16-inch guns. I gave her my grid position. Then:

"Armageddon, this is Iwo, two-six Charlie. Urgent fire mission. Target, Japanese headquarters. Large reinforced concrete blockhouse. Main Battery. One gun. High-capacity. Terrain obstructing. Prep armor-piercing." I gave them the grid numbers. "One round. At my command, over?"

Her Main Battery Plot radio operator repeated it verbatim, and then said out.

Ninety seconds later, they came back with the Ready transmission. Somewhere out there on the darkened sea, an enormous battleship, bigger than *Nevada* and with significantly heavier guns, was creeping along a course roughly parallel to the coast, with one turret trained out and a single barrel elevated to send a 2,700-pound projectile ten miles into the canyon.

"Ready, break, fire, over."

"Shot, out." Six seconds. "Stand by, out."

I didn't need binoculars to see the impact point. The round hit at the end of the straight part of the canyon, just before that dogleg turn to the right. The entire canyon lit up and the sound overwhelmed the rattle of gunfire to my right. In fact, the firefight stopped entirely when that single round went off down in the canyon, as if the Japanese had been momentarily shocked at the size of the explosion on the other side of the ridge.

"Spots follow: Right one hundred. Up fifty feet. Add one hundred, over."

They read back, and in less than a minute: "Ready, over?"

"Ready, break, fire, over?"

We danced the dance for the next three minutes while I tried to ignore the rising volume of small-arms fire behind me, even as a succession of sixteen-inch rounds slowly walked around the dogleg below. But it was also becoming clear that there was no way I could get a direct line of fire onto that blockhouse. I'd also seen a possible unintended consequence of hitting the rim of the canyon above the blockhouse: the debris might bury the structure, thus saving it and anyone inside. Then I had an idea: the overhang above the blockhouse wasn't the real problem—the vertical wall of rock which defined the interior edge of the dogleg was the problem. I needed to knock down that obstacle in order to open up a direct line of fire.

Wait one—all this shooting must have dulled my brain bone, because there was yet another way to do this. There were two ways for a big naval gun to hit a target. You could fire from long-range, using an arcing trajectory, or you could move in much closer and shoot at a really high angle, giving up the protection of distance from your enemy for a trajectory that could come almost, but not quite, straight down. Since the blockhouse couldn't shoot back, the *North Carolina* didn't need that protection.

I requested Armageddon to close the island at best speed for high-angle fire and to report ready for fire mission, with the target at approximately the same grid position. I would then re-call the mission. They acknowledged, but they requested the target's position in lat-lon, not grid, this time. For a moment, I panicked, but then remembered I still had that badly scrunched-up navigation chart from our little swim-meet around the LCI, and it included this canyon. It didn't have the blockhouse, of course, but I could wing that for the first spotting round.

The melee on the northeast path had subsided, but then mortars started coming up from somewhere down there in the darkness, probably some deep pit or even a cave entrance. The two Marine teams behind me quickly set up their own 60mm mortars and started exchanging love notes with the gloom. If I could've seen the mortar flashes I could have put the *Pensacola* to work on the mortars while waiting for *North Carolina* to get on station, but I wasn't about to stick my head over that rim and invite a sniper to take his best shot.

I calculated an impact point down in the bottom of the canyon and two hundred yards *back* from the actual turn into the dogleg and went back to *Pensacola* while the beast was still en route. Maybe she could help me shave some stone off that corner. I called for three rounds. They landed in the canyon, but were long. I thought hard: I needed to raise that trajectory about a hundred feet into the air and bring it right one degree, no more, and then to drive the impact point directly toward me. I gulped, tried to ignore the ruckus behind me, and made the call.

As I waited for them to apply the spots I heard, or thought I heard, yells down on that path that we had first come up. Enemy? Or Marines? Then I heard the words: Hold fire, hold fire.

The ship came back with: Ready, over. I went back with: Check fire—danger.

They repeated that and waited. Danger close meant friendlies close to the impact point. Danger meant the spotter was too close to what he'd just called. Sometimes you had to do that—there were incidents where spotters had called for the firing ship to aim right at them if their position was being overrun. Waiting wasn't a problem: the Mark One-Able could wait all night, coldly maintaining the solution, and still obliterate everything in sight.

Suddenly there were Marines everywhere, dozens of them. I pointed them to where I thought my guys were fending off Japanese, but that wasn't necessary. The volume of small-arms fire rose precipitously, and I knew I was probably safe. Then I called the CP and told them Marines had come forward into the canyon. Their carefully planned, early morning, coordinated general offensive plan had just fallen apart.

Now, let's go do some good work for the Lord, I said to myself, although I had to wait for Armageddon to get into position.

There were more and more indications of a general engagement down below my perch on the eastern canyon rim. The brass at the CP must have realized they were no longer in control of the battle and just sent everything forward, even at night, in an effort to finish this mess. I was glad I wasn't down below, because there were definitely going to be some friendly-on-friendly incidents in a melee like that. There must have been a couple hundred Marines up on the rim with me, awaiting orders. The CP probably had no damned idea of where they were. Being Marines, they were digging in. It was hard going, with shovels clanging off volcanic rock. It wasn't granite, but it wasn't dirt, either. I knew they'd be breaking out the C-4 cubes pretty soon. Meanwhile, the faithful flares kept popping. I knew it was ridiculous, but they seemed brighter up here.

A familiar face appeared at my spotting station. It was Major Murphy, fully equipped for field operations.

"Remember me?" he said with a grin.

"What are you doing up here?" I asked, truly surprised.

"I snuck three Navy medics in and they snatched Wreck from the

CP. Just in time, in their opinion. Three hours later Sitting Bull came back from a headquarters meeting. Where's Wreck. I 'fessed up."

"Good God, that must have been loud."

"Indeed it was," he said with another grin. "That afternoon I was sent to the front to join a line infantry unit. As an observer, no less. No command. No troops. No job. But up front. *Way* up front."

"And the colonel—really, how was he taking it?"

"That's the sad part," he said. "After the blow-up when he found out what I'd done, we think he had some kind of incident. Maybe even a stroke. He just went to a chair, sat down, and put his head down. We later found out from the medics who came for him that his injuries were more serious than he'd let on. Arm shattered, not broken. His eye socket was infected and hurting. And he was physically exhausted—you know he never quit, rarely slept. In the end he just collapsed. Did you know he was fifty-two?"

"Well, maybe he'll see Wreck on the hospital ship, then," I said. "Back together after all."

"Wouldn't that be nice," Murphy said. "Can I help out up here?"

"Yes, sir—take charge of all these volunteers and get ready to repel boarders."

"Aye, aye, Captain," he said. "Great working with you."

Murphy took charge and organized the mob. Some were put to digging, others in sentry positions, and a couple sent down the paths about fifty feet to watch for attackers. I saw Goon lie down behind a big rock. I thought he went to sleep.

"Iwo, two-six Charlie, this is Armageddon. In position and ready, over?"

"Armageddon, Iwo, two-six Charlie: fire mission. Large concrete blockhouse." I gave him the position in latitude-longitude, as he'd asked. My position unchanged. "One gun, high-capacity, high angle trajectory, at my command, over?"

They did the read back, and then reported ready.

"Ready, break, fire."

"Stand by, out." That came sooner than I expected and then I heard that *wa-wa-wa* of a 2,200-pound, sixteen-inch-diameter projectile coming down. Close. Much too close, I thought, and flattened myself just as the projectile hit the extreme edge of the canyon rim perhaps eight feet below the edge and went off. Fortunately, most of that explosion vented out into the canyon below the rim, or everybody up there would have been dead. As it was, we were all stunned and deaf. My teeth were humming. Many of the Marines were on the ground, having been knocked flat by the blast.

"Spots," I croaked. "Left one hundred, down two hundred feet, add four hundred, over?"

I wondered if they could hear the bruising in my voice. I couldn't hear a fucking thing, but I could see a lot of Marines looking right at me, as if to say: Loot: you do that?

"Ready, over?"

"Ready, break, fire."

This time the round landed against the wall of the canyon well below us, thankfully, and closer to the dogleg, but still shaking the entire ridge.

"Repeat," I called.

They fired again. Just beyond the base of the dogleg.

"Spots: no change, down two hundred feet, add two hundred."

They fired again, and this time the round landed about two hundred yards in front of that concrete building.

"No change, no change, add two hundred," I called. "Stand by for Able Peter."

This round landed right alongside the building. If there'd been a door it would have blown it in. Another flare popped in approval, giving me a really clear view.

"No change, no change, add fifty."

"Ready, over."

"Ready, break, fire. Over?"

This round landed on the front face of the blockhouse. When

the smoke cleared there was a fifty-foot-wide dimple in the face of the blockhouse, with rebar clearly showing. That was seriously reinforced concrete.

"This is Iwo, two-six Charlie. Target. Three guns, armor-piercing, nine rounds, fire for effect, over?"

No more at my command. They had the solution. I wanted them to clobber that thing before something changed. By now, all the Marines up there with me were on their bellies at the rim, dying to see what happened next.

What happened next was that the blockhouse disappeared, but in two stages. First there were three hits all along its upper face, producing big holes and a lot of dust. Dark red glares bloomed inside those holes and then big, punching explosions that first lifted and then dropped the entire structure in boils of fire.

"Target. Go on, three guns, armor-piercing, nine rounds. Stand by for high-cap."

They read it back and then proceeded to flatten that blockhouse headquarters building with the last three rounds mostly blasting debris into smaller and smaller pieces while making the hole in the ground bigger and bigger. The center of the explosions seemed to be migrating a little to the east, so I sent a spot.

"Spot: left fifty, no change, drop fifty. Three guns, one round, high-cap."

They'd understand that, I hoped. You're opening the crater and killing anybody who got out of that, which, from my perspective, had to be nobody. The Marines lining the rim were clearly in awe of what was happening, and there were no more mortars coming up the hill, either. There was a slight delay, probably because of the ammunition change, but then three more rounds came hurtling down from above the flares and that appeared to finish the job. I blew out a big breath and called both *North Carolina* and *Pensacola*.

"This is Iwo, two-six Charlie: cease firing, target destroyed. Request remain on station. Our troops are moving up, over?"

An older, Southern voice came back from Armageddon: "Ain't goin' nowheres, there, Charlie. Nice workin' with you. Out."

I dimly heard small-arms fire coming from behind me, possibly down on that canyon path.

Wait. Wrong path.

A moment later far too many Japanese burst into view from the *original* path we'd taken up, which nobody had been guarding at the top because they'd been too busy sightseeing. Screaming like banshees, a couple dozen vicious-looking small men covered the distance between the top of the path and my little stone saucer at the speed of heat.

My entire body seized up in cold panic. I knew I was done for. I scrambled to twist sideways to pull out my .45 and promptly dropped it. Two of the banshees raised bright steel swords over their heads, but then dropped them as rounds from a Thompson cut them in half. Marines were up now, running, and screaming, stabbing with their bayonets, and shooting in a blaze of mayhem. Then I saw Goon step out from behind a rock, holding *my* Chicago typewriter and grinning like a fool as we both watched the massacre going on in front of us. That was until the eastern path vomited *another* crowd of screaming banshees who arrived shooting. I saw Murphy go down and then something smacked the helmet off my head, followed by a sledgehammer hit to my right side. The chaotic scene before me began to fade to black, and I finally got that nap I'd been just dying for.

TWENTY-EIGHT

Doctor, one-sixty-seven is regaining."

I tried to open my eyes. They seemed to be glued shut to just a bare crack, but there was truly bright light in those cracks. Then there were hands doing things around me as I tried to rise up out of that chemical fog. There was a thing in my mouth and my arms and legs were restrained. I felt a moment of absolute panic until a woman's voice said: "Easy there, Captain Bishop, we've got you, we've got you. You've got a breathing tube in your mouth; we're gonna take it out. Can you open your eyes?"

I tried to say, no I can't, somebody's glued 'em shut, but speaking with a tube in wasn't possible. She should know that, shouldn't she? I thought. I made an unh-unh sound.

"Okay, relax, lemme irrigate."

A wet cloth pressed down on my sticky eyelids and then I could open my eyes. All I could see were the silhouettes of three or four figures standing around me against a blaze of painfully white light.

I quickly closed my eyes and tried not to cough, then tried to see again.

Someone was fooling with what felt like a paper tag attached to my neck. "Okay, I think we can pull it," a man's voice said from somewhere. "It's been five days. Remember, slow but steady—don't stop."

"That's what all the girls say," said another man's voice.

"Really, Doctor," the nurse said in an annoyed voice, as someone put what felt like a stethoscope on my chest, which I realized was really sore. I still could see them only as silhouettes so I just gave up and closed my eyes. But then that thing came up out of my throat from somewhere down in my chest like a big, warm snake. I took a breath and then another. That hurt, too, but I could talk now.

"Where am I?" I croaked. Even croaking hurt. Shit, everything hurt.

"You, sir, are aboard USNS *Solace*, a US Navy hospital ship. We're somewhere to the west of the island. They brought you aboard five days ago, with a crease bullet wound to the skull and another in your right side that lodged in your right lung, stopping just short of your aorta and heart. God was with you, I'd have to say."

"Not when all those Japanese showed up, He wasn't," I grumbled. "Is Goon here? Twitch? Monster?"

"Um, it's possible," the voice replied, sounding puzzled. "We'll be sure to go check that out in a little while. But right now, we're kinda busy, okay, Captain?"

Why were they calling me Captain, I wondered. A strange sensation bloomed in my right forearm. I guessed that the effort of talking had invited that mist back to my head, and I began to feel really sleepy again.

"Okay," the voice I associated with a doctor said. "I'm putting him back down for another twenty-four hours."

"The restraints?" the nurse asked. I could hear, even as I started back down.

"Leave 'em on while he's out. Remove them when he resurfaces. Keep those other two IVs going. Give him a little ice water to loosen up his throat when he resurfaces, and then start him on some liquid sustenance. He's way underweight, just like all the others. Check the lung drain once an hour for bleeding. Call me, even if it's just a tincture, but I think he's good for now."

I wanted to ask a million questions right then, but that mist was insisting that I go to sleep like a good captain. My last thought was that I'm a lieutenant, not a captain, dumbass. Tell 'em, Goon.

The next time I woke up the bright white lights were gone. I tried to sit up but my legs and arms wouldn't move. I looked around. I was in some kind of ward. There were portholes along the bulkheads and sunlight coming in. The ward was overcrowded. There were three rows of beds instead of two, with the third row where the central aisle should have been. A hospital corpsman in whites came by, saw that I was awake, and wormed his way through the beds. He glanced at the chart hanging from the foot of my bed. He was wearing the chevrons for an E-5, but looked much too young for that rank.

"Morning, Captain Bishop," he said. "How do you feel?"

"Shot at and missed, shit at and hit," I said, weakly. My voice still wasn't ready to go back to work.

He grinned. "That's good," he said. "I'll get somebody to get those straps off. Let you sit up."

"Why the straps, anyway?" I asked. Other patients were looking over with interest. Apparently, someone coming-to was an event. I guessed not everyone on the ward came to.

"Sometimes patients under induced sedation start flailing around; pull out IVs, disturb bandages, open surgical wounds. It's standard procedure. But your orders say to pull the IVs when you wake up—get you sitting up and becoming human again."

"Don't feel human, though," I said.

"Take your time," he replied, making some notes on my chart. "Then look around. It'll make you feel better, I promise. Rounds are in one hour. Docs will tell you more. In the meantime, lemme find some scissors."

"One question, Corpsman?"

"Sure."

"Why's everybody calling me captain? I'm a Navy lieutenant, from the *Nevada*."

He seemed surprised, and again consulted my record. "Says here you were brought in with a bunch of Marines, what, six days ago? Dog tags gave us your name. O-3 stamped on the tags. Were you on the island?"

"I certainly was," I said. It seemed so long ago. "Are we still here? I mean, at Iwo?"

"Yes, we are, but not for long. Another hospital ship is due in five days. Then we'll head for Guam and then, eventually, Tripler. Back in Pearl."

He went to find scissors, came back, and cut me free. Physically it didn't feel all that much different, but knowing I was free to hit the deck and start digging in made a big difference. Then I realized how ridiculous that thought was. Still. Free was better. I had to force myself not to look around for my typewriter. He helped me sit up on some pillows and then left.

I did look around and pretty quickly understood what he'd meant about feeling better. My chest wound was serious, but some of the other men on that ward had been maimed beyond belief. Hideous burns. Missing limbs. Heads completely swathed in bandages, with only small holes where their noses and mouths should have been. Legs elevated on slings, but with nothing below the knee. Or thigh. Two guys with no eyes, shuddering as they tried to cry.

Then I got a tiny whiff of what had been that overwhelming stench of death on the island. Gangrene. One guy two beds over who looked dead to me. Eyes partly open but unseeing; no breathing movement under his blanket. A nurse came by, saw him, and quietly pulled the blanket over his head. The guys on either side of him blinked a couple of times and then pretended not to notice. Those horrific casualty numbers began to take physical shape around me, and I found that I could weep, too. I went back to sleep. It seemed the safest thing for me to do just then.

Four days later I was in a different ward, where men who'd been wounded but were on the mend were berthed. I had to admit I was glad to leave that other ward. I was walking by then, learning how to breathe with one point three lungs. It was such a relief to be clean and breathe fresh sea air. They'd taken out the drain and now the thing that hurt the most was the wound that had been the least serious, that eighth-inch furrow across the top of my scalp. A tiny bit of hair had started to grow back, and it was snow white. I was eating two times a day and spending far too long in the shower, gently but firmly scrubbing the death-stained grime of Iwo Jima off my skin long after that was really necessary. I found out that hot water and all the soap in the world couldn't get Iwo Jima out of my soul, though. And I was homesick for my ship.

That afternoon a buzz went around the ship. We were leaving the next morning around noon for Guam and points east. Two, not one, hospital ships were coming in that night to absorb the still-sobering number of casualties coming out of Iwo. There was some place called Bloody Gorge where the battle had finally, really ended. I wondered if that was my canyon.

My canyon. Jeezus.

We got teletype-printed daily news bulletins from home. The Japanese had stood true to their orders, to take ten Marines for every one of theirs. The generals had been declaring increasingly large parts of the island "secured," but had forgotten to inform the Japanese, who had apparently died to the last man. There were times that the sadness of Iwo Jima overwhelmed me, and I wasn't the only walking wounded on that ship who suddenly sat down on a topside bench and wept. And yet, strangely, I didn't want to go back to Pearl Harbor, or even the States. I wanted to go find Goon and the guys, Sitting Bull, and even Wrecked. I'd never be able to do that from here on a hospital ship, especially one that was going to leave the active war zone. What

I really wanted was to get back to *Nevada*. They had a good sick bay. They'd take care of me better than some Army hospital, I was sure of it.

Then I had an idea. I made my way up to the bridge of the ship. There was an officer of the deck and a couple of lookouts, but nothing like the crowds of people I'd seen on warship bridges. They were apparently used to having walking wounded come up and look around. The view forward was expansive. The sea was slate gray with tiny lines of whitecaps. I hadn't been aware of how big a hospital ship was. The deck forward was emblazoned with a giant red cross. I wondered if this particular enemy would respect that. As if to make that point, there were two destroyers patrolling ahead of us. I wasn't just a tourist, however. I was, once again, in search of a radio.

There was one radio circuit up on the bridge that seemed to be the general admin circuit for all the ships around us. We were in the Service Force formation, which contained oilers, cargo ships, transports, an ammo ship, and the hospital ships. It wasn't much of a formation, by Navy standards, but there were at least two dozen ships out there, and more destroyers, too. They were using ships' names instead of call signs, and when a call came in for *Solace*, the OOD picked up a handset on a center console and answered it. When he went back out to the bridgewing, the bridge was unattended. As was that radio. I saw my chance.

I picked up the handset. "Armageddon, Armageddon, this is Lieutenant Lee Bishop. I was Iwo, two-six Charlie, and now I'm on the *Solace* and I want to come home, over?"

There was no reply, not even an annoyed call from whoever was Net Control.

Well, I thought. I tried. I hung up the handset and went below. The OOD hadn't even noticed that I'd done it. Service Force, I thought. Try that on a warship tactical or even admin net and someone would have been jumping down my throat.

I went back to my ward and took a nap. When I got up it was dinner time. I wasn't hungry, but the docs had told me to eat. I sat on the edge of my bunk and wondered about Goon and his amazing sidekicks. How could I ever find out what had happened to them in that sudden firefight on top of the canyon? Had they been killed by that second bunch of bad guys? I prayed that one day I could track them down, although as a mere lieutenant in the Navy, that seemed like an insurmountable task. I missed those guys so much.

I left the ward and headed aft, where the mess decks for patients were. There were an unusual number of people in the passageway, all seemingly excited, all going to the outside hatches as if something was happening out there. I didn't mean to but I got swept up in the crowd and ended up on one of the outside gallery decks, which were crowded. I looked out to sea and saw why.

Coming alongside, like some kind of floating mountain, was *Nevada*, in all her haze-gray glory. Her massive bulk, even at an almost stopped speed, nudged the hospital ship sideways. The ship took on a port list as more and more personnel, staff and patients, crowded out onto the weather decks to catch a glimpse of a real live battleship that loomed ever bigger as she came closer alongside. Those great fourteen-inch guns were laid flat, which made them even more menacing. I stared in absolute amazement.

Back on her starboard quarter a boat was being lowered. It was the captain's gig, and it splashed down into the water alongside. There was a brief puff of smoke from its stern and then the boat cast off and headed for the hospital ship's port quarter. The hospital ship's general announcing system lit off and announced: Lieutenant Bishop, lay aft to the quarterdeck. There was a hospital corpsman standing next to me. "How do I get to the quarterdeck?" I asked.

He stared at me for a moment, and then said: "That you? I'll take you."

We made our way aft through the throng of spectators, went down two ladders, and then aft again along the main deck. I felt really conspicuous in my hospital PJs and slippers. By the time I got to the quarterdeck, there were several ship's officers standing around, including the hospital ship's captain. The *Nevada*'s gig was alongside, bobbing gently to the sea-painter provided by the *Solace*. The ship's captain saw me. I caught a whiff of stack gas coming from the beast's funnel.

"Are you Lieutenant Bishop?" he asked.

"I am, sir," I said.

"Your chariot awaits, young man," he said. I couldn't tell if he was annoyed or impressed. The whole of the horizon was dominated by that castle of steel, waiting four hundred feet away. I didn't know what to say, but he just smiled and pointed me to the accommodation ladder.

I went down the ladder, almost tripping over myself in my haste, then slowing down, rung by rung, grabbing the wire handrails, as my chest began to complain. A corpsman was right behind me in case I tripped and fell. At the bottom, an officer I didn't recognize helped me aboard the gig and then down into the rounded cabin at the back. Captain Henderson was there, helping me to the leather bench at the back of the cabin, with a big, proud smile on his face. Commander Willson grinned at me from the other side. I couldn't contain myself and burst into tears of gratitude as I heard the boat crew topside cast off the sea-painter and then rev the engine for the return trip. Here I was, going home, and bawling like a baby. I was going home. I only wished Goon and the boys were going with me.

TWENTY-NINE

*N*evada left Iwo the day after I returned aboard and headed back to Guam. After that, she was destined for the upcoming invasion of Okinawa. I'd been taken down to sick bay and given a bed, diagnosed with malnourishment, sleep deprivation, and a variety of small nuisance infections from not having bathed during my entire time on the island, just like everyone else there. I'd lost twenty-seven pounds and a good part of my hearing, and had the beginning symptoms of scurvy, all in addition to the damage to my right lung, which apparently wasn't cooperating with all the meds.

All of *Nevada's* Marine patients had been transferred to that second recently arrived hospital ship, so the sick bay was empty except for a couple of the usual shipboard earaches and other domestic maladies. Compared to those brutal days when Marine casualties had overwhelmed the hospital ships, the place was a veritable ghost town, much to the visible relief of the ship's medical staff. They had to be as tired as I was. Commander Willson visited me twice a day. On our way back to Guam he told me that he had been ordered to command a new construction destroyer that would be waiting for him in Guam. Our skipper was also moving up. He'd been selected for flag rank and was going back to Pearl to become the deputy for battleship operations on that part of the CINCPACFLT staff that had remained behind when Admiral Nimitz moved out to Guam to finish this war. The new captain was rumored to be something of a screamer, which news was doing the ship's morale no good at all.

The various medicines the docs were using to reconstitute my overall health and especially the remains of my right lung kept me in a lethargic state, pain-free but fully aware that the absence of pain was entirely artificial. I could feel it coming back to feed on me at the end of each six-hour pill cycle, a deep, this-is-serious burning in my chest that seemed to be timing itself to each labored breath. I was also just generally beat up, but not, of course, anywhere near as beat up as the Marines on Iwo were—because they were still there. The end was in sight, as the Navy and Marine Corps publicists proclaimed hourly, but that was small comfort to the small units still out there in the stinking sands, hunting down the unknown number of enemy soldiers who'd gone to ground. Much was being made of the fact that damaged B-29s, coming back from Tokyo bombing runs, had begun landing on Iwo. There were even crowing newsreels, as if the big brass knew they needed to justify the horrific losses before the American public absorbed how bad Iwo had become. Willson told me an entire Army Air Forces fighter wing was supposedly setting up on Airfield No. 1 so they could escort the big bombers on their missions to burn Japan down, out and back.

I saw about two hours' worth of Guam when the ship pulled in and then I was transferred to yet another hospital ship for the passage back to Pearl. The vastness of the Pacific became clearer and clearer as, for day after day, we made our way east through seemingly unchanging seas. At Pearl I underwent more surgery, this time to take a little more of my right lung out and quash the infections it was spreading once and for all. That took two lonesome weeks, after which I was officially sent home, but not before being invalided out of the Navy on a medical discharge, like hundreds of other servicemen at the huge Tripler Hospital up on the hill above Pearl Harbor.

I kept asking every Marine I ran into, and there were many, how I could find out about Goon, Twitch, and Monster, but with no luck at all. It didn't help that I couldn't remember their real names. One badly maimed lieutenant colonel told me I'd have to wait for this goddamned war to be over before I'd ever be able to find out anything. "Japan is done," he said, with a sad smile. "But apparently it's gonna take a million troops to go tell 'em, face-to-face, know what I mean?"

I knew exactly what he meant. By this time, I was feeling like a small wood chip bobbing down that vast river of human casualties being sent back to the States for their families to deal with, since they were no longer of any use to that enormous military machine that was gearing up to go to Japan and smash it flat, at whatever the cost.

It wasn't as if we were being discarded like a bunch of empty shell casings—the docs, the nurses, even the admin people were hugely solicitous and did their best to handle telegrams back to the States and make sure we had a suitable mode of transportation home. But it was clear that everyone else was focused hard on the upcoming Okinawa invasion, and after that, Japan itself. Everyone somberly understood that taking the home islands of Japan would make Iwo look like that proverbial walk in the park.

Looking out the hospital windows that overlooked Pearl Harbor, I often wondered if the Japanese ever regretted the colossal strategic mistake they'd made right here in Hawaii way back in 1941. Based on what I'd seen of the size of the American fleet that was gathering to obliterate them, if they hadn't, they soon would. And yet, I now knew that what would have deterred Americans into a pre-invasion peace conference wouldn't faze those very alien people.

Once I'd gotten back to Pearl, I'd telegraphed my father that I was coming home, sometime, since I didn't know when Tripler would release me. He replied he would meet me in San Diego or wherever they dropped me off and then escort me back to Georgia by train. I then got a second telegram, one day later, from my sister, who told me that Dad was in no shape for a transcontinental trip, and that she would come instead. I wired back that neither of them had to come; I had a surprising amount of back pay coming, and I'd get a compartment in a Pullman car and sleep my way back across the country. I hadn't told them of my injuries, and they hadn't asked. My sister didn't come right out and say it, but I suspected my father's weak heart was coming back to finally harvest him. That was a sad thought, but I'd had enough of sadness just then and put it out of mind.

Home. Just get your country ass home, Lee-boy, before anybody notices and calls you back. And that's what I'd done.

There were lots of delays. There were hundreds of more urgent cases who were being *flown* back to the States for specialist care. The hospital staff was being decimated to man up yet more hospital ships, many of them quick passenger liner conversions, who everybody knew were going to be needed soon. I was wounded, but walking wounded, so I just had to wait my turn for a slot home. I didn't mind. I used the time to build back my strength and endurance. I had to get all new clothes, too.

One day I helped a gaunt-looking older man in a wheelchair get down to the dining area in Tripler. His eyes, framed by deep black circles, were set so far back in their sockets that they looked like those well-known headlights in a tunnel. I could just about see every bone in his face and wondered how often he did get down to the dining room. We exchanged the obligatory where-were-yous. Turned out he'd been assigned to the Fifth Marine Division headquarters staff. I took a shot: you ever hear of the Goon Squad? I asked. He stopped the chair in its tracks and then I had to maneuver him out of the stream of people headed for chow.

"How do you know about those boys?" he asked, sharply.

I told him. He stared back at me. "Holy shit," he said. "*You* were Iwo, two-six Charlie? The Navy guy with the new grid? Man, excuse me, but you're famous, you know that?"

I sighed. "I don't feel famous, but I'd sure like to know what happened to them after the fight at that canyon."

He nodded. "The staff people called that canyon Bloody Gorge. The chief of staff explained that that name had two meanings. It was a hot fight, and bloody was the right word. But the other meaning was that a whole bunch of officers ended up in deep shit when their troops took it upon themselves to go up there and completely disrupt the plan for the next day's general assault."

"I figured as much," I told him. "But isn't that what Marines do: they hear there's trouble, that Marines are in trouble, and they goddamn come running."

He nodded. "I'd like to think so, Lieutenant. But this fucking war's become so big that people all the way back in Washington think they need to control everything. The grunts ask: where were they when we hit the beaches on the 'Canal, you know?"

"So: Goon, Twitch, and Monster?"

His face sobered. "Goon survived Iwo. He got hit the day after the Gorge, but it was a million-dollar wound. When they asked him if he wanted the ticket home, he said yes. Where to, I don't know, but he'd had enough and I think he knew what was coming next. Twitch got killed in an accident. He was so tired he fell asleep at the front of the Gorge and a tank ran him over."

I blinked, hearing that. He saw it. "Happened more times than you wanna know, Lieutenant," he said. "People were dead on their asses and just lay down. Sometimes in the wrong damned place."

"And Monster?"

He shook his head. "Never heard from again," he said. "Listed as missing in action. Probably down in some damn cave or tunnel, lookin' for eyeballs to fry. At the end, we quit going into holes. We'd burn 'em with a Zippo, then blow the front door down. God knows how many bad *and* good guys are still out there on that goddamned, stinking island. Or up inside that volcano."

My knees went weak. I suddenly had to sit down and put my back to the wall, hold my head in my hands, and just weep. You'd think that might be something of a spectacle at Tripler, but I'd seen the same thing happen dozens of times since I'd been there. Nobody stared or asked why. They didn't have to.

My companion didn't say a word. He just waited. I finally got ahold of myself, stood up, and we rejoined the chow line. Then I remembered I didn't recall Goon's name. I asked him. He shook his head.

"It was just Goon," he said, his own eyes tearing up. "That was what everybody called him." He hesitated. "You're gonna want to find him when this is all over, aren't you."

I nodded.

"Don't do that, Lieutenant. Let it go. We've all gotta learn that. Let it go. He sees you, you see him, it's all gonna come back to both of you like a goddamned avalanche. Don't look back. Don't ever look back. It'll just break your heart. I just *hear* the name, Iwo. Breaks my heart, every time."

"What was your job there?" I asked.

"I'm Major Paul Whiting, USMC, and medically retired. I was Number Two at the Graves Registration post on Iwo."

My heart almost stopped. Great God Almighty. I couldn't imagine how bad that must have been.

"Lemme tell you something, Lieutenant," he continued, his voice tight with emotion. "There are somewhere near seven thousand Marines who'll have to be dug up and sent back when this thing's over, and maybe more if they start searching the caves. I was the officer who had to verify and record each name, wherever we could. I had to see each one. I see them every night, now. Every goddamn night, which is why I look the way I look. I have to stay here or in some other facility until that stops. I told them I was never wounded. They're telling me my mind was. So: for God's sake, don't go looking back. You don't know what you might disturb—up here," he said, pointing at his head. "Okay? Take it from me, you can break more than just your heart doing that. Let it go. Let it all go."

EPILOGUE

It was two-thirty in the morning, and my darling wife was sound asleep in my arms on the porch swing. I was tired, but somehow I felt better for having told the story. A great horned owl started cackling in the nearby woods. My chest was complaining again. Whenever I sat for long periods my chest would begin to hurt. The remains of my lung had failed again when I got back to Georgia, so I'd had to go up to Augusta to the Lenwood VA Hospital for yet more surgery, and now I was a one-lung choo-choo. No more cigarettes, that's for damn sure. My scalp wound never did stop hurting; I swear it felt as if it had become an open fissure that moved, back and forth, every time I opened my mouth to speak, even though the docs assured me it had rewelded itself long ago. The white stripe in my hair went from ear to ear, like some kind of earphone rig. My wife called it my Pacific tiara, but never in public.

I looked out over the near fields and the long driveway. I was home at last, and I was determined never, ever to leave. I'd tried hard to banish all my experiences on Iwo, but I just couldn't do it. Like the guy said at Tripler: it'll break your heart. Every time. So don't do that. Think of the present. Think of the future. And yet, something deep in my psyche did not permit it and subconsciously scolded me for even trying. I believe that anyone who was there, who was actually on that island, ended up spiritually scorched, especially the Marines. I'd tell myself I was being overly dramatic, but I often recalled the face of that walking ghost who'd been at the Graves Registration station. I shivered at the thought. My wife stirred.

"Whatever became of Sitting Bull, and Wrecked?" she asked.

I was startled. Had she listened to the whole tale, after all? I wanted to tell her I just didn't know, except that I did.

I'd asked as I transited through the Balboa Hospital in San Diego if either of them was a patient. They had no patients named "Wreck." I guessed that, without any identity, he'd been relegated to a psych ward pending treatment and, hopefully, eventual rehabilitation. Major Murphy had done the right thing and had paid for it up on that ridge.

Colonel Sam Nicholas survived his "incident" but had sought medical retirement at the end of his treatment at the hospital. He'd been discharged two weeks before my arrival. His home of record according to his medical file was listed simply as: unknown. The admin clerk told me that the Marines would know, but that I might want to wait a while to make the inquiry. He'd done the colonel's paperwork, and thought that, while he'd survived whatever had happened to him, he had left unhealed. I told him I understood.

Boy, did I.

So: both of them had essentially disappeared. At least they weren't still on that island or in that vast cemetery. I couldn't imagine a sadder scene than Iwo Jima after all the fighting forces had withdrawn to go get ready for the next bloody expedition, or a sadder bunch of troops than those who'd been left behind to care for that cemetery. The casualty numbers had been kept quiet, but anyone could see from pictures that there must have been several thousand or more temporary graves.

I discovered the real numbers when I later read a commentary in a newspaper as I made my way home, from one of those bespectacled armchair warriors in New York who'd never served. The Japanese won on Iwo, he pronounced. They lost the island, of course, but that was pretty much a given when it started. But we had three whole divisions wrecked by "only" twenty thousand Japanese soldiers. A hundred thousand Marines committed, nearly seven thousand killed in action, and twenty thousand more wounded or still missing in action. Yes, Iwo was used as an emergency airfield and saved a lot of planes and aviators. But one had to ask: were such losses truly necessary? I couldn't answer that question. Bare casualty statistics take some of the sting out of what they represent. But conjure up some faces and see what happens, every time.

Tears. That's what happens. Like right now. I knew that somehow I'd have to get past all that. I wondered, as we went back inside, if I ever would.

AUTHOR'S NOTES

Tarawa, Peleliu, and, to a lesser degree, the Marianas (Guam, Saipan, Tinian) wrecked Marine divisions in terms of being an effective fighting force. The Iwo battle nearly *destroyed* the Third, Fourth, and Fifth Divisions as fighting forces. The stark casualty figures don't tell the whole story: about seven thousand killed in action and twenty thousand wounded in action, out of one hundred thousand committed to the battle, but the fact is that once you kill and maim a certain percentage of any division, Marine or Army, it ceases to exist as a cohesive fighting force. That's what happened to the Third, Fourth, and Fifth Marine Divisions. They came off the battlefield and went into reserve, which is to say they had to be refilled with manpower, then retrained, and then deployed, with your fingers crossed. In fact, at Okinawa, it was the Navy who suffered the most casualties from the kamikaze attacks offshore, with some 4,907 sailors killed and 4,824 wounded, and with 368 ships damaged in addition to the 36 ships sunk.

Peleliu, Saipan, and Iwo Jima were the first clear demonstration that the Japanese had recognized that they simply couldn't "win" this war that they'd started with America, not in the conventional sense. Just as the American high command began to accept that the Japanese were never going to surrender and seek terms, the Pacific war transmuted into a war of extinction. People thought the European war was total war—and it was, in the sense that there were minimal rules, in the ancient meaning of the Rules of War. Although: once the depravity of the Germans became obvious when the first death camps were overrun, it became very difficult for the Allied generals to hold their soldiers back from executing every German involved.

The Pacific war was a collision between two military powers with totally different warrior cultures. The Japanese fought to the death in every case. The Western soldier fought until the "enemy" gave up and laid down his arms. The Japanese didn't do that and thought that the Western soldier was defective in expecting mercy if *he* did that. Once the Western soldiers and their officers finally absorbed that bloody fact of life, things changed. American troops *hated* their Japanese opponents, hated them for their barbarity, their strangeness, and for loving death in battle more than life itself. In Europe, each side took prisoners of war. In the Pacific things were quite different.

As I've described in this book, the Japanese changed tactics at Iwo. Once they saw that the American pre-invasion bombardment was having little or no effect on the preparations they'd made, they let the Americans land without any more than token resistance. The American generals and admirals, lulled by previous "victories," shortened the pre-landing bombardments and landed anyway, piling thousands and thousands of troops onto the beach to achieve that all-important force advantage, without even knowing precisely how many Japanese were waiting for them or what they had planned.

Amphibious warfare theory had long been: rapidly concentrate your forces on the shore, and then move inland to overwhelm the enemy's defenses. The Japanese, who fought this entire battle from the perspective that "we're all going to die here anyway," simply waited until they had enough warm bodies in their gunsights on the beach, and then killed just about all of them.

I personally think it never occurred to the American high command at the time what the Japanese mission on Iwo really was, namely to convince the Americans that when you come to Japan, proper, you are going to suffer *unimaginable* casualties. So will we, but we exult in such casualties as a mark of honor. And if you don't learn that lesson here, come to Okinawa and we'll administer yet another dose of reality. General Kuribayashi told his twenty thousand troops that they had to think of this island as their grave. It would be a grave of great honor as long as they each took ten Americans before they died. Twenty thousand true believers saluted and went to work.

But here's the thing: the Japanese strategy on Iwo made everything personal. The reaction of the average GI on the beaches as he watched thousands die was—hey, this isn't fair: come out of your holes and fight like men. The Japanese said: no, we're going to stay in our holes and *die* like warriors. You're going to die out there in the sand like the stupid dogs you are. Once the GIs figured that out, the battle turned into one driven by pure hate. Marines began to find dead Marines out on the battlefield with their severed genitals stuffed into their mouths. Or obviously wounded, but not yet dead, Marine POWs strangled or impaled. And then the older sergeants would start telling tales from when the Japanese army invaded Chinese cities, like Nanking, and used pregnant women for bayonet practice: stab them shallow until you feel the baby, then skewer the baby, but leave the woman alive.

The Japanese justified such actions by professing a self-serving theory about such barbarity: make war so horrible, so painful, so complete, that no one will ever even think about taking Japan on in battle. That way you make war shorter, which is better for everybody. Cruelty is the order of the day—the worse you make it, the less likely you will see your opponent ever again.

The American Marines reacted just like you'd think they would. The Japanese were not human. Utter barbarians. Bring me my flamethrower and let's burn them to cinders in their caves like cockroaches. Then drag 'em out and burn them again. I feel that, in one sense, the dropping of the atomic bombs was the ultimate expression of how the armed forces felt about the Japanese. And yet today, they are probably our staunchest allies in the western Pacific, especially in the face of growing Chinese imperialism.

The surviving veterans of Iwo have mostly died out. There are some who have been able to reconcile with their Japanese counterparts in the battle of Iwo Jima. There are photographs of Japanese vets and American vets weeping together as they revisited the island to pay homage to those who died there and to those whose bones still lie out there in all that volcanic sand. Nothing quite embodies the horrible scourge of war as a scene like that, two old men standing on the black slopes of *Suribachi*, weeping for what they lost there. I must admit that I teared up sometimes just thinking about what happened there while writing this story.

I'm not a Marine, and thus I don't rate saying it, but I still take a lot of pride in pronouncing the Marine Corps motto: *Semper Fi*. Semper fidelis. Always faithful, to your duty, to your comrades in arms, and to the Corps.

PTD